A PLACE FOR
Miss
SNOW

OTHER BOOKS AND AUDIO BOOKS
BY JENNIFER MOORE

Lady Helen Finds Her Song

Simply Anna

Miss Burton Unmasks a Prince

Lady Emma's Campaign

Becoming Lady Lockwood

A Regency Romance

A PLACE FOR

Miss SNOW

JENNIFER MOORE

Covenant Communications, Inc.

Cover images: *Woman* © Lee Avison / Trevillion Images; Vathia, Mani, Greece © ilbusca, courtesy istockphoto.com

Cover design copyright © 2016 by Covenant Communications, Inc.

Published by Covenant Communications, Inc.
American Fork, Utah

Printed in the United States of America
First Printing: September 2016

22 21 20 19 18 17 16   10 9 8 7 6 5 4 3 2 1

ISBN: 978-1-572440-036-1

For Dave-bey, my brother and friend.
There is no chicken.

Acknowledgments

I CANNOT SAY THANK YOU enough to those who helped bring about this book. First, and most of all, I have to thank my brother, Dave Lunt. This book was his idea. He told me stories about the Maniots and the klephts and the Filiki Eteria, brought me books, and even met me in Greece, where he had an entire trip planned out where we could see Areopolis and Limeni and the Taygetos mountains firsthand. Not everyone gets to have a professor of ancient history for a brother, and I thank my lucky stars that I'm one of the lucky ones. Thanks to Dave and his wife, Jana, for planning the adventure, and to my sisters, Allison Harris and Amanda Lunt, who came along for the ride. You all made it one of the best experiences of my life.

Thank you to Themis Sokratous, our waiter in Limeni Village, who made us laugh and told me all the insider tips about the Mani.

Thank you, Father Matthew and Bill Rekouniotis, for taking the time to show me the cathedral in Salt Lake City, for giving me a personal tour of the Greek History museum, and for answering so many questions. I cannot imagine a more touching way to spend a Sunday morning than attending the Holy Liturgy. Thank you for explaining the beauty of your church and for your kindness and patience with all my questions.

As I have been working and researching, so many lovely Greek people have come into my life, willing to share family stories, traditions, and recipes. Thank you to Jodie Sanders and her father, Nolan Karras, for telling me about their grandpa, Ionnis Karakalios, and letting me use his name in the book.

Thanks, Helen Mellos, for your family recipes.

Thank you, Tiffany Schwebach, RN, for answering baby-delivery questions.

Thanks, Fred Luedtke, DDS, and Renn Veater, DDS, for teaching me about teeth problems, old-fashioned dentistry, and the healing properties of myrrh.

Thank you, Jen Geigle and Dave Lunt, for reading through my rough draft and helping me tighten up the story and get the Greek words right.

As always, thank you so much, Covenant, for your work: publishing, editing, marketing, cover design, and everything that goes into making my story into a beautiful book. Stacey Turner, I am so grateful that you're my editor and that you are patient with deadlines and know how to talk me down when I get crazy and stressed.

Thank you to my wonderful husband, Frank, and my awesome sons for all your support while I work so hard to follow my dream. I know it's a sacrifice for all of you.

And last of all, thank you to my Heavenly Father for putting such wonderful people in my life and giving me the chance to be a writer. Every day I'm grateful for it and the blessings, people, and experiences that enrich my life through it.

Chapter 1

ALEXANDROS METAXAS GLANCED OVER HIS shoulder and cursed under his breath when he saw two British soldiers following him. The large parcel he carried must have aroused their curiosity. He maintained a casual gait despite the tightness in his shoulders and the burden weighing him down. He did not wish to attract further attention by quickening his pace along the dock. Those who had sent him warned that the mission would be dangerous, but he hadn't expected trouble the moment he stepped off the ship. His eyes darted around the island harbor, looking for a place to shake off his pursuers, but he saw only fishermen unloading nets full of the day's catch on the rocky beach. Turning his path toward the noisy center of town, he lengthened his steps and hoped to find concealment in a crowd.

As he approached the Corfu City marketplace, his gaze traveled over his surroundings. Pastel-colored Venetian-style buildings with slate roofs were interspersed with open squares and church steeples. Red geraniums flowed from window boxes, and ornate iron railings decorated upper-level balconies. The sight was very similar to his home of Nafplio, even down to the Byzantine citadel atop a hill high above the city, and he was not prepared for the wave of nostalgia that clogged his throat.

He gave himself a hard jolt. This was no time to be sentimental. His training took over, and he paused, pretending to admire figs at a fruit stand and glancing back the way he'd come. The red-coated soldiers were still following about fifty meters behind. If they judged by his clothing and the origin of his ship, they probably assumed he was a Turk—which was reason enough for suspicion. He could easily convince them otherwise, but if they stopped him, they'd undoubtedly search his bundle. And if they did so, his mission—along with years of planning, months of preparation, and most likely his very life—would end in a matter of seconds.

Shifting the bulky weight on his shoulders, he ducked behind a group of scarf-wearing old women, switched direction to follow a heavily laden donkey cart past an inn's outdoor taverna, and turned immediately down a small alleyway. Dashing around the next corner, he spotted a plain door at the rear of the building. A delivery entrance for the inn—precisely what he was looking for. He hurried inside, closing the wooden door behind.

Alex stood in a dimly lit passage and waited for his heart to calm. Along the walls, boxes and crates were stacked in orderly piles. Ahead, he could hear the sound of voices and the clanking of dishes. He took a few steps and opened the first door he came to, just enough to peek through the crack and see that the room was deserted. He slipped inside, thanking St. Christopher, the patron of travelers, that nobody had stopped him.

The small chamber was filled with old barrels, broken furniture, and odds and ends. There were no windows, so with the door closed it was nearly impossible to see. But after a moment, his eyes became accustomed to the darkness, and the light filtering through the boards of the ceiling helped him to distinguish the shapes around him.

He pulled a bundle of clothing from his pack, took off his embroidered vest and loose breeches, and stuck his legs into fitted trousers that he hoped covered his scuffed boots. He tucked in his cotton shirt, slipped on a waistcoat, a cravat, and a jacket. The heavy woolen clothing immediately made him sweat, and he thought, not for the first time, how strange it was that urban Europeans copied the British style of dress—especially in the humidity of the Mediterranean. After dressing as a peasant for the past week to blend in with the other travelers on the ship, the woolen clothing felt restrictive and thick. As he slipped off the worn cap and tied his hair back with a leather cord, he worried about his lack of a top hat. With the limited amount of space in his belongings, he'd left behind his fine boots and hat, hoping if he carried himself with confidence, nobody would question his poor fashion. After all, he was on a Greek island not in a London ballroom.

His disguise complete, he concealed his clothing with the remainder of the parcel behind a dusty shelf where it would be unnoticed until his return. He paused only a moment as he exited the room. If the parcel was found, the entire mission would be terminated. But being discovered with it would produce the same result. He stepped into the hall, then strode straight through the kitchen and up the stairs. A few servants looked at him with a confused expression, but none inquired as to what he might be doing in their domain. He knew they would not have hesitated to throw him out if he wore peasant garb, but the people of the Ionian Islands still did not know what to make of their new British rulers. And Alex used their uncertainty to his advantage.

He walked through the dining area and crossed the open patio. When he was about to step onto the street, the sight of the two soldiers made him pause. The men were heading directly toward him. Alex did not have time to consider whether they had gotten a good look at his face earlier or if his costume had changed his appearance enough that they would not recognize him. He veered back among the diners.

Taking a quick appraisal of the patrons, he saw two young ladies at a table with an empty chair. He assessed them in a glance as he made his way toward the table. Sisters, he thought, one not yet twenty, and the other perhaps a few years older. They seemed the best choice among the diners, harmless and pleasant. Alex said a quick prayer that the young women would not be distressed to be joined by a stranger. If his luck held, his charm would win them over instead of arousing their suspicion.

He approached and saw the elder sister was listening to the younger. Her eyes were kind, but her mouth turned in a smile that seemed a bit forced. A patient listener, he thought. He overheard a snatch of their conversation as he drew near.

"And did I tell you, Lieutenant Ashworth is paying me a visit tomorrow morning?" The younger sister clasped her hands together. "He sailed with Captains Drake and Fletcher on the HMS Venture, you know, and he was with Brigadier-General John Oswald, as the army invaded Cephalonia and forced the French garrison to surrender within a matter of hours."

"I believe you did tell me, Molly," the elder sister said. Only the slightest tick of her mouth told Alex she'd likely heard these facts numerous times. "Lieutenant Ashworth is quite a hero."

"You are too right. And he did dance with me at—"

Alex glanced once more at the soldiers and slid into the empty seat, stopping the young lady's words. "Good afternoon."

Both women turned toward him with wide eyes.

The younger sister, Molly, drew in a fast breath. She sat up straight in her seat, smiling.

The elder seemed to recover from her surprise quicker. She cleared her throat. "Sir, you have made a mistake."

Alex furrowed his brows. "A mistake?"

She did not appear to be amused by his feigned innocence. Squaring her shoulders and lifting her chin, she narrowed her eyes. "This is not your seat. Kindly remove yourself."

Molly looked back and forth between the two, biting her lip. Her nervous expression told Alex that she would not make trouble. The elder sister was the one he needed to win over. And the task wasn't going to be as easy as he'd hoped. He studied the woman. Chestnut brown hair pulled back and pinned in a simple twist at the base of her neck. Her skin was fair, a sight he was not used to in the Mediterranean. In spite of the hot sun, she did not have a single freckle. She had likely never ventured out of doors without a parasol or bonnet. Based on her rigid posture and the way no lock of hair escaped its pins, he had the thought that a freckle would not be bold enough to blemish her face. Her lips were pink, pursed at the moment, but full and nicely shaped. Her eyes shone with intelligence. She sat perfectly straight in her seat with raised brows, looking down her nose at him as though he were a naughty school boy.

The naughty school boy inside him would have loved to tease a reaction from her. Had they both been fifteen years younger, he would have pulled her braids or untied her shoes. But his current task unfortunately did not make allowance for goading the overly proper woman. For a fleeting moment, he wondered whether she was prone to anger or laughter when caught off guard. The former seemed the more likely, and Alex wondered exactly what it would require to make her smile. He stopped himself before his mind wandered too far from his mission. He realized he'd been staring too long.

"I beg your pardon. I simply meant to make your acquaintance." From the corner of his eye, he saw the soldiers speaking to a man he thought might be the inn's manager.

"A gentleman should know, it is an *extreme* breach of etiquette to speak to a lady before he is introduced."

Alex expected her to wag a finger at him in disapproval. "Then if you will allow me to introduce myself—"

She cut him off. "A gentleman does not introduce himself. He waits until the lady expresses an interest and approves the acquaintance." She folded her napkin and set it beside her plate. "Now if you do not vacate the seat, sir, I shall report your conduct to those British officers." She lifted her chin in the direction of the soldiers.

Molly's gaze still moved between them. She looked as though it took all of her effort not to interrupt.

Alex shrugged a shoulder and pulled off his gloves, finger by finger, without showing the slightest bit of trepidation at her threat. "By all means, miss. I believe that is the precise reason the army is stationed in Corfu, to enforce proper British etiquette on those not suitably familiar with the customs. They are probably patrolling this very moment for ladies who sip their tea too loudly or gentlemen with untrimmed fingernails." He set his gloves on the table and turned to the younger girl. "Now, miss, did I hear your name is Molly?"

Molly's sister's mouth opened and closed. "This is highly improper," she muttered, running her finger over the fold in the napkin.

Molly hurried ahead and answered, the curls on her forehead and around the sides of her face bouncing as she nodded. "Yes, Molly Campbell. My father is Sir James Campbell, inspector-general in Zakynthos. We arrived in Corfu last week from London to meet him for an extended stay.

The elder sister let out a huff and with the tips of her fingers, lining up the ends of her silverware, exactly spacing apart each utensil.

Alex held back a smile. If nothing else, he had managed to silence her protests, and her prim mannerisms amused him. "A pleasure, Miss Campbell, and this lovely lady, who may or may not wish for my acquaintance, she is your sister?"

Molly looked at the other woman and put her fingers in front of her mouth to hold back a giggle. "Oh no, Miss Snow is my chaperone."

Miss Snow lifted her face toward him. She gazed at him steadily, but he noticed her cheeks had colored the smallest bit. Though she held her emotions tightly, he could see that the label embarrassed her.

Alex did not fully understand the British customs, but he knew some British ladies were eligible for a man's attention while others weren't. He'd thought the distinction had to do with age and had been under the impression that chaperones were much older women who were widowed or had given up hope of marriage all together. But Miss Snow couldn't be older than twenty-three.

He shrugged again, pretending to look as if he was not completely confused by the strange rules, and employed his most teasing tone. "Well then, Miss Campbell, if Miss Snow does not wish for my acquaintance, we will simply have to converse among ourselves, won't we? And without a chaperone to keep us in line, who can tell what sorts of mischief we might get into?"

Molly pressed her fingers to her lips, giggling again. Her blonde ringlets, small pink lips, and bright blue eyes were the very picture of British beauty. Although she did not look like the most intellectual person he had ever met, she was cheerful and her manner set him at ease. She shook her head. "Oh, you are a tease, sir." Turning to her companion, she tipped her head and opened her eyes wide. "Miss Snow, you will allow me to introduce our new friend, won't you?"

Miss Snow moved her saucer a few inches to the side and turned the cup so the handle was in line with her napkin. "Very well." She lifted her gaze, and Alex was struck again by her eye color. A dark blue line around the iris surrounded a lighter color that he could not name as either blue or green. Gray, he decided, like the goddess Athena's. A fortunate omen for his mission.

"Diana Snow, I am pleased to introduce—" Molly lifted her hand toward him. "I'm sorry, sir, you never did tell me your name."

"Alexandros Metaxas." He closed his eyes and bent his head forward in a small bow.

"A pleasure, sir." Miss Snow's brow furrowed. "*Metáxi?*" She pronounced each syllable. "Silk?"

Alex pulled back his chin in surprise but wished he hadn't when the stiff collar and tight cravat practically choked him. "Yes, my family is descended from silk merchants. *Miláte Elliniká?* You speak Greek?"

"*Ochi*, no. But I am learning. Modern Greek is much more difficult than the ancient language I learned in school."

"Extraordinary. I have never met an Englishwoman who studied my language."

"Perhaps you should improve your circles of acquaintance. I know of quite a few very well-read women. Many of whom speak multiple languages."

Alex again felt a ripple of amusement. Where Molly's laughter and joyful manner had made him like her immediately, Diana Snow was an enigma, a puzzle he wanted to solve. "And, if I might ask, is there a particular reason you chose to study modern Greek?"

"Obviously because I was traveling to Greece." She blinked and looked at him through partly lidded eyes as if his question was absurd, but she did not fully pull off the expression. He could tell by the way she could not hold his gaze and the spots of pink in her cheeks that she was secretly pleased at his notice. He did not think Diana received much attention with Molly and her contagious joy taking center stage. Did she wish for attention? He again felt a pull to know more about Miss Snow.

Molly shifted in her seat, recapturing his attention. "And what about yourself, sir? You speak English very well. Where did you learn?" She must worry that he would be put off by Diana's manner and thus sought to change the subject.

"My parents sent me to school in Italy when I was very young."

"Oh." Molly's face lost some of its light. "Being away from family can be very difficult. I do hope you were fortunate as I was to have a teacher like Miss Snow." The women exchanged a smile that indicated a close relationship. Small wonder he had assumed they were sisters. "You see, she was my finishing school instructor before my father enlisted her to accompany me to Greece."

Miss Snow's eyes tightened in a slight wince, and she darted a glance at him. Apparently the information was something she had not wished him to know.

"You are very lucky to have such a person who cares about you." He glanced once more toward the street, but the soldiers had apparently either lost interest in pursuing him or decided to search elsewhere. "I apologize, ladies, but I must cut our visit short."

Molly's brows drew together. "Will we see you again, Mr. Metaxas?"

"I'm afraid not. I plan to be on Corfu for only a few more hours." He was quite enjoying his new acquaintances, but if he didn't leave now, he might miss the messenger who would deliver his contact's rendezvous point.

"Oh, what a pity. I'd hoped we would become great friends." Molly's lip pouted.

Did he see a flash of disappointment in Diana Snow's face as well? Or had he imagined it? He rose and bowed over each lady's hand as he bid them farewell.

Striding along the street, he attempted to look like he knew where he was going as he studied the street signs and concentrated on the map he'd memorized. Just as his leader had predicted, moving about the city in British clothing would attract less suspicion. If only his movements did not feel so constricted. But there was work to do, and too much depended on Alex fulfilling his mission. He did not have time to dwell on uncomfortable trousers. For that matter, he needed to stop wondering about a particular gray-eyed woman and her prim behavior. Her tidy habits and curt manners were a barrier, designed to keep people at a distance, but he'd seen the gentle way Diana had acted to her young charge. And though she'd tried, she'd not been fully able to conceal her reactions when the conversation had become personal. There was more to this woman than coldness and rules, and Alex wished circumstances were such that he could discover what secrets she protected.

Chapter 2

DIANA STOOD WITH THE OTHER women at the conclusion of the evening meal. She was relieved that supper had ended and the ladies could withdraw, leaving the men to their port and conversation. The two wives of the officers Sir Campbell had invited for supper accompanied her and Molly to the parlor belonging to the suite of rooms Molly's father had rented for the months they were visiting Corfu.

The room was small and cozy. Diana found the Greek furnishings comfortable and much more practical and sturdy-looking than those found in an English drawing room. Dark, solid wood chairs stood around the edges of the room, and the few upholstered pieces were covered in light beige fabric with brightly embroidered pillows giving a burst of color. No yards of patterned silk covered the plain walls. The plaster was a clean white decorated with an occasional colorful painting. A cool sea breeze stirred the sheer curtains that hung in front of the windows. Rich rugs lay over the stone-tiled floors, and the dark wooden beams showed on the walls and ceiling. Tidy and unassuming, Diana thought. Nothing extravagant or unnecessary—excepting perhaps their guests.

Diana studied Mrs. Wheaton and Mrs. Kerry as they took their seats. Both were young—much younger than their officer husbands—and their hairstyles, clothing, and jewelry were more costly than she'd have expected from a military man's salary and seemed extremely gaudy for a simple dinner party. She'd noticed throughout supper that, though the women claimed to be the very best of friends, their actions tended more toward competition, each attempting to best the other, no matter the topic. The evening could not end speedily enough to suit Diana.

The women perched next to each other on a settee, facing Molly on the sofa. Between them, instead of a low table, stood a large wooden chest holding a pot of red flowers.

Situating herself in a straight-backed chair, a bit away from the others, Diana found her polite smile and prepared for another conversation about fashion, soirees, and handsome suitors. Luckily, she was not expected to contribute much to the discussion because nobody would direct the conversation to her. She could simply nod or add an occasional thought.

A servant brought tea, and as soon as Molly had finished pouring out, Mrs. Wheaton accepted the offered cup and saucer. Leaning forward, brows raised and thin lips puckered, she said, "My dear Miss Campbell, now that just ladies are present, do tell us about Lieutenant Ashworth. If I am not mistaken, he danced with you twice at the Lord High Commissioner's ball."

Molly's face lit up, and Diana couldn't help but smile at the happiness she saw in the expression. "Oh yes. Isn't he the most agreeable gentleman? So thoughtful. And very handsome. He has asked to pay me a visit tomorrow morning." She tipped her head, and her eyes softened while she let out a sigh.

The women on the settee exchanged a look.

"I shouldn't be surprised if he were to make you an offer, my dear." Mrs. Kerry did not smile but raised her brows in a knowing manner, precisely as her friend had done a moment before.

Molly pressed her palm against her chest. "An offer? Do you really think so?"

"Why wouldn't he?" Mrs. Kerry glanced at her fingernails and regarded Molly as if she were the expert on all matters concerning matrimony. "You are pretty, young. He seems to have taken a liking to you."

"A royal marine. One could certainly do worse." Mrs. Wheaton set her cup into the saucer on her lap. "And so connected. His uncle is the Duke of Southampton, you know. And his father, Lord Vernon, is apparently quite wealthy in his own right."

Molly's cheeks grew red as the women talked, and her eyes brightened further. She twisted slightly in her seat to face Diana. "Miss Snow, do you think Lieutenant Ashworth truly thinks to propose marriage? And if he does, what then? Should I accept?"

Diana thought for a moment before she answered. "I cannot speculate as to the man's intentions. But as for you, I think you would be wise to know him better before making a decision of that magnitude. Learn more about what sort of person he is, then consider if he is the type of man you wish to marry."

A line grew between Molly's brows, and she nodded slowly as if thinking about what Diana said.

The other women, however, looked anything but thoughtful. Mrs. Kerry's nose wrinkled as though she'd smelled something foul, and Mrs. Wheaton blew out a puff of air.

Mrs. Kerry set her teacup and saucer onto the wooden chest with a clatter. "What kind of advice is that, I ask you? Did you not hear?" She turned toward Molly. "He is *wealthy, connected,* and in a position for *military advancement.*" She spoke slowly, drawing the words out, as if Molly may have a difficult time understanding.

Molly nodded. "Yes, but, I think Miss Snow is right. I do not know him well. I should—"

Mrs. Wheaton spoke right over her words. "Trust me, the less you know about a man before you marry him, the better. He is at his best behavior before vows are said. But not to worry. Once you are married, you will make friends with the other officers' wives and not have to give more than a few minutes of thought to your husband each day."

Diana could not believe what she was hearing. True, she'd not had any experience with courting or marriage herself, but the advice of these women seemed perfectly ludicrous. Molly deserved a person who respected her. She clenched her hands tightly in her lap.

Mrs. Kerry made a show of appraising Molly from head to foot. "Make sure you look your best tomorrow, and do not do or say anything that might make him think you are considering his character—or considering anything seriously at all for that matter—or he may turn his attention elsewhere. A man does not want to know his wife thinks too deeply."

Heat filled Diana's chest as she watched Molly soaking up the advice. She knew she could wait to speak to her young charge in private, but she did not want her silence to be taken as agreement. She turned her full attention to Molly, lest the other women see the annoyance on her face. "Miss Campbell, I hardly think Lieutenant Ashworth would fault you for considering either his nature or your own feelings before you enter into an arrangement as consequential as marriage. It shows a strength of character." The idea that Molly would think to "catch" a man because he was wealthy and pretend to be a brainless buffoon to do it made Diana ill. Though Molly was a bit silly and entirely too romantic for her own good, Diana cared for her, probably more than she ought, and it worried her that her charge would listen to these women and their horrible advice concerning a matter that would affect the remainder of her life.

Mrs. Kerry leaned to her friend and whispered something from the corner of her mouth. Both women turned toward Diana. Mrs. Kerry smiled, though her eyes were so cold that Diana thought the temperature in the room may have dropped. "Miss Snow, I do not believe I asked about your background. I believe I heard you are an instructor at Elliot School for Young Ladies in London?"

Diana nodded. "Yes, that is true."

"How nice. And how did you come by that position?"

An icy chill rose in Diana's stomach, but she did not flinch. "A church man from St. Luke, Chelsea, recommended me.

"A Christian charity orphanage?" Mrs. Kelly's eyes hardened further, and an ugly smile pulled her lips. "Oh. How fortunate that they would take you with your workhouse background." She shrugged her shoulders as if making pleasant conversation. "I'd thought Elliot School was a more reputable institution."

Mrs. Wheaton nodded. "You must be so grateful for the mercies shown to you in your . . . circumstance. And you must realize you are in no position to give advice to a *refined* young woman."

Diana held her feelings tightly, not permitting the turmoil inside to show on her face. After years of practice, she'd become an expert on not revealing her emotions. People thought her cold, and she'd even heard some of the students refer to her as "Stone Heart," but to let the feelings out was unbearable, and she'd pushed them deep inside for so long that she'd become an expert at maintaining her mask.

Mrs. Wheaton tapped her finger on the side of her chin. "I wonder, does Sir Campbell know the pedigree of his daughter's companion? Indigents do so tax society . . ."

Molly bounced in her chair, her hands clenched into a ball on her lap. "No, no. You are completely mistaken. Miss Snow is an elegant lady and very accomplished. She speaks French and German and is now learning Greek. Lady Stanhope herself considers her an expert in matters of etiquette, and she is quite respected in London Society."

"An oversight, I would think," Mrs. Kerry said under her breath, though it was certainly loud enough for the entire room to hear.

Molly stood, her arms trembling and tears in her eyes. "Madam, I'll not have you speaking of my companion in such a way. It is intolerable to—"

Diana rose and placed a hand on her arm. "Thank you, Molly, but there is no reason to be upset. Please do not allow me to spoil your evening. If you'll excuse me, I have a bit of a headache."

"There is no need to leave, Miss Snow. I—"

"Good night." Diana squeezed Molly's arm and smiled reassuringly.

"Miss Snow, please, do not . . ."

Diana shook her head as she walked to the door. Her heart pounded, and her muscles ached with the effort of maintaining her calm. "I am sure Mrs. Kerry and Mrs. Wheaton would love to hear about our visit to Venice."

Mrs. Wheaton clapped her hands together. "Oh, we certainly would. Venice is so lovely this time of year. Tell me, what did you think of the Piazza San Mar—?"

Diana closed the door behind her and leaned against it. The backs of her eyes stung, and her throat was tight. Drawing in a shaky breath, she raised her chin and pushed down her shoulders, forcing the emotion rising inside of her back into the depths where it belonged.

The two women were unhappy and petty, and she would not let their mean-spirited words affect her. And Molly . . . When Diana thought of the young lady's defense of her, a fresh wave of feeling surged up, but with a self-control developed over years of practice, she stifled it.

She heard men's voices. Before the gentlemen happened upon her in the hallway, she hurried to her bedchamber, closing another door behind her and not missing the symbolism in her action. Shutting out anything that could hurt her had always been her best method of protection.

In a moment her breathing had calmed, and she could think of the conversation objectively, without the painful tightness in her throat.

The women had been right. Diana was not a lady, or anything close, no matter the gracefulness of her deportment, the perfect spacing of her embroidery stitches, or the number of languages she spoke. A child who taught herself to read and spent every moment devouring the books in the kind Reverend Delaney's library did not have much hope of enduring the physical rigors of an orphan's workhouse. Few alternatives for a woman in her position existed, and she could imagine surviving none of them. Diana truly believed Lady Stanhope had saved her life by offering her a position at the finishing school.

She stepped across the room and opened the curtains, carefully sliding the sheer fabric along the rods to leave the same amount of space between the folds. The evenness of the arrangement helped calm her. As there were few things in her life over which she had power, she took immense care to make them impeccable. Having the ability to manage her emotions and her surroundings gave her some semblance of control.

She lined up the shoes in her closet, moved a few gowns along the hanging rod into a more satisfactory pattern and felt relieved when everything was in order. She turned back toward the room, and her eyes fell on the nightstand, specifically on the pair of men's gloves that looked so out of place in the room. A tremor fluttered in her middle.

She sat on the bed, turning the gloves over in her hands. It had been so unlike her to take them. Of course, when she realized they had been left behind, she'd thought to hand them over. Perhaps the owner would return to the inn and inquire about them. But for some reason, once she picked them up, she'd not wanted to surrender them. The gloves were a link to an incident she could not quite understand, and turning them in would somehow mean the experience was over before she had time to fully contemplate why something as ordinary as a conversation with a stranger had felt so significant. And if she were to be honest with herself, she hoped to see him again, though she knew she would not. He had probably already left Corfu. But she liked the idea of having something tangible that had belonged to him.

She smoothed the gloves on her lap, tracing the stitching around the hollow thumb with her fingernail, thinking of the man to whom they belonged.

Alexandros Metaxas had worn scuffed boots, a poorly tied neck-cloth, and no hat. Not to mention, he'd forgotten his gloves. Such a disorganized person was so unlike her. But his manner had interested her. Why was he in Corfu for merely a few hours? Whence had he come? Why was he dressed as an Englishman? And even more confusing was the fact that he'd seemed interested in *her*. He'd held her gaze, asked questions—she'd even thought he'd been staring. Aside from the minister at the orphanage, no man had ever taken notice of her at all—especially not a handsome man with an accent.

Though she knew it was silly and romantic, she'd thought perhaps he'd enjoyed speaking with her. Had he truly been impressed with her study of language? Or was he simply acting polite? She thought of his dark hair, his tidy mustache. He had straight, white teeth, tanned skin, and coffee-colored eyes that studied his surroundings sharply. His gaze seemed very astute. She'd wondered what he'd seen when he looked at her. Had he known she'd admired his appearance? The fluttering she'd felt earlier returned.

The exchange had left Diana so flustered that anything she would have liked to say had flown from her head. She wished she could have chattered or teased like Molly to dispel the fluttering in her stomach. But she had the feeling Alexandros would have seen right through any attempts at falsehood. When he'd turned his intense gaze on her, she'd felt flattered at his notice, and at the same time, horrified that he saw more—understood more—than she wanted to reveal.

She paced to the window, allowing the ocean breeze to cool her, embarrassed that her skin had been heated by her thoughts. Streetlamps cast pools of yellow light on the darkened cobblestones. The sound of the waves and the feel of the night air had become familiar to her as she'd strolled around the streets near the inn after dark. As Diana was not a gentlewoman, walking alone was one of her freedoms, and she found she enjoyed the small indulgence. She'd been assured by the hotel manager that, unlike London, Corfu was safe at night. "The British soldiers, they patrol the streets," he'd said, his eyes narrowing but he returned quickly to a smile as if he remembered to whom he was speaking. "You have only to worry about cats, miss."

She loved the wide open squares and fragrant flowers. And she smiled, with not a little envy, as she heard the sound of bouzouki music and Greek voices spilling out of tavernas well into the early hours of the morning. It was nearly impossible not to compare the booming laughter to the shallow conversation of the dinner party she'd just attended.

Diana leaned forward, closed her eyes, and let the whispering of the waves work its magic, lulling her into calm. She scolded herself for the ridiculous way she'd allowed her mind to meander. Alexandros Metaxas was certainly not interested in her.

A man educated abroad was obviously not without means—despite his lack of fashion sense. He must have simply intended to be courteous in his conversation. If he knew her true circumstance, she was certain he would not give her another look.

The officers' wives were right—though it was hurtful to admit. She was fortunate to be accepted on the edges of a society she was not a part of. Though she loved Molly, she was not Molly's friend. Diana was her chaperone, her father's employee. They didn't move in the same circles, nor would they ever, and she would do well to remember it.

"Do not forget your place, Diana," she said aloud, slapping the gloves against her hand. She left the room and walked down the corridor. The sound of the group in the drawing room was enough to hurry her on her way to do what she should have done in the first place—give the misplaced gloves to the hotel management in case Alexandros Metaxas came looking for them.

When she arrived downstairs, she saw nobody at the reception desk and turned toward the dining room, hoping to find assistance there. Though the doors to the outside patio were locked, the shutters were open and the curtains pulled aside to allow in the night air. At this hour, the streets were silent, and Diana could hear the waves from the sea that surrounded the city on three sides.

Finding no one in the restaurant, she decided to knock on the door of the hotel offices. She stopped, whipping her head around when someone walked on the street past the window. Not merely someone— Alexandros Metaxas. She was certain of it.

She hurried to the front door, pushing it open and rushing outside. Alexandros—there was no doubt about it—turned down an alleyway next to the hotel. Diana took a step but halted when she heard someone calling to her.

A man dressed in a doorman's livery was hurrying from the direction of the hotel offices. "Miss?" The sound of the door opening must have alerted him to his negligence. "Miss, shall I send for a carriage?" He spoke with a thick accent.

Diana looked back toward the corner of the building. "No, thank you. I only mean to step out for a bit of air."

"Surely you need a cloak. The sea air will chill you." He had obviously been trained to anticipate the needs of British patrons, and Diana realized how ridiculous she was acting, running outside with no bonnet, gloves, or wrap.

She glanced back toward the place she'd seen Alexandros disappear. Curiosity burned inside her. What business did he have at this hour? If she returned to her bedchamber and came back properly dressed, she would lose the chance to catch him.

When she returned her gaze to the man, who stood patiently holding open the door, she realized she was standing in the street in the middle of the night, improperly attired, carrying a man's gloves, and staring out at the darkness. What had gotten into her?

"Yes, of course." She nearly rolled her eyes at her foolishness and took a step back toward the building. "I'm sorry—"

At the sound of voices from inside, the man looked over his shoulder. The officers and their wives were leaving the dinner party and headed right toward them.

Diana's chest tightened. "Excuse me," she said, and instead of stepping through the open door, she ducked her head and rushed away. Mrs. Kerry and Mrs. Wheaton were the last people she wished to meet, especially caught in such an improper circumstance. She darted to the corner of the building and turned down the dark alleyway. Now that she was here, she realized finding Alexandros would be impossible. The scant moonlight barely lit the narrow lane. She crouched down behind a potted tree, grateful for the dark shadows that concealed her. She could not imagine what would happen if she were discovered. Once the party departed, she would return to the hotel, turn over the gloves to the doorman, and put all of this nonsense behind her.

She watched from her uncomfortable crouching position as the carriage arrived and the two couples climbed inside.

Once the sound of hooves and the rattle of wheels on cobblestones receded and Diana could hear the whisper of the waves again, she rose, brushing off her skirts. "That is quite enough adventure for one lifetime," she muttered. She stepped around the large pot, but the sound of a door closing echoed down the alleyway.

She crouched back in the shadows as footsteps approached. A man walked out of the blackness carrying a bulky pack on his shoulder. Though it was dark, she could see the outline of his loose clothing. He walked with quiet steps, and she got the distinct impression he did not wish to be seen.

Diana shrunk back. Her heart pounded, and she prayed the stranger would not notice her. What sort of man crept about the streets at night? He was obviously up to no good. Should she alert someone?

The man paused at the entrance to the alley and glanced in either direction before walking into the street and turning his steps away from the hotel.

Diana gasped when the moonlight shone on his face. Alexandros Metaxas!

Chapter 3

ALEX DARTED HIS EYES BACK and forth as he walked through the city's winding streets. His ears strained for any noise, most precisely that of soldiers' marching feet. The tall buildings cast strange shadows over the narrow streets, and more than once he'd been startled by a stray cat. He did not let down his guard, but the longer he walked, his confidence in the success of his mission grew.

Aside from the soldiers who had followed him from the waterfront, he'd not drawn a second glance the entire day. He'd harbored a bit of worry that he'd not find the man he was to meet. Not only had he not been told the man's name, Alex knew nothing about him. The Filiki Eteria operated under extreme secrecy—essential for a secret society—and members seldom knew the identities of more than a few others. Alex himself had met only three members besides his leader Xánthos and the intelligence man who had provided disguises and maps and information about the mission.

In spite of Alex's worry, the contact had met him precisely on time and informed Alex that all arrangements had been made. Everything was progressing according to plan. The Mavromichaleis awaited him.

A roll of nausea moved through his stomach, but he breathed deeply. The Mavromichalis clan was the very strongest of the Maniots. Their leader was also the *bey*—a local chieftan—Petros Mavromichalis. Petrobey was the man Alex had been sent to recruit to the cause. But even *meeting* with the man would be difficult. The last few beys had been tricked by the Turks into leaving their strongholds and were then executed. The Mavromichaleis would undoubtedly guard their patriarch carefully. Alex must not give them any reason to question his intent. He did not doubt for an instant that they would have no qualms about throwing his body into the sea if they believed the bey to be in danger.

An audience with Petrobey was not Alex's only worry. The Maniots were isolated, unpredictable, naturally suspicious of outsiders, fierce warriors, and, with few natural resources in their remote homeland on the southernmost tip of the Peloponnese, ruthless pirates. They had successfully managed to remain the one small region of Greece able to resist Ottoman rule. The well-guarded harbors and mountainous terrain deterred the Turks, so with little outside interference, the people of the Mani were left to govern themselves, which suited them perfectly.

At the sound of a rock skittering over the cobbled road, Alex whipped his head around, peering into the shadows, but he saw nothing. Likely another cat. He was getting jumpy. He said a quick prayer to St. Nikolaos and stepped off the road onto a dirt path that wound down a hill. Cicadas shrilled from the scrubby trees around him, and prickly bushes snagged at his trousers. He was soon walking in a sort of gorge between two mounds of earth. He shifted the bundle he carried when it no longer fit through the narrow space, making sure to place his feet carefully on the loose gravel. As he continued down the steep hill, the sound of waves grew louder.

The path emerged between two large rocks into a small cove. In the moonlight, a ship bobbed in the harbor nearly hidden by the cliff's shadows.

The face of the rock split off, and Alex realized the dark shadow was in fact a man walking toward him. Behind the man, a flick of light grew into a flame, and a companion bearing a torch followed closely.

Alex remained still, knowing that any wrong move could be taken as a threat. He studied their silhouettes. One was tall with broad shoulders, the other smaller and softer around the waistline. But both carried themselves—and the short-bladed Turkish yataghans in their hands—in a self-assured way that let Alex know neither would permit him to leave alive if they sensed a threat.

The torchlight was behind the first man, keeping his face shadowed, but the flickers of the flame revealed the shorter man's features—round cheeks and a thick mustache that lifted in a sneer.

The tall man spoke, "You are the Phanariot."

Alex was surprised at the term. He and the other Greeks in Constantinople had often been referred to in this way, but he'd not expected the Maniot to use it. Perhaps the secluded people were not as ignorant of the larger world as he assumed. "*Naí.* Yes. My name is Alexandros Metaxas."

The man grunted. "Constandinos Mavromichalis."

He held out his hand, but when Alex took it, Constandinos spun him around, twisting his arm behind his back and holding it so tightly Alex was certain he'd hear the pop of his shoulder any moment.

Alex did not offer any resistance, though his natural reflex was to fight back. He could sense that a struggle was exactly what they hoped for. These men seemed to be itching for a confrontation.

The other man thrust the base of the torch into the pebbly beach to hold it in place. He patted his free hand up and down Alex's torso, discovering and removing the pistol from the sash at his waist and then poking his fingers into the tops of Alex's boots. Once they were assured he concealed no other weapons, his arm was released.

Sliding his saber back into the sheath at his waist, the shorter man loosened the fastenings of Alex's parcel, opening it and lifting out the rifles carefully packed within. He hefted one, testing its weight and sighting down the barrel.

Alex took a step back, rolling his shoulder and massaging the ache. "Satisfied?" he asked.

Constandinos nodded. He moved around to face Alex. His face was hard and proud with a strong nose and heavy mustache that stretched over his cheeks to join the hair above his ears. His eyes were intelligent and expressive. Alex didn't think it would take more than a small change for them to become either fiercely cruel or extremely kind. Alex knew immediately that Constandinos was the man to impress. He was a natural leader, and his stance indicated a seasoned fighter. The air around the man seemed alive with energy. Xánthos had been correct. The Maniot warriors were just the kind of men the Filiki Eteria needed.

Constandinos flicked the tip of his weapon toward the other man. "Themis, my cousin." He did not re-sheathe his yataghan but held it at his side. "You are alone?"

"As you see. Only the messenger knows I am here."

Themis continued to remove firearms from the parcel and dig through a sack of ammunition.

Constandinos held Alex's gaze. "A strange request the messenger brought, Alexandros Metaxas. Why do you wish to visit the Mani?"

Alex knew his answer would decide his fate. He'd been recruited for this mission for the very reason that he could read people, understand what they kept hidden by the movement of their bodies and their subtle expressions. The skill had been developed and refined for years, and now he realized just how valuable it was. Constandinos would know in an instant if he were lying, and Alex knew the truth was the only option if he wanted to leave this beach alive.

"As you can see, I have access to merchandise that would be beneficial to your family and your people."

"Why do you bring us weapons?"

Alex drew his brows together. This man was smart. Testing Alex by asking questions he already knew the answers to. "Why do you think?"

Constandinos scratched his neck. "We do not share the same enemy as the rest of Greece. The Turks do not rule the Mani."

"But for how long?" Alex asked. "Do you think they will leave you alone forever? They already have a toehold in Laconia. The Outer Mani is plagued by the sultan's armies, and soon they will not be satisfied. Even now, the Turks feed the feuds, hoping to weaken the Maniots as you kill off your own warriors."

Themis snorted. "The Turks cannot manipulate us."

"Silence, Themis." Constandinos's voice was barely heard over the flow of the water, but it carried a strength that sent a sliver of fear into Alex's heart. "Alexandros Metaxas, why do you want to go to the Mani?"

Alex's heart pounded. "I would like to meet with Petrobey." He managed to push the words out through his dry mouth. He froze, waiting for the reaction that would determine whether he was run through with the Turkish blade.

At the sound of his leader's name, Constandinos's eyes widened ever so slightly. He stood still, his gaze on Alex. Finally, he lifted his chin. "Can we trust you?"

Alex felt a wave of relief that nearly made his knees weak but kept his face impassive. "I have told no falsehood."

At the sound of loose gravel sliding, the three men turned their heads.

Themis darted toward the source of the noise with a speed that Alex would not have expected from the thickset man. He reached behind a boulder and seized what appeared to be a woman. Pulling her to her feet, he dragged her toward them and thrust her to her knees in the circle of light.

Alex's gut compressed. *Diana Snow!* What on earth was she doing here?

Diana gasped as her knees hit the rocky ground. Her fair skin had lost any bit of color, but she did not weep or struggle. She held her chin up, her eyes moving between the men. "Unhand me at once, sir," she said, and though she tried to conceal it, Alex heard a quiver in her voice. "Mr. Metaxas—"

A shove from Themis stopped her words.

Alex fought to keep his breathing steady and his face from betraying any sign of recognition. If only she would remain silent. Their lives depended on it.

"Who is this? Your spy?" Spittle flew from Themis's mouth as he pulled his saber from its sheath.

Alex felt Constandinos's gaze on him. A moment earlier, he'd been certain the man would see through any untruth, but now, Alex knew both his and Diana's lives depended on his ability to deceive.

Alex curled his lip. "A woman?" He scoffed. "Surely I have better judgment than to trust a woman as my spy."

"Who is she?" Constandinos's voice was low, but Alex did not miss the threat contained in the tone.

Alex lifted a shoulder and drew down the corners of his lips. "I have never seen her before." He did not know how much of the conversation Diana understood and did not dare look too closely to try to gauge. He prayed she would remain silent.

Themis stepped closer to Alex until his face was merely a few inches away. "She said your name."

Alex sighed and with effort maintained his casual posture, though his pulse pounded through his ears. He waved his hand, as if exasperated. "She must have heard me introducing myself to you." He moved his gaze over her in an unconcerned manner. Though the night was cool, beads of sweat stood out on Diana's forehead. She appeared tensed, as if holding her emotions tightly, but he saw her lips tremble. Her gray eyes were wide and pleading.

Alex's chest was tight. He turned away, shaking his head. "She appears to be *British*." He smirked. "Probably does not understand a word we say."

Themis tapped the tip of his saber beneath Diana's chin. "Then if she is no friend of yours, it would not upset you if I were to *dispose* of her."

Diana's breath sped up, and she closed her eyes.

Alex's chest seized, and he fought to keep his stance relaxed, even though every impulse screamed to jump to her defense. He wished she understood. *I do this to save both of us.* He wrinkled his nose as if the thought of murder was merely bothersome. "I could not care less. However, you should ensure that you do not leave any evidence on the beach."

"He is right," Constandinos said. "A dead woman would be cause for an investigation. We do not want anyone paying close attention to this harbor, and I'll not chance the anger of the British navy."

Cool relief slacked Alex's muscles. He darted a glance toward Diana. She still looked terrified, but her gaze was fixed on him and anger had joined her expression. The betrayal in her eyes pierced him. He hoped for an opportunity to explain his actions.

"Should we sell her to the Venetians?" Themis slid the sword back into its scabbard.

Now that her life was no longer in peril, Alex's thoughts returned to his mission. He could not allow Diana to go free, not knowing their names. "She has seen us together, seen the weapons, and cannot be allowed a chance to tell the tale, either in Italy, or here among her people." He tapped his finger on his lip. "Perhaps she is most valuable as a hostage. She surely has friends or relations who would pay for her safe release. By the time she is returned, our deal will be complete, we will have gone our separate ways, and there will be no risk of interference." He raised a brow. "And if you tell the story right, you will be heroes for rescuing her."

"Take her to the Mani?" Constandinos pursed his lips and squinted. He remained silent for a moment before nodding once. "Yes, this is the best course. Petrobey will know what is to be done with her." He left Alex's side and strode to Diana, reaching out a hand and lifting her to her feet. "Do you speak Greek? What is your name?" Diana clasped her hands together. "I speak a bit. My name is Miss Snow."

"You will come with us, *Missno*." He said the name slowly, as if the sounds felt strange in his mouth. "And you will not make any trouble. Do you understand?"

Diana nodded. She followed Constandinos toward the small boat that would take them to his ship. She held her skirts, taking unsteady steps on the rocky beach. Alex wondered if her knees were bruised from the rough treatment.

Themis indicated for Alex to follow, then lifted the parcel of weapons onto his shoulder and pulled the torch from the ground.

As the firelight moved over the beach, something white caught Alex's eyes. He squinted and moved closer until he recognized his white gloves. His throat thickened as Diana's reason for following him became clear. *Surely she did not follow me all this way to return my gloves.*

Her expression of fear and betrayal had been painful to watch, but there had been something more—a courage and determination had shone through in the slight tightening of the skin around her eyes and way she'd held her chin high. He felt a surge of admiration. She'd been taken prisoner by pirates and did not plead or weep. She managed to speak firmly and somehow kept herself from falling to pieces. There was more to her than met the eye, and perhaps a journey to the Mani would reveal to Alex exactly what sort of woman Miss Diana Snow was. And he had to admit, the idea of getting to know her better did not bother him a bit.

Chapter 4

DIANA HEARD A NOISE IN the passageway outside her quarters in the ship's hull and glanced up. But the door didn't open. She felt relief that Themis, the stout pirate, had not returned, and if she were honest, she also felt a bit of disappointment. The small room where she was confined was extremely dull. The only furnishings were a narrow bunk that was little more than a shelf protruding from the wall and a crate that she figured was to be used as either a table or a chair. The sailors had provided her with a blanket that she folded and refolded until it was perfectly wrinkle-free, then stowed beneath the bunk. While she supposed the gesture was to ensure her comfort, the square of wool was old, full of holes, and extremely pungent. She didn't need a blanket anyway in the heat of the stuffy closet.

The terror that had spiked through her at being taken prisoner and remained pulsing in the nerves just below her skin had long since mellowed. She'd spent the first two days aboard the ship with her mind in a whirl: startling at every sound, thinking of plans to escape, wondering if she could get a message to Sir Campbell, and pondering on her fate. Moments of despair had almost broken down her defenses, but she'd held tightly to her emotions and not given them any slack. Doing so had, at times, taken every bit of her self-control, but she did not permit herself to weep or panic. And she especially did not allow any of the men to know how frightened she was. Now that days had passed, she felt nothing but sheer boredom. The pirates were by no means friendly, rather indifferent to her presence. But if they intended to harm her, she thought they would have done so by now.

The most difficult moment had been on the beach when she'd realized Alexandros Metaxas was not going to help her. She'd not fully comprehended the men's conversation, but she'd understood immediately that he was on *their* side. He denied even knowing her and did not spare her another glance while they casually discussed her fate as though they were deciding whether they'd prefer to play cards or billiards. His betrayal and subsequent failure to even glance her way stung so strongly she'd felt tears push against her eyes. It had taken an immense amount of discipline to force the emotion down and keep her chin up.

Her stomach rolled over. What had come over her outside the inn? Why on earth had she behaved so rashly, following a stranger through the dark streets in the middle of the night? At first, it had seemed the proper thing to do—returning his gloves. But his path had been unfamiliar, and a few twists and turns took her away from the streets she recognized. She could not return to the inn, as she had lost her bearings. But the longer she followed Alexandros, the more ridiculous she felt about calling out to him. She'd finally decided once she discovered his destination, she'd certainly be able to ask someone for assistance or find soldiers to return her to the inn. At least that was her rationale at the time. She'd nearly convinced herself of the wisdom in her decision, but if she were to be honest—and sitting in a musty prison aboard a pirate ship was no place to sugarcoat the truth—she knew her actions had been the product of curiosity about him.

Though it made her stomach burn, she forced herself to think of it, made herself feel the cold twist of humiliation in her chest and heat of embarrassment over her skin to ensure she'd never behave so foolishly again.

She drew a jagged breath, remembering his sneer as she knelt on the hard rocks with a blade against her neck. Heat and cold had shaken her from the inside, and her mind had gone blank as inky fear stole her thoughts. Until that moment, she'd never known how truly vulnerable a person could feel—or how wounded. And the reason his disdain had hurt so badly was that she'd fooled herself into believing there had been a connection between the two of them, something unique that they'd shared in the short moments she and Alexandros had spoken.

But the truth was painfully obvious. Any feelings had been hers alone. Frustration tightened her fingers into fists. She knew better than to allow silly romantic nonsense to shape her actions. Diana's fate was decided nearly at the moment of her birth, and if she had only remembered her place in society, she would at this very moment be listening to Molly sigh over her handsome marine. But instead she was a prisoner of Mediterranean pirates, aboard a filthy ship, with no idea of her destination.

She planted her feet on the boards of the deck, wishing she could pace, but the room did not have space for more than two tiny steps in any direction. Even if the floor were larger, her bruised knees would not be pleased with the exertion. So she stood in the murky evening light that filtered between the boards of the bulkhead, shaking her head, wishing there was something to straighten or to tidy, absolutely disgusted that her life's path had been altered by a pair of men's gloves.

Diana brushed her hands over her skirts. In the heat, her gown had become damp with sweat. She longed to remove it when she slept, but the thought of one of those men coming in while she wore only her chemise was enough to banish that idea.

As it was evening, she expected the door to open at any moment. So far on the voyage, her only visitor to the tiny room had been Themis, and he only came twice a day to give her a plate of hard biscuits and salted fish, then escort her to the privy.

It was beyond dreadful that the highpoint of her day involved taking care of her personal business in a horrid little chamber with no roof, where the necessary consisted of a rough wooden bench with a hole through which she could see the blue ocean.

She thought of the sea voyage merely a few weeks earlier. She and Molly had considered their cabin upon the passenger ship to be a ridiculously diminutive size for two adults, but now Diana thought the space had been downright luxurious.

A noise sounded again, and the door opened to reveal Themis.

Out of habit, Diana took a step back. Though she had expected him, she still felt uncomfortable in such a small space with the man. "*Geia sas*." She spoke the greeting carefully, enunciating each syllable.

"*Sas*," Themis muttered as he set the wooden plate, spoon, and a mug of water on the crate. His heavily lidded eyes gave him the appearance of a person perpetually bored. Which he probably was, she thought. Delivering food and accompanying a woman as she tended to private matters could not be a very entertaining duty for a pirate. He held open the door and motioned with a jerk of his head for her to set off toward the upper deck.

Diana could not help but feel a bit offended at his brusque manner. She had not spoken to another person for days, and even though he was hardly a person she wanted to converse with at length, exchanging a few pleasantries would not be entirely unwelcome.

She centered the plate on the crate, moving the mug to a better position—with the handle facing outward and the wooden spoon lined up between—then walked past him, along the passageway and up the companionway stairs, clinging to the hand ropes.

The blast of crisp sea air that greeted her as she stepped onto the deck was fresh and cool. The sun was low on the starboard side, indicating a southern course. She'd rarely stepped outside without a bonnet and gloves since she was a small girl, and she felt strangely exposed. The warmth of the sun on her hair was a sensation she did not know if she'd ever get used to, and would she develop freckles on her cheeks?

A few men were engaged in various duties around the deck. She recognized Constandinos speaking to a man at the helm, but she was relieved that Alexandros was nowhere to be seen. Diana breathed a deep breath of fresh air as she followed the usual path toward the bow of the deck, savoring the salty smell of the sea since she'd soon return to the stale air of her quarters. A shabby screen made from worn boards gave a small amount of concealment to anyone using the privy.

She completed her business quickly, but when she returned, Themis was not waiting in his regular position. She spotted him speaking with Constandinos and a few other men, and she decided she would enjoy the moment of freedom. She walked to the bulkhead and leaned her arms on the rail.

The sea was a deep turquoise. Varying depths of ocean floor gave a dappled blue effect with new shades of color everywhere she looked. On the voyage from England, she'd often thought it would be impossible to tire of the changing sight of the Mediterranean waters. The sea seemed to have a life of its own.

The setting sun made yellow and pink glimmers on the tips of the rolling waves. The breeze left salty moisture on her skin. Diana closed her eyes and listened to the whisper of the surf and, for just a moment, almost forgot her circumstance didn't particularly lend itself to appreciating the beauty around her.

The sound of a clearing throat pulled her back to the present. Themis tipped his head toward the companionway, and Diana's shoulders sagged as she blew out a breath.

He didn't seem at all apologetic at her disappointment at having to return below.

She glanced around the deck once more, and her stomach lurched when she saw Alexandros leaning against the far rail. His gaze locked on hers, then moved on as if he were simply looking about, watching the activity on the deck.

Anger rushed up her neck and flooded her cheeks. Even the rudest pirate nodded his head when their paths crossed. Alexandros Metaxas did not show the most meager bit of courtesy. How could she have ever thought him interesting—or handsome? Arrogance surrounded him like an odorous cloud. The man was a liar, involved with illegal activities, consorting with pirates, and he was surely an absolute scoundrel. Diana wished he would turn back toward her so she could fix him with the glare he deserved, but he appeared to be inspecting his fingernails.

The angry flames grew inside her as Themis closed the door to her chamber, leaving her in near darkness with her supper. She blew out a very unladylike breath through her nose, rather like a charging bull at a matador fight, she thought, though she had never actually seen such a thing. An hour later, as she squirmed around on the wooden bunk and tried to make a pillow out of her arm, she drifted into a fitful sleep where she dreamed of Alexandros waving a red cape while she glowered at him with fire in her eyes.

❦

Diana woke to the sounds of activity on the deck above. She could tell by the noise of rushing feet and voices calling out that something had changed. Had they reached their destination? Where were they? She peered through the cracks between the bulkhead boards but saw only blue sky. The creaks and bumps of heavy items being moved around above her led her to assume cargo was being unloaded. The fear that had been eased by boredom and a predictable routine returned full force, and

Diana's chest felt tight as she wondered what her fate would be. It was no secret that the slave trade was alive and well in the Mediterranean. Turks, Venetians, Greeks, North Africans—all captured and traded human cargo with little regard. She hoped her small understanding of Greek and the fact that she was British would work in her favor. She smoothed back her hair and wished for a hairbrush. What sort of impression would she make in an evening gown she'd sweated and slept in for three days?

The hours moved past, and her anxiety grew when Themis did not fetch her. Had she been forgotten? Her stomach made a noise, and her mouth felt sticky and dry.

Just as she started to fantasize about the taste of salted fish and dried biscuits, the door opened.

Themis's face was more animated than she'd seen before. He spoke rapidly, motioning toward the passageway with a sweep of his hand.

Diana tried to concentrate on his words. "I'm sorry. I do not understand."

He gave an impatient snort, pointed at her then the passageway, speaking another stream of foreign sounds.

Diana could not believe he spoke the same language she had been studying for the past months. Whether it was his muffled way of speaking or his accent or the speed at which he spoke, she did not know. The only word she understood was "Petrobey," the same name Alexandros and Constandinos had spoken.

"Petrobey? Is that who I am to speak with?"

Themis's expression looked as though Diana's confusion made his life that much more difficult to endure. He spoke again, then reached for her arm with his meaty hand. But she twisted, pulling it away.

"I am quite capable, sir." She walked past him with quick steps, hoping he would not try to grab her again.

When she reached the main deck, she saw that her supposition had been correct. The ship was docked in a small harbor with rocky hills all around. A village of rectangular stone houses with small windows and towers clustered at the water's edge. Men were hard at work carrying crates and barrels from the hull down the gangway and stacking them on the dock. She saw Alexandros and a gathering of men inspecting firearms, but he did not notice her.

A group stood on the deck, supervising the unloading of the ship's cargo. Constandinos was speaking to an older man she hadn't seen before. She estimated the man to be near fifty. His clothing was clean, and she decided he must have just come aboard. He wore a black vest embellished with colorful embroidery over a loose shirt and wide-legged trousers. A red hat that looked like a Turkish fez sat atop his graying hair. He had a long, stiff moustache that stretched out to the sides and drooped down at the ends. Fists on his hips, he scrutinized the proceedings around him with a shrewd eye. As his gaze wandered, watching men unload the cargo from the ship's hull, he nodded, occasionally saying something to Constandinos.

Diana could see a resemblance between the two. They were certainly related—perhaps father and son? Where she'd thought Constandinos carried himself with an air of command, his manner was nothing to the man standing next to him. Absolute authority exuded from every movement and expression. She was certain he must be the owner of the ship, if not the town. Perhaps he was the governor. Though his gaze appeared cunning and intelligent, he did not look unkind.

When Themis led her closer, both men turned their attention to Diana. Constandinos stopped speaking as the older man studied her.

"*Anglicá?*" he asked, lifting his chin in her direction. Is she English?

"*Naí.*" Constandinos nodded.

The older man took a step toward her and bowed, then placed a hand on his chest. "Petrobey Mavromichalis."

Diana was surprised at his gallantry and, out of habit, curtseyed. "Diana Snow. Pleased to meet you."

Petrobey asked her a question that she did not understand.

"I am sorry. I only speak a bit of Greek. *Lígo.*" She held up her finger and thumb, slightly apart to illustrate. "Perhaps if you spoke slower. *Vradýs.*"

He spoke to Constandinos, who shook his head.

Themis said something, then walked toward the group with the firearms. He returned with Alexandros.

"*Milás angliká?*" Do you speak English? Petrobey asked Alexandros.

"*Naí.*" Alexandros replied with a nod.

Neither of the younger men looked at Diana, but Petrobey continued to watch her. She felt as if he were studying her through a quizzing glass. He spoke to Alexandros but kept his gaze on Diana.

She twisted her fingers together, counting the boards of the deck in an attempt to calm herself.

"Petrobey asks if you have been treated well," Alexandros said.

"Yes. I mean *naí.*" She spoke directly to Petrobey, doing her best to ignore his traitorous translator.

Petrobey nodded once. He spoke again to Alexandros.

"He asks if you can write."

"Of course I can write." Diana shot a furious glare toward Alexandros, but he was not looking at her.

Petrobey continued to speak, but his words were directed to the other men. Themis left them and walked down the gangway toward the town. Constandinos answered once. Alexandros simply listened.

Diana kept her face turned firmly away from him. Though she did notice from the corner of her eye that he did not once glance in her direction. *What a horrible man. If only someone else spoke English, or I had studied Greek more thoroughly, he would not be involved in my affairs.*

After a moment, Petrobey stopped talking and turned toward Alexandros as if he were waiting.

Alexandros spoke to Diana. "You are to write a letter which will be taken by the next ship and delivered to a British settlement. Tell your people you have been treated well and that you are under the care of Petrobey Mavromichalis in Limeni, who will return you unharmed when a British ship arrives."

Diana's heart pounded. Write a letter? Would anyone come for her? She didn't think Sir Campbell would be bothered to set sail to rescue a finishing school instructor. She was no one of consequence, an orphan. Not a lady whose capture would be of sufficient concern to launch a military ship. And what did it mean to be under the care of Petrobey Mavromichalis?

When she didn't answer, Alexandros cleared his throat, and though his expression did not change, the tone of his voice lowered and increased in intensity. "The Maniots are not known for bestowing favors. You should acknowledge his kindness."

She certainly did not need an etiquette lesson from Alexandros. "Thank you, Mr. Mavromichalis. *Efcharistó.*"

Petrobey's mustache lifted a bit. "*Parakaló.*" He nodded with a blink of his eyes.

Rushed footsteps hurried up the gangplank as a young woman ran toward them followed by Themis. Petrobey's entire countenance changed. His eyes softened, and the small lift of his mustache Diana had seen earlier grew into a smile. "Elena." He held out his arm toward her, then turned her by the shoulders toward Diana, speaking in a gentle voice and motioning with a curl of his fingers for Alexandros to listen also.

Elena was about seventeen years old. Her hair and eye color were dark, and her skin was the warm golden color of one native to the Mediterranean. The young woman was absolutely beautiful. She nodded as she listened to Petrobey and looked at Diana with wide, curious eyes.

When Petrobey was finished speaking, Alexandros translated. "Petrobey's son Hektor is away at sea. His wife is in need of assistance with her home and family. You will go with her daughter Elena, first, to Petrobey's home to write your letter, then to Tsímova to assist the family."

"Tsímova?" Diana said.

"The main town in this region," Alexandros said.

"And I don't— What am I to do?" Even though she hated the ship with its cramped quarters, salty food, and ghastly privy, the thought of leaving it for the unknown made her breath come in short gasps that she fought to control.

A flash of concern moved through Alexandros's eyes. "You will be safe. I will make sure of it." His tone was low and soft.

Diana lowered her shoulders, frustrated and embarrassed that he'd seen her worry. Her panic was replaced by the anger that had been simmering since that night on the beach. "You are the last person I trust with my safety."

He drew his brows together and looked as though he would like to say something, but his lips tightened and he remained silent.

Just as well, she thought. She calmed her breathing and raised her chin. "Mr. Metaxas, please ask Mr. Mavromichalis if there is a library or somewhere I can borrow books. I should like to improve my knowledge of Greek." She cocked a brow, hoping he understood that an objectionable translator was further motivation for her request.

The corner of his mouth lifted the slightest bit before he spoke to Petrobey.

Petrobey opened his mouth to answer, but Elena burst in with a stream of words. She clenched her hands together in front of her chest as she talked.

The two conversed for a moment, and Petrobey pinched his lower lip, looking back and forth between his granddaughter and Diana. Finally he spoke to Alexandros.

"Petrobey said Father Yianni at the church has books. He teaches a few of the boys in the village, but Elena wishes to learn as well. He asks for you to teach her to read, and she will in turn help you to learn Greek."

A familiar calm feeling settled over Diana as she looked at Elena. Instructing young ladies, watching them feel pride in their learning and recognizing their own intelligence was the task that gave her the most joy. Planning lessons, organizing books and paper, and writing implements were what she knew best. And she loved it.

She'd studied enough to know the Greek alphabet and modern Greek phonetics. And with Elena to translate the words they read, each would benefit.

She lifted her gaze to Petrobey. "Yes. Thank you," she said in Greek.

Elena nodded her head and grinned. She kissed her grandfather's cheek and stepped closer to Diana. "My name is Elena," she said.

Diana was glad she at least spoke enough Greek to introduce herself. "Very nice to meet you, Elena. I am Miss Snow."

"Missno." She flapped her hand in a motion for Diana to accompany her.

Petrobey patted Elena's shoulder, and Diana followed her from the ship, stepping onto a rocky land where trepidation and hope fought inside her, making her fingers tingle.

Chapter 5

ALEX STUDIED THE PICTURE ON the wall of Petrobey's office. The lithograph nestled between religious ikons was one he'd seen before. Two men, who Alex knew to be the scholars and philosophers Adhamántos Koraís and Rígas Pheréotos, supported between them a beautiful young woman dressed in rags. The picture symbolized Greece being lifted up by forward-thinking, educated men—revolutionaries, like himself.

He smiled as he continued around the room, looking at the books on the shelf behind Petrobey's desk. Recently translated volumes by Voltaire, Montesquieu, and Rousseau stood next to a classical volume of Harmodius and Aristogeiton—ancient Greek heroes who overthrew the tyrant Hippias.

Alex could not have found better indicators that Petrobey was exactly ripe for the cause if he'd planted the items himself.

A fleeting thought entered his mind. Why had Petrobey not loaned *these* books to Diana? Perhaps because he was still studying them. Or was he afraid that word would get out about his reading habits? Such literature could be considered treachery. If that was the case, was Petrobey not worried about Alex seeing them? The idea did not bode well for Alex's future if he was not able to earn the bey's trust.

He strolled around the room, pausing to admire a gilded curved saber that hung on the outer stone wall, and a painting of a mountainous landscape. Red blossoms dotted the scrubby ground and cypress trees poked up like long spindles between well-ordered olive groves. His throat tightened, and he swallowed hard, surprised at the deep ache in his chest. This was Greece, his fatherland. Glancing back to the lithograph, he made a silent pledge to the young peasant girl that he would do all in his power to free her.

The door opened, and Alex cleared his throat, schooling his face to conceal his emotions. He remembered his duty, his mission, and the cause he was fighting for.

Petrobey entered and tipped forward his head in a bow. "British rifles. A gift such as this does not come without conditions."

Apparently the bey did not bother with small talk. "The condition was simply the opportunity to speak with you," Alex said.

"Then speak." He lowered himself into a carved wooden chair, clasping the armrests as if he sat on a throne. Somehow he managed to look relaxed and alert at the same time.

Over the last weeks, Alex had imagined various conversations with Petrobey, and had always assumed the discussion would progress gradually from pleasantries and introductions, ultimately arriving at his purpose. Not once had he thought he would be asked his business so bluntly, and he considered exactly how to go about explaining himself.

He said a prayer in his heart and began. "You are a student of French Enlightenment philosophy." He lifted his palm toward the books on the shelf. "And an admirer of Koraís and Pheréotos with their concepts of education and reform." Petrobey watched without changing his expression, so Alex plunged forward. "I too am a believer in freedom. Though it will be hard bought."

"I could have you killed for the mere insinuation." Petrobey's voice was low.

Alex kept his gaze steady. "I know."

Petrobey's brows arched. "You are not afraid? Why?"

"I believe you and I want the same thing." He crossed the room and pointed to the lithograph. "Freedom for the land we love."

Petrobey raised his chin and pursed his lips. "My son Dino tells me you are from Constantinople, but your accent sounds to me like you hail from perhaps Athens?"

"Nafplio." Alex did not let his surprise show at the sudden change of topic.

"And educated abroad?"

"Yes, mostly in Italy."

Petrobey pinched his lip. "Education—I believe education is key."

"You wrote a letter to Kapodhístrias expressing your interest in establishing a school in the Mani."

"You know Kapodhístrias?"

"Yes." Alex did not know if he would have much longer in the bey's presence, and the man had given him an ideal opening. "Kapodhístrias is a member of the group that sent me. This group—society—operates in secrecy with the ultimate goal of freedom from our Ottoman oppressors. Liberation for our fatherland." He felt a pinch inside his chest as he said the words. Whereas his statements before could have been argued to be off-handed observations, this was pure treason. "I have here a letter from Lycurgus the Logothete." Alex pulled the crumpled envelope from an inner pocket.

"Lycurgus also?" Petrobey's brows rose.

"He is one of us."

"And this group has sent you to me because . . ."

"Because we need you. We need the Maniots if we are to have any hope of success. I do not need to tell you that your people are the fiercest warriors and most brilliant strategists in all Greece."

The muscles around Petrobey's eyes tightened, and his cheeks lifted. He was pleased with Alex's compliment and knew it was the truth, not empty flattery.

Alex pushed ahead on the momentum of his words. "Isolated uprisings are quickly squelched, but a coordinated attack on multiple fronts will strengthen our hope of success." He raised a fist. "*Eleftheria i thanatos.*" Freedom or death.

Petrobey continued to scrutinize him.

Alex's impassioned speech left him breathing heavily. Did it have the desired effect? Surely Petrobey felt the same fervency for his fatherland as he did.

"The Maniots are free," Petrobey said with a shrug. "The Turks do not rule us.

"Or so they want you to believe." Frustration made Alex's hands shake. He wanted to throw something. How could Petrobey not see the truth? "What happened to the beys before you? What happened to your father, to your grandfather at the Orlov Revolt?"

Petrobey's eyes narrowed at the reminder of the defeat.

"The Turks leave the Maniots alone as it suits their purpose, but do not be fooled into believing they are above inciting clans into vendettas and blood feuds. Even as close as Outer Mani, there have been incidents of *devşirme*."

Petrobey cringed at the mention of the Turks' dreaded child collection—stealing young Christian boys to serve in the sultan's army and girls for his harem. The practice had taken place for centuries with the penalty of immediate death for anyone who protested or tried to prevent it.

Alex could see his words had hit close to the bey's heart. He imagined Petrobey was thinking about his granddaughter Elena. "We sought you because you have brokered peace between feuding clans. You are the man to unite the peoples of the Mani, to show the Turks the descendants of Sparta will not bow down to their oppression."

Petrobey pinched at his lip, staring at the patterned rug that stretched over the stone floor.

"A ship at Corfu, filled with weapons and supplies, awaits my word. You and I will speak to the kapetans of the klephts and leaders of the other clans. If they're willing, recruit them to the brotherhood." He leaned in close, speaking in nearly a whisper. "When the time is right, the Maniots will lead the Greeks to victory, and you will lead them as the commander in chief of the Spartan forces."

Petrobey glanced up, but he did not answer. He continued pinching his lip, his brows furrowed.

"Greece needs all of us." Alex pointed again to the defeated young woman in the lithograph, then turned to face Petrobey. "She needs *you*."

"I must speak to my family," Petrobey said at last.

⤛∼⤜

Hours had passed since Petrobey's dismissal. Alex had been treated well, shown to a room and fed, but even though he'd been shown nothing but hospitality, he knew he was not a guest. The door to his room was locked, and a man stood outside beneath the window.

He gazed at the rocky hills that rose above the city. Cicadas and other insects keened and chirped a symphony that was as familiar to him as if he had not left these very shores twenty years earlier. The whispers of the waves in the harbor were a perfect accompaniment to the sound. He breathed in, smelling the sea as well as spiced meat—*souvlaki*—being cooked on sticks somewhere in the village. If he closed his eyes, he could almost imagine himself a young boy of eight, sitting on the balcony of his parents' home in Nafplio. The only things missing were the smell of his father's pipe and his mother's voice humming softly while she stitched. He turned away from the window as an ache grew inside his chest and his eyes burned.

From within the house, he heard the muted sound of the *Gerondiki*—the family council's—voices. Sometimes rising as men spoke over one another, fighting to be heard, and sometimes quiet as they listened.

Alex paced over the stone floor. His muscles were tight with anticipation. What were the men saying? He thought Constandinos—Dino, as his father had called him—likely stood quietly in the room, listening first to Petrobey and then to the other men's discussions with hardly a word. If his father believed revolution to be the right thing, Dino would join. Alex had not been certain the man trusted his intentions, but he seemed to be a person of honor.

Themis, he assumed, would follow what his cousin recommended, but Alex thought once his mind was decided, Themis would not waver. Though he seemed to be easily angered and slow to trust, Themis was a loyal man and, Alex had observed from their few interactions, a skilled warrior.

The other men in the family could be saying anything at all. No doubt, from the cadence of their voices, some were displeased with the idea while others tried to convince them. He wished he could have the chance to speak to all of them, assure them that, though the risk was great, it would be worth it in the end when their beloved fatherland was freed.

He did not think the Mavromichalis family would allow him to leave if his proposal was rejected. And he did not think they were the sort of people to care for a prisoner. If his words had not managed to convince Petrobey, Alex was confident that he would be killed.

For an instant he felt a pang of regret, and when he focused on the cause, Diana Snow came to mind. He had hoped for a chance to explain himself, to apologize for the way he'd treated her and tell her why his callousness had been necessary for both their sakes. He was grateful Petrobey had shown her compassion, though he most likely did so out of hopes to ingratiate himself with the British after being Napoleon's ally. Thinking of Diana's and Elena's heads bent over books in the church brought a smile to his face. She would be valuable here as a teacher. He'd hoped—

The door opened, breaking off his thoughts.

A young man Alex had not seen before stood in the doorway. "Come."

He followed his escort through the hallways, past closed doors and finally into Petrobey's chamber.

He estimated nearly twenty men stood in the room; their ages varied from elderly to barely older than a boy. Each watched him somberly. The men moved aside, making a path to Petrobey.

Alex's skin stung, and his lungs could not draw a full breath as he awaited their verdict.

Petrobey rose from his chair and walked to Alex. His expression was grave. He clasped Alex's hand and laid the other on his shoulder, holding Alex's gaze solemnly. "For *patrídha*." For our fatherland.

The men of the Mavromichalis clan raised their voices in a cheer.

Alex's heart pounded, even as relief flowed over him. He clasped a hand on Petrobey's shoulder. "*Eleftheria i thanatos.*" Freedom or death. He spoke the Greek motto with pride, his voice catching in his throat.

Petrobey shook his head. "I told you, Maniots are already free. *Niki i thanatos.*"

The other men repeated the words.

Victory or death.

Chapter 6

DIANA WOKE TO THE SOUND of children's voices. Glancing at the window, she could not see any light between the slats of the wooden shutters. The day began early, she realized just as a candle flared to life on the wooden table.

Elena had already begun to dress.

Diana rose from her cot in the small room they shared, shivering in the cool of the autumn morning. She felt nervous at the new surroundings and the unfamiliar noises of the house. What would be expected of her in this place? Would she be a servant here? The family had not been unkind to her, but she was obviously expected to earn her keep.

As soon as she'd arrived the day before, Diana realized why Petrobey had considered his daughter-in-law to be in need of assistance while her husband was away. Sophia Mavromichalis's stomach was swollen, and she walked with rocking steps, wincing as she stood and breathing heavily at any exertion. Elena had only been in the house for a few moments before insisting that her mother sit down and helped raise up her swollen feet to rest on a cushion.

Although Diana's exposure to women in a family way was nearly nonexistent at the orphanage and the finishing school, she thought Sophia's stomach was exceptionally large. Perhaps she carried twins.

The candlelight illuminated an elaborate golden cross on the blocks of the stone wall. The sight was so unfamiliar compared to the simple Anglican crosses she was accustomed to, but somehow, seeing it there gave Diana comfort.

She studied the clothing Sophia had provided for her since her dinner gown was filthy and, of course, unsuitable for working on a farm. First, she pulled on a white underdress, admiring the embroidery that decorated the collar and the cuffs of the sleeves. Then, long woolen socks. Over the white underdress, she wore a pleated dark skirt and a long burgundy vest that fit like a tunic, with a strip of blue fabric tied around her waist. The clothing was bulky, but she was grateful for the extra warmth.

She straightened the blanket on the cot, lining up the seams with the edges of the thin mattress and spread her hands over it, smoothing out any wrinkles, then followed Elena down the stairs. Warm air filled the stairway along with the comforting smell of baking bread as they entered into the main area of the house.

Like the other structures in Tsímova, the house was built of stone. Diana had thought the shape appeared like a creation a child would make with building blocks. One section was four stories tall—a tower. Next to the tower was another section with two levels. The bedrooms were on the second floor above the main living area. And finally, the last area, behind the house, was only one level. The door to this section was low with stairs leading down to it from the kitchen. Though she hadn't been inside, Diana assumed it was for storing food. Stone stairs ran up the outside of the building and onto the flat roof, giving the home the feeling of a small castle.

In the kitchen area, Diana saw Elena's three youngest brothers had already dressed and now sat at the table, talking with sleepy voices.

Sophia smiled when the other women entered, and she pushed a long wooden paddle into the open-brick oven to remove a round loaf of bread. Diana was struck by the woman's beauty. She was a young mother, in her midthirties, Diana thought. She shared Elena's thick hair, high cheekbones, and full lips, but her characteristics were more pronounced than her daughter's. In a few years, Diana thought Elena's round cheeks and soft features would look just like her mother's.

Elena spoke to her, and even though Diana recognized only a few of the words, she knew the daughter was scolding Sophia for not waking her earlier. She took the paddle from her mother's hands and motioned toward the sofa near the table.

Sophia's lips spread in a grateful smile as she crossed the room to sit. A string of stone beads hung from her waist and clicked together as she walked.

Another son, the oldest of the boys, entered the house with a bucket of fresh milk. Georgi, Diana remembered from the day before.

Diana and Elena sliced the bread and covered it with honey, then poured the warm milk into wooden cups. Elena sat at the table with her brothers, scolding them and rolling her eyes at the things they said. She motioned for Diana to join them.

Diana ate her warm bread and honey and drank the milk. The flavor was strange and the consistency thicker than any she'd had before. She'd seen goats outside the house and wondered if she were drinking their milk.

The family talked together, the boys teasing and laughing. As she watched them, she couldn't help but smile. She glanced at Sophia and saw her wince as she shifted her position on the wooden sofa. She lifted the string of beads and worked them through her fingers as she laid back and closed her eyes.

While the children ate, Diana slid a low table across the floor, close to where Sophia reclined, then brought over a plate of breakfast.

"*Efcharistó.*" Sophia's eyes closed for a moment as she took a deep breath.

"You must rest today. Elena and I will manage everything."

Sophia opened her eyes, drawing her brows together. Her expression clearly showed that she did not understand, and Diana searched through the brief list of Greek vocabulary in her mind, finally coming up with the words: *sleep*, she turned over her palms, making a motion as if pressing downward; *us*, then motioned between herself and Elena; *finish*, then finally swept her arm around the room.

Understanding dawned in Sophia's eyes, and she moved as if she would rise.

Diana repeated her pantomime, glancing behind when she heard children's voices repeating the words, "*sleep, us, finish,*" and mimicking her motions. They all performed the routine with laughter, embellishing with their own flourishes. But instead of mocking, she saw sincerity in their faces, a concern for their mother that made her heart warm.

After the chanting had repeated a few more times, Sophia threw her hands into the air and tipped her head back, laughing as she looked to the ceiling, clearly surrendering.

The boys cheered, and Elena ran up the stairs, returning with an armload of pillows. Sophia kissed each of her boys on the forehead before they bid her farewell and left the house.

Diana wondered what type of work young boys did. The oldest, Georgi, was tall, but she did not think he was above thirteen or fourteen years. She guessed the youngest was perhaps four. All had similar coloring—golden skin and chocolate-brown eyes. She would have to work hard to distinguish between the younger boys and learn their names.

Sophia leaned forward while her daughter slid pillows behind her and then settled back into the sofa. She motioned toward a chest on the other side of the room, speaking too quickly for Diana to understand.

Elena lifted a sky-colored dress from the chest and brought it, with a basket of thread and needles, to her mother.

Diana looked closely at the gown and saw that Sophia was embroidering a colorful design onto the hem and sleeves of the cotton damask fabric. "Beautiful," she said.

Elena smiled. She pointed to the dress and then to herself, sweeping her hands down and out as if she wore the full skirt.

Diana did not understand the words she said but knew from her actions and the way her eyes sparkled that this must be part of her trousseau. Her wedding gown. "It is so lovely, Elena."

"Lovely," Elena repeated.

Diana nodded. She lifted the skirt. "This *dress*"—she released the fabric, clutched her own dress, and then motioned toward Elena's—"is *lovely*." Clasping her hands in front of her chest, she let out an appreciative sigh as she said the last word.

Elena nodded. She imitated the motions, indicating the dress. "*To fórema*," then clasped her hands, "*eínai ómorfo*."

Diana repeated the sentence, and Elena grinned.

She smiled at the girl. A clever young lady who was thoughtful to her mother and kind to her younger brothers would be a delight to spend time with. Many at the finishing school were spoiled and selfish. She'd observed the happy mood this girl brought to those around her. Yes, she liked Elena very much. For just a moment she was reminded of Molly, and a pang tugged at her heart. She missed her friend.

Diana pushed down the sentiment and cleared off the breakfast dishes, smiling as she thought of the children joking with one another as they ate. She'd not shared a meal with children since she was one herself, and thinking of mealtimes at the orphanage made her shudder. Her memories of that place were always accompanied with feelings of hunger and cold. A small, skinny child was a victim, and she'd learned to push food into her mouth as quickly as she could, knowing it would be stolen from her if she didn't. Her instructors at the finishing school had been disgusted, and they scolded her for the appalling table manners. But the habit had been a difficult one to break. Years had passed before she stopped hiding food in her bedchamber.

Elena joined her in the kitchen area, explaining patiently the tasks for the day and repeating herself in a game of charades until Diana understood. They straightened the kitchen, prepared for the evening meal, tossed corn outside for chickens, then Diana fetched water for the house while Elena searched for eggs.

Diana found the routine and the completion of chores brought a calmness she craved. Everything in its place. After ensuring that Sophia had what she might need for the next few hours, they gathered soiled clothing and washed it in the stream behind the house.

As they moved around the house and yard, Elena would point to an object, saying its Greek name and waiting for Diana to repeat. A few times, Diana surprised her by knowing the word before she was told, and Elena clapped and praised her student. Each time she did, Diana's heart warmed.

Once the wet garments hung from a line between two trees, they returned to the house and packed meals of bread, cheese, and pears to deliver to the boys for their midday meal. From what Diana understood, the younger boys were in the hills tending to the goats. In his father's absence, Georgi helped with the harvest at his uncle's olive orchard.

Following Elena's lead, Diana placed a large, triangle-shaped kerchief over her head, crossing the corners beneath her chin and tucking them over her shoulders. Though it was not a bonnet, she was grateful for the scarf. She'd felt exposed and vulnerable without a head covering.

The pair walked through the town. Sophia's family farm was near the edge of the village, surrounded by rugged mountains, and so on her arrival, Diana had not seen much of Tsímova. The roads were so narrow she did not think a wide carriage could pass through. Everything, from the street to the buildings to the walls along the roads, was made of the same light-colored stone, but Tsímova was far from colorless. Vivid flowers poked between the paving stones, and trees shaded the road, growing from behind garden walls in soil surrounded by low curbs. The flowers were the most brilliant shades of pinks, purples, and yellows she'd ever seen.

Many of the buildings were constructed in the same style as Sophia's house, stacks of different-sized cubes with stairs leading up the outer wall to a flat roof. Some included an attached tower, making them look like small fortresses. Other shops and village homes were built more simply with a red-tile roof.

All around them, villagers called in friendly welcome to one another as they went about their days. Donkeys brayed, cicadas keened, and birds chirped. Tsímova was tidy, with painted doors and flowerpots adding even more color to the view and a charm that showed the pride the people felt in their home.

They passed through the main square, where Diana saw a well and a stone church with its large, round dome; bell tower; and heavy double doors.

A plant Diana did not recognize seemed to grow everywhere. It had no leaves, but pink flowers grew atop flat, rounded pads that looked like swollen stems and were about the size of a saucer. Diana reached to touch the plant and felt a prick of pain. She yelped and pulled her hand away. A drop of blood grew on the tip of her finger. Looking close, she saw needles poked out of the green discs.

Trying again, more carefully, she rubbed her finger over the smooth flesh of the strange plant. *Is it a vegetable?* she wondered, but when she turned to ask Elena, she saw the girl's gaze was upon a house on the other side of the road.

"Is this your friend's house?" Diana asked in halting Greek.

Elena's cheeks turned pink, and she looked down, shaking her head with a small smile. She opened her mouth to reply when they heard a shout.

A young man waved from the doorway of the house Elena had been watching, and Diana could see precisely what—or whom—had brought about Elena's blush. He walked toward the wall separating the house's garden from the road.

"Spiros Sássaris," Elena whispered.

Diana read volumes in the way she said the name.

He was a few years older than Elena, possibly nineteen or twenty. Spiros's eyes were dark, his nose straight, and the casual way he leaned his arms against the gate and smiled gave the impression of an easygoing person.

"Elena." He waved.

The two spoke for a moment, and Elena introduced Diana, explaining that the Englishwoman didn't understand much of what was being said. Spiros greeted her. His smile was friendly enough, but it was clear he preferred speaking with Elena.

Diana listened to the conversation, unable to pick out more than a few words. Elena seemed to ask about a family member, and Spiros's smile faltered as he answered. A moment later, a woman's voice called from within the house. A young girl came outside and motioned to him, and he bid them farewell.

Elena watched as he departed, her head tipped and her eyes soft.

Diana smiled to herself, remembering Molly wearing the exact same expression when she thought of Lieutenant Ashworth. Diana waited a moment before touching her friend's arm. "Elena?" She raised her brows.

The girl blinked and pulled back her head as if awoken from a dream. The pink returned to her cheeks. "Georgi." She pointed toward the olive grove on the hill beyond the village. "He is waiting for his lunch." She walked at a quicker pace, and Diana did not tease over her obvious fondness for the handsome young man.

They hurried toward the orchard, stopping only for a moment at a roadside shrine. They had passed another shrine when they'd entered the town the day before. Diana did not want to seem disrespectful and so did not examine the monument too closely. From what she could see, it was about the size of a birdhouse, built on a stone pillar. Inside the glass door was a cluster of candles before a miniature painting of Mary and Jesus. Golden halos surrounded the figures. Elena paused, bowed her head reverently, crossed herself, and then continued on— just as she had done the day before.

They left behind the village and climbed up a hill toward the orchard. Diana recognized the silvery oblong leaves of the olive trees. She had never seen more than one olive tree here and there in Corfu and along the shores of Italy. The grove was beautiful. The trees grew in orderly rows, their branches gnarled like an old woman's knotty hands.

Some men were picking ripe olives, others sorting them into sacks. Diana picked Georgi out with a sack on his shoulder. He lifted it into a donkey cart, then straightened and wiped his brow. When he looked up and saw Diana and his sister, he waved, then jogged over to join them, placing a few purple-black olives in both their hands before taking the parcel of food from Elena. He sat in the shade, stretching out his legs with a sigh. The women sat beside him.

Diana took small bites of the tart olives, eating around the pits, while she watched the men working in the orchard and listened to Georgi and Elena.

Elena inquired about his work and asked a few more questions that Georgi answered with grunts and one-syllable answers between mouthfuls of food. Elena did not seem put off by his manner, and Diana did not think he was acting rude, simply tired. She envied the comfortable way the brother and sister had with one another, and she let herself wonder, as she ran her fingers through the pleats on her skirt, how much different her life would have been if she'd had a brother.

Once Georgi was finished, he rose, bidding the women farewell and thanking them for luncheon before he returned to his labor.

Elena rose also, pointing at the rocky path that led past the olive grove and up into the hills.

After just a few steps, Diana realized "path" was a relatively loose term for the route. She felt as though she were stumbling the entire way up the hill. Small rocks slid beneath her feet, and more than once she caught herself before falling. The light-colored stone around them was not smooth, and the scrubby bushes caught on her dress. She was grateful for thick stockings and a woolen dress. Above them, they heard the jingle of the goats' bells, and Diana followed Elena from the path, toward the sound.

Stepping carefully over and around rocks, Diana kept her eyes on the ground. When she lifted her gaze to locate Elena, she saw that she'd nearly walked into an enormous spiderweb. A black-and-white spider—larger than any she'd seen before—sat in the very center. Diana gasped and stepped back. Her foot landed on a loose rock, and she lost her balance. She fell hard, hitting her knee and her palms on the rocky ground.

Elena rushed down the mountain. "Missno!"

Diana stood, wiping dirt from her palms and wondering if her knees were destined to be eternally covered with bruises. She raised her skirt and touched her knee, but it wasn't bleeding. "Do not worry, Elena. I was simply startled by the . . . the *aráchni.*" She pointed at the disgusting web and its vile inhabitant.

Elena looked at the web and nodded solemnly. She glanced at the sun as if determining the time. "*Mágisses,*" she muttered, knitting her brow and pursing her lips together. She motioned for Diana to hurry after her.

What is Mágisses? Diana wondered, glancing back at the spider. And why did Elena look so worried? Was the spider poisonous?

A few moments later, they found the boys, sitting in the shade of a sparse tree as the goats around them climbed over the rocks, chewing on the scant blades of rough grass and scrubby bushes.

The boys cheered when they approached. They sat together, happily eating their lunch and sharing with Diana and Elena.

Elena spoke to the boys, and between the words she understood and Elena's actions, Diana knew she was telling them about the spider and her fall.

"*Mágisses,*" one of the boys—Mikhail—whispered.

Elena nodded.

The boys' mood dampened, and Diana wished she hadn't been the one to discover the dangerous spider and frighten the children. But maybe knowing it was there would help them to avoid it.

After they had eaten, Diana stood, ready to descend the hill and return to the town, but Elena stopped her. She pointed to the sun and motioned for Diana to sit. "*Mágisses,*" she said again as if a poisonous spider were an explanation for remaining where they were.

Diana was tired, her hands stung from washing the clothes in cold water and then scraping them on the rocks. Her thighs hurt from climbing the steep hill, and she thought it would not be unpleasant to remain in the shady spot for a bit longer if it made the children happy.

She searched around briefly for a stick then indicated for Elena to slide closer to her. Diana tucked her legs beneath her and brushed her hand over a patch of reddish dirt, smoothing it out as well as she was able; then she used a stick to draw an *A*. She pointed to the letter. "*Alpha.*"

Elena's face lit up. "*Alpha,*" she repeated.

Diana brushed away the letter with her hand, then gave the stick to Elena. She pointed at the smooth dirt. "Alpha."

Elena drew the symbol.

"Very good," Diana smiled and nodded, brushing away the letter. "Now *Beta . . .*"

When they left the hills an hour later, Elena had drawn and said the names of all twenty-four letters in the Greek alphabet. She sang to herself as they walked toward the village, and her excitement was contagious. She linked her arm through Diana's.

Diana pushed down the urge to sing herself. She realized that in merely one day, her entire outlook on her situation had reversed. She'd left the pirate ship full of discouragement and feeling rather sorry for her misfortune, but after only a little time with this family, her feelings had changed. She felt needed and valued. She wanted to help Sophia with her household, to teach Elena to read, to make sure the boys were fed and their clothes clean. She felt glad to be in Greece where she could make a difference and be appreciated. Even if the entire situation was temporary.

A tendril of worry wound its way through her chest. She did not know how long she'd be permitted to remain. What would happen when Petrobey realized a ship was not coming for her? When Sophia's husband returned? When the baby arrived and Diana's help was no longer needed?

The joy that had seemed like sunlight in her heart was now tempered with a rain cloud. They passed the church and Spiros Sássaris's house, and the anxious feeling that she could not control her situation made Diana's hands clench, and she itched to straighten a curtain or rearrange a dressing table.

As she fought against the fretfulness inside her, the pair rounded a corner, and her unease grew into a torrent of apprehension.

Alexandros Metaxas was approaching from the other direction.

Chapter 7

ALEX FELT A RUSH OF relief when he saw Miss Snow walking arm in arm with Petrobey's young granddaughter, Elena. She appeared happy and unharmed. Even though she'd rejected the offer, he would keep his vow to protect her. Her angry words had both amused him with her stubbornness and struck him with unexpected force. The lump of guilt he carried ever since she became involved—he smiled wryly at the term—in this business grew heavy inside his chest.

Although she'd tried to hide it, he'd seen terror in her face when she'd left the ship the day before. But Petrobey appeared to have kept his word, and she was being treated well. She appeared almost—happy. But he knew she would do all she could to conceal the emotion from him. Alex was no novice at reading people, at discovering their secrets or earning their trust. He knew how to peel away layer after layer, to learn what they hid deep inside. Diana Snow held her mask in place like few he had met before. If he didn't know better, he might think she was a spy herself. The desire to understand why she concealed so much of herself intrigued Alex for reasons he himself did not understand. A challenge, perhaps. But that did not fully explain his need to learn more about this woman.

"Good afternoon, Miss Snow." Alex bowed when he reached them. He greeted Elena in Greek.

Elena responded cheerfully, but her gray-eyed British companion merely raised her chin and looked the other direction.

He fought a smile of amusement at her reaction. "Have you been learning to read, Elena?"

"Missno taught me the letters. Alpha, Beta, Gamma, Delta . . ." She rattled off the entire Greek alphabet, ending with, ". . . Psi, Omega."

"You learned this all today?" From the corner of his eye, he saw Miss Snow watching her student. She did not smile, but her eyes were bright.

Elena grinned proudly.

"Very impressive." Alex raised his brows and nodded his head.

"And I have practiced writing the letters too. But only with a stick on the ground. Soon, we will read books from the church." Her smile grew.

"Elena is very fortunate to have such a capable teacher," he said in English.

Miss Snow made a *hmph* sound. "We don't mean to keep you, sir. I'm certain you must have business to attend to." She started walking, pulling Elena with her.

The girl looked back and forth between them. Alex pivoted and kept pace with her quick steps. "You are correct. But, you see, I am attending to that business even now."

Miss Snow darted a look toward him. "Harassing innocent women is your business?"

"I came to find you."

Her step faltered, but she continued her quick march.

"How are you treated?" He lowered his voice even though he knew Elena could not understand what he said.

Before Miss Snow could make an answer, a gypsy woman called to them from the gate of a house at the edge of the village.

At the sight of her, Miss Snow drew in a gasp and moved slightly in front of the young girl beside her.

The old woman's appearance was indeed startling. She wore dirty, tattered clothing, and beneath the torn scarf on her head, the sun-darkened skin of her face was weathered and heavily lined. One of her eyes was clouded, and sores spotted her lips.

Elena released her companion's arm and hurried toward the woman, opening the gate and leading her into the yard.

"Oh." Miss Snow was clearly surprised by the girl's actions.

"Greeks consider caring for the poor to be a duty," Alex said in a low voice.

Elena settled the woman on a bench in the shade of a tree and hurried into the house.

Miss Snow moved as if to follow her, but he caught her arm just before she stepped through the garden gate. "Do they treat you well, Miss Snow? Are you all right?"

Instead of jerking away, she turned completely toward him, and he received the full effect of her gray-eyed gaze. "I do not know why you bother to ask, Mr. Metaxas; it is because of *your* actions that I am here."

Alex felt a spark of anger at her accusation. It *was* thanks to his actions that she was here and not floating in the sea. He had done everything in his power to keep her from danger. "Are you saying that I kidnapped you and dragged you away from the city? Or that I had any knowledge you were at the beach?" He fisted his hands. "Might I ask, what were you doing there in the first place?"

She turned her eyes downward and rubbed her fingers over the stone of the garden fence. "I meant to return your gloves. I . . . It was foolish, I know."

The regret in her voice was not enough to ease his frustration. "In the middle of the night, in a hidden smuggler's cove? Surely you have better sense than to—"

Her eyes snapped to his, and no remnants of apology remained in her glare. "Do not turn the blame on me, sir. I am not at fault." Her voice did not get louder, but each word was clipped and clear. "You told those men you did not know me and conspired to have me carried away as a prisoner in that horrid ship. Do not deny it was your idea." She folded her arms, breathing heavily through her nose.

"Yes, it is true, and for that I must apologize. And explain myself."

Her brow raised a slight bit, but the fire did not leave her eyes.

"The Maniots are suspicious of outsiders. It took a great deal of persuasion, but that night, they agreed to meet me, and I assured them I was alone. When they discovered you, they would have killed us both in an instant if I had revealed that we were acquainted. Persuading distrustful men they were not being deceived would have been impossible."

Miss Snow pursed her lips and appeared as though she were considering his explanation.

"As for kidnapping you and bringing you here, I convinced them not to murder you on the beach and as a British woman, you were much more valuable as a hostage than a slave for the Venetians. I give my word, Miss Snow, I acted only to protect you."

The tension left her face and shoulders. She lowered her arms and clasped her hands at her waist. "Well, it is certainly ungentlemanly to consort with pirates. And not acknowledging a person when you encounter her on the deck of a ship is simply rude."

He realized Diana was no longer angry, but his behavior had hurt her. He also realized she had shared a very brief glance beneath her mask. She had been afraid and upset on the ship, even though she had tried to conceal it. And whether she realized it or not, she had just confessed her desire for a friend. "Quite so on both counts. And I apologize for any lack of decorum. You certainly did not deserve such treatment, though it is preferable to death, I would think."

Elena returned from inside the house with a cup and a slice of bread. She sat on the bench as the old woman ate.

Miss Snow watched the pair silently and then glanced toward him. "Petrobey and his family seem happy with the weapons you brought."

Alex was surprised but realized she had changed the subject once she started to feel vulnerable. "Yes. I believe they are."

"I am sorry to have taken your time, Mr. Metaxas." Diana dipped in a curtsey and stepped again toward the gate in a move intended to signal him to step aside.

Alex shifted his weight in the other direction so that she would have to squeeze past him to get through the opening. "I will leave once I am assured that you are well taken care of."

She looked up, and when their eyes met, she took a step back, as if she had not known he was standing so close. "I am well. The family is kind, and I am happy here." She pushed past him through the gate.

"Miss Snow?"

She turned back.

"It occurs to me that I have never seen your smile."

Pink spots grew in her cheeks, but she held an aloof expression. "You've hardly given me a reason to smile, sir. Neither inviting yourself to tea nor conspiring in my capture with pirates warrants a positive response."

He was starting to recognize Miss Snow's manner of speaking grew increasingly less polite in an effort to prevent emotion from showing.

She was protecting herself, hiding behind a curt, almost rude reply in hopes to ward off anything or anyone from getting too close.

"It is a sight I should very much like to see."

She looked toward Elena and then down to the ground, twisting her fingers together. "You would be disappointed."

Her voice was soft and her words so vulnerable that he realized he'd gotten a glimpse of her true feelings. Her reasons for protecting herself stemmed from insecurity, and possibly fear. Alex's curiosity was further piqued. "I very much doubt it."

He had the pleasure of seeing her face flush red. She darted a look up at him and fled into the house.

Alex walked slowly toward the center of town. His recruiting mission to the Mani had been something he'd planned and worked toward for years, and now that he was here, another task had inserted itself in his heart. What was Diana Snow protecting herself from? And why had discovering the answer become so important?

⥽⤫⥼

Three days later, Alex stood in church. The smell of incense and the chanted words of the Divine Liturgy were like a balm to his soul. He let the familiarity of the ceremony fill him with comfort.

His gaze traveled around the church interior. A screen painted with ikons of saints, partitioned off the holy altar, where the priest prepared the Eucharist. The smell of incense rose from burners, and candles flickered from their braziers. He lifted his gaze to the colorful depiction of the Most Holy Theotokos and her son, Jesus Christ, painted with golden halos surrounding their heads.

He looked over the congregation and recognized the few men he'd met, patriarchs of their clans. In the rows ahead of him stood the Mavromichalis family. Dino stood beside his father, and his cousin, Themis, a row behind.

Themis's eyes narrowed as he met Alex's gaze. In the few interactions they'd had since the Mavromichalis clan had pledged to join Alex, Themis had not-so-subtly indicated that he would follow Petrobey's orders, but he wasn't happy about it.

Alex moved his gaze to the row behind Themis. The priest had provided Elena's mother with a chair before the service began. She had waved it away at first, then sank gratefully into it when the priest insisted. The poor woman looked swollen and miserable. His gaze traveled over her daughter and the four boys then locked with Diana's.

She quickly turned her face forward, but Alex smiled, knowing she'd been watching him. The priest and altar boys made their processional with the Holy Gospel through the narrow aisle of the church, and Alex turned his attention back to the ceremony. Memories washed over him as he remembered the priest in Nafplio cutting his hair symbolically before he began his duties as an altar boy. It had been so far away and such a long time ago, yet the ceremony was the same, even here in this small village.

He recited the words of the Lord's Prayer, stealing a glimpse at Diana. She stood quietly, hands folded in front of her, and her brow furrowed in concentration. He wished he could read her mind. Did she find the Liturgy beautiful and sacred as he did? Or was the entire ceremony strange to her?

His eyes traveled over the gathering, and his heart was full. The Turkish taxes were crushing, and the simple solution was to renounce Christianity. Muslims were not taxed nor forbidden to own weapons or ride horses. Greek peasants bore the brunt of the burden, yet these people held tightly to their beloved faith. The level of sacrifice required for them to worship in this holy place caused tears to sting his eyes.

As he listened to Father Yianni's voice rising and falling melodically with the prayer, Alex drew in a sharp breath. Though he'd heard the words hundreds of times, today they struck him with a force that surprised him.

The priest offered a petition for the people of God. He prayed for a "Christian end to our life, painless, unashamed, and peaceful, and for a good defense before the dread judgment seat of Christ."

Alex looked again at the members of the congregation, especially the men and older boys. Before he left Constantinople, he'd hoped for men, warriors. And here, in the Mani, he'd found them. But being among these people, spending time with them, seeing them interact with their children and wives . . . They were no longer merely weapons to use against the Turks but actual people with homes and families. Alex was asking them to risk their lives, to believe in the cause, and to be willing to die for it. His throat tightened as his gaze traveled over the beautiful women and children that would be left behind, but a warmth filled him.

Father Yianni had blessed his mission and reassured him that the cause was just. A Christian ending to a Christian life, Alex thought. And what more could he ask for?

His gaze landed again on Diana, and a dull pain grew in his stomach. He attributed his reaction to hunger. He and the rest of the congregation had fasted since the evening before in preparation to partake of the Holy Gifts. He enjoyed Diana's company, was fascinated by her, worried about her safety, found her extremely beautiful, and thought of her too often. But he was a revolutionary. His goal was to start a war, and dragging a gentlewoman into the equation would do no good for anyone. Best to leave her alone and let her people come for her. Once she'd departed these shores, he'd not worry about her any longer. If only the ache inside agreed with him.

Chapter 8

THE DAY AFTER THE SABBATH, the boys left early to tend the goats and pick olives. Elena and Diana hurried through the business of morning chores. Sophia had spoken to Father Yianni the day before, and he'd agreed to allow Diana and Elena to come to the church and read in the afternoon.

Diana made certain Sophia was comfortable and had her sewing nearby, then went outside to find Elena. She found the girl in the yard attaching a cart to the family's donkey.

"Today, we must gather wood," Elena said. "Then after the boys eat their lunch, *mitéra* says we can go to the church." She clapped her hands together, grinning.

Diana felt herself caught up in the girl's enthusiasm. Elena had practiced her letters at every opportunity, and with only a bit of instruction, she'd begun to string the symbols together in an attempt to make simple words. Diana had no doubt Elena would be reading within a few weeks, and the thought filled her chest with pride in her student. Perhaps Petrobey would see the benefit and send other children to learn.

The pair led the donkey along the road away from the town. At the crossroads, instead of turning down toward Limeni, they continued upward, higher into the hills. The buzzing of insects grew louder as they climbed. Tall, jagged mountains rose around them, and Diana thought if they did not have the road to follow, she would most certainly be lost. She had only ever lived in London after all. How did one keep track of directions among all these rises and drops with no buildings to use as landmarks?

Leaving the donkey tied to a low bough near the road, the pair climbed up even higher into the dusty hills, over rocks and around thorny bushes. Elena tugged on a scraggly, dead-looking bush and held up a branch that was thin, twisted, and hardly thicker than her arm. "Brushwood burns fastest. Olive wood burns longest." She started a pile, and Diana climbed in the opposite direction to do the same, keeping a watch for spiders as she went.

Half an hour later, Diana carried an armload to the cart, grateful for her thick sleeves. At least her arms were protected, though she couldn't say the same for her hands. A week ago, the thorns would have torn her palms to pieces, but farm work had made them tough, and gathering wood only added to the crisscross of scrapes over her once soft skin.

As she climbed over the rocky mountain, wrestling rough brushwood branches from the scraggly undergrowth, her mind turned to the service the day before. She'd been surprised to see the church held no pews, only a few chairs for people who were too ill or too old to stand for the entire service. She'd expected a sermon, and the smell of incense and the chanting voice of the priest had surprised her. At first, she'd been frustrated, trying to distinguish the words, but once she stopped and let herself *feel* instead of understand, the reverence of the ceremony filled her with peace. She watched the people around her and saw the devotion in their faces as they worshiped.

Without her permission, her mind conjured an image of Alexandros. She'd not expected to see him at church. She didn't realize criminals attended Sunday service. But the thing that had surprised her the most was the reverence in his expression. His eyes were soft, at times wet, and his face peaceful. The meeting was holy to him, and for some reason, the knowledge started a burn of guilt in her middle. Was he not the scoundrel she assumed?

She squelched the thought as soon as it arose. After all, the pirates were at the Divine Liturgy too, and she'd seen firsthand their unlawful ways. But the burn remained, making her squirm uncomfortably, and she couldn't justify it away.

Best to ignore it, she decided.

A few hours later, the cart was full, and the pair began the walk back to Tsímova. Elena sang as she led the donkey, and Diana found herself humming along to the tune.

When they reached the fork in the road, Elena waved her arm over her head, calling out to a trio approaching from Limeni. The two young people carried large, covered pots, and they were accompanied by an older woman with a basket hooked over her arm. "My cousins," Elena said to Diana.

The relatives joined them, and Diana saw the younger people were near Elena's age, maybe a year or two younger. The boy was stocky with heavy eyelids, but his sister seemed to be the very opposite, slender, almost to the point of frailty, with wide eyes and long limbs. The woman was thin, like her daughter. She bent forward her head in greeting when she reached them. Diana's initial impression of the woman was a person who was cordial but not exactly warm.

Elena kissed her aunt's cheeks and embraced the young woman. "Missno, this is my father's cousin Agatha and her children, Stella and Kyros." She indicated each in turn.

"Nice to meet you," Diana said, pronouncing each word as correctly as she could.

"We are bringing *avgolemono* soup to your mother," Stella said. "And of course to poor Costas Sássaris."

"Thank you. She will be so happy to see you." Elena smiled brightly. "She gets lonely. Come, help me make a spot in the cart." Kyros and Stella shaped the pile of branches into nests to hold their pots.

Diana held the donkey's rope while the others adjusted the load. She found it strange that women in a family way walked around the village, attended church, and now, Sophia was accepting guests? In London, such a woman would remain in confinement as she waited for a baby to be born.

Agatha glanced up the mountain road, and her eyes squinted into a scowl. "Let us be on our way." She started toward Tsímova, motioning with a swipe of her hand for the other to hurry.

Kyros's face darkened as he looked back up the road.

Diana stepped around the cart, following his gaze, and saw two men walking toward them. They wore thick stockings beneath white kilts. Each man had a saber at his waist and a musket over his shoulder.

"Klephts," Kyros muttered, glancing at the girls.

Diana didn't understand the word or their reaction. Were the men strangers? Perhaps it was their weapons that caused the reaction. She walked faster, catching up to Elena and Stella. The girls' arms were linked, and they chattered. The men on the road didn't seem to bother them. But they were certainly not making an effort to be friendly.

Diana glanced back. The men maintained their original pace and didn't seem to be threatening.

"What is a klepht, Elena?"

"*Klephtopólemos,*" she said.

Elena shook her head to show she didn't understand.

"It is wise to leave them alone." Agatha joined the group, pursing her lips. Diana wasn't sure if the expression was typical of the woman or if the men were the cause of worry.

When they entered the house, Sophia was delighted to see them. She rose up from her bed on the couch, but Agatha motioned for her to remain. It was a testament to how poorly Sophia felt that she did not argue.

Kyros moved the wood to the storage building, then took his leave in order to finish a few hours' work at the olive orchard with Gregori before it was time to accompany his mother and sister back to Limeni. Diana and Elena quickly made up a meal for the two cousins to share at the orchard. He thanked them and departed.

Diana scooped the creamy soup into smaller bowls while Elena sliced warm white bread. When Sophia insisted on joining them at the table, Agatha assisted her across the room, placing a pillow behind her as she eased into a wooden chair. Stella brought a stool for her feet.

Diana moved back and forth between the cooking area and the kitchen table, carrying bowls, the butter dish, and the honey pot. Elena took wooden spoons from the drawer and poured goat milk into cups.

Once she was certain the women had everything they needed, Diana walked toward the door, but Elena called her back.

"Please join us, Missno."

Diana hesitated, glancing at the four women. She was certain the relatives did not want an outsider intruding on their luncheon. "I thought to feed the chickens," she said. "And we did not fetch eggs this morning."

"Of course you will join us." Sophia motioned to a chair. "The chickens can wait." The woman's smile was tired but genuine.

"Thank you." Diana scooped some soup for herself and sat at the table, wishing Agatha and Stella were not studying her. She did not like to be the center of attention.

Sophia prayed over the food. She took a spoonful of soup, then let out a contented noise. "Agatha, you knew exactly what I needed today. I do get lonely, and you make the best avgolemono in Laconia."

Agatha's face warmed into a pleased smile. "Stella baked the bread."

Sophia lifted a slice, inhaling deeply, then spread on butter and honey before taking a bite. Her brows rose, and she nodded while she chewed. She swallowed and smiled. "Delicious, Stella. You'll make a fine wife."

Stella grinned and Elena giggled.

"But not too soon," Agatha said. "Her father would be very sad."

Sophia smiled as she nodded. "True. Themis acts strong, but a daughter softens a man's heart like nothing else can."

Diana lifted her wooden spoon, attempting to look dainty as she scooped the creamy soup with the thick utensil. She sipped carefully at the edge of the rounded wood. Chicken soup with *lemon*? She chewed the bits of chicken and rice as she thought of what the women had said and tried to keep shock from showing on her face. *Themis* was Stella's father? This lovely young girl was the daughter of the pirate that had kidnapped her? She did not think the father's heart had been soft when he'd held a blade against her neck.

She studied Stella, searching for a resemblance to her father. Diana took another bite. Now that her mouth was prepared for it, she found the mixture of flavors less shocking and actually rather delicious.

"Stella, perhaps your father will allow you to learn to read," Elena said. "Missno is teaching me."

Diana smiled at the look of interest in Stella's eyes. She seemed every bit as bright as her cousin.

Agatha's expression grew tight again. "This is her grandfather's doing, no doubt?" she said to Sophia.

Sophia took a drink of milk. "The idea was Elena's. But, yes, Petrobey did agree to it."

"What possible use could she have for such a thing?" Agatha rubbed her brow as if the very idea were giving her a headache. "She would do much better to learn skills that will make her a good wife."

A familiar burning started in Diana's chest. The circumstances were so different but the advice nearly identical to that given to Molly by the officers' wives.

"And reading will not?" Elena asked.

Sophia darted a look at her daughter, who lowered her eyes in apology. "Elena knows that if her household duties suffer, she will need to stop."

"And perhaps a husband will have need of a wife who reads." The words popped out of Diana's mouth before she had even finished thinking them.

The four women looked at her, and she felt her face flame with heat. Diana held herself tightly looking at her soup as she waited for a reprimand. *Why can I not keep my mouth quiet?* When the reprimand didn't come, she risked a peek at Agatha.

Agatha regarded her for a moment. "I had not thought of that." She turned down the corners of her lips as if she were considering Diana's words. "But, still, her father will not allow it." She took a bite of soup, swallowing before she spoke. "Less than two weeks remain before Calantha Michalakiáni and Socrates Grigorakiáni's wedding." She turned to Sophia. "I cannot imagine you will feel up to making *kourabiedes*."

And just like that, the moment passed. Nobody was angry with Diana's opinion. Agatha, in spite of her curt personality, had even considered it and, though she didn't agree, had responded politely. Diana was more surprised than when she'd tasted lemon in the chicken soup. Did these women actually care about what she said?

Sophia's laughter brought Diana's thoughts back to the conversation. "No, I am nearly certain I will not be making wedding cookies for a few months. Perhaps Stella could come help Elena and Diana with the baking?"

The cousins grinned and shared an excited look. Whether it was because of the wedding or their opportunity to spend time together, Diana wasn't certain. She listened to the women's discussion as they continued their meal. They gossiped and argued, and even though she was not able to follow some of the conversation, Diana was coming to recognize the direct talk was not intended to offend. Arguments and disagreements were natural, and she decided she quite preferred this blunt honesty to manipulation and backhanded compliments.

After an hour, Agatha assisted Sophia back to the couch. "We should not have kept you so long. You look tired."

"I am tired." Sophia adjusted the pillows and rested back, lifting the beads at her waist and clicking them together absentmindedly. "But never too tired for a visit."

Diana took the bowls from the table and stacked them in the washing basin while the young girls whispered and giggled. She thought she heard the name Spiros Sássaris mentioned in their conversation.

Agatha sat on the edge of the couch and brushed a lock of hair from Sophia's forehead in a tender gesture. "We go to the Sássaris house now."

Sophia's expression fell. "And young Costas? He remains ill?"

"Yes."

"Poor Daphne. She has only her daughter, Theodora, and one healthy son, Spiros." Both women crossed themselves.

Diana did not miss Elena's glance darting across the room at the sound of the name.

After saying their good-byes, the relatives took their leave.

As Sophia slept, Elena and Diana delivered lunch to the young goat tenders and then made their way back through the village toward the church. In anticipation of her reading lesson, Elena walked quickly with bouncing steps.

Inside the church, Father Yianni showed them the shelf where the sacred texts were kept. Diana studied the small selection of books. Eusebius, a book of etymology by Nikolaos Glykis. Neither seemed appealing to a young girl. She looked at the next volume and smiled, glad to see the familiar lettering of a Septuagint Bible. She had studied a Greek Bible in Reverend Delaney's library and knew the language of the Gospels was simple enough for Elena to learn.

She reached for the book, but the priest put his hand over hers, stopping her from removing it. He shook his head, pushing the book firmly into the shelf, indicating the Bible was not an option.

Diana knitted her brows but did not argue. She touched the spine of a book of Psalms and glanced at him with a question in her eyes.

Father Yianni nodded.

Diana pulled two straight-backed wooden chairs into the dim light of a small window and sat in one, patting the other for Elena to join her. Luckily the sun was bright today, but in the future, they would need to either read outside or bring a lantern.

The two bent over the book, Elena carefully pronouncing each sound, and Diana studying the sentences, using Elena's help and her own knowledge of the verses to decipher the words.

After an hour, Elena rubbed her eyes. "We should see to supper."

"You did wonderfully." Diana slid the book of scripture back into its spot on the shelf. She could tell reading had been more difficult than Elena had anticipated, and she didn't want the girl to become discouraged. If only they had access to the level primers Diana taught from at school.

Stepping outside, Diana closed the heavy wooden door behind them. When she heard her name, she whirled around. The sound of Alexandros's voice brought a flutter of agitation that muddled her mind and heated her cheeks.

He approached across the square. "Good afternoon, ladies." He bowed when he reached them. "Have you been reading?"

Elena nodded. "Yes. Father Yianni let us practice with the Psalms and Patristic Writings." Her eyes dimmed. "They are a bit difficult."

"And I can't imagine very interesting," he said.

Elena's eyes opened wide at his irreverence regarding sacred texts, then she laughed.

"How is the other student's progress?" Alexandros tipped his head as he directed his words to Diana.

"I am understanding quite a lot when I listen and read," she said in careful Greek, "but speaking is not as easy." She lifted her gaze and saw that he watched her thoughtfully. His eyes were soft, sending a shiver over her skin.

"You speak my language beautifully," he said in English. The low husky sound of his voice made her heart flip over.

She took a step back, practically pressed against the door. Enough was enough. Diana straightened her shoulders, feeling as though she needed a barrier between herself and this man whose every word and expression disconcerted her to the point of distraction. "Excuse us, Mr. Metaxas." She dipped in a curtsey. "We must get home."

"I'm looking for Father Yianni," Alexandros said. "Is he within?"

"You've no doubt come for confession," Diana said in English. She knew her words were rude, but self-protection was her driving force and pushing him away felt safer than allowing him to get close.

Instead of looking offended, one side of his mouth lifted. "You truly think I'm a villain, don't you?"

"How could I not?" She lifted her chin, looking down her nose at him, hoping her expression showed disdain instead of the uncertainty she felt.

Elena looked back and forth between them as they spoke in English, her brows pulled together. "Father Yianni may be with the Sássaris family. Their son Costas is very ill."

"I see." Alexandros pushed his fingers through his thick curls. He glanced at the church behind them, squinting his eyes.

A man strode into the square. Diana recognized him as one of the pair from the hills. Now that she had a better view, she saw he was still a youth. Certainly, he was as young, if not younger, than Elena. His face was dark from the sun, and a white scar ran down his cheek. She tried to remember the word Kyros had used. "Klepht," she said in a quiet voice.

When she said the word, Alexandros turned toward her. He raised his brows. "You know of the klephts?"

Diana dropped her gaze, embarrassed that she'd spoken aloud. But she was curious about the men in their strange uniforms. "Just the name. I do not actually know who they are."

Alexandros glanced across the square. "Guerillas, independence fighters hiding out in the hills. To the Turks, they are outlaws."

"They sound dangerous."

"Their reputation is not flawless. Most consider them heroes but still keep a distance—and a close eye on their daughters." He turned and lifted his hand, waving to the man.

The klepht returned the gesture.

"He is here for you," Diana said. It was not a question. She reverted to her scornful mannerisms, not wanting him to see the disappointment that grew heavy in her stomach. "I should have guessed." A part of her wanted Alexandros to be honorable, but wishing wasn't enough to make something so.

"I am meeting with his *kapetan* at their camp in the hills."

"Of course you are."

He ignored her sarcasm. "I must go now, but I will return in a few days."

Diana glanced around the square, afraid to look at his face. She was frustrated that her heart had begun to beat faster and terrified that he might notice—and worse, know his words had caused the reaction. She pulled down the sides of her mouth, thinking of something to say to cover her discomfiture. "Use caution in the hills, lest you meet *mágisses.*"

Alexandros's eyes widened, and his chin dropped in a look of surprise.

Diana couldn't help but feel a bit of triumph. He may be a scoundrel, but he did not know the dangers of the Greek wilderness as she did. "Elena and I had an encounter just a few days ago."

His brows pulled together. "You saw . . . *mágisses?*"

Elena heard the word and began to speak rapidly.

Diana hardly understood what she said, but by her hand motions, she knew Elena was speaking about the venomous spider.

He turned back to Diana. "And you believe this?" He spoke in English.

She stared at him. "Believe? In a spider?"

Alexandros's face fell slack. His lips quirked, and laughter burst from his mouth. "A spider? Miss Snow, *mágisses* are witches."

"Witches? But . . ." Her words trailed off as her mind turned over the information. Did the children believe witches put the spider in her way? "Surely . . ."

"Maniots are quite superstitious. Misfortune during the noon hour is often blamed on witches."

Diana opened her mouth, then closed it, not sure what question she would even ask. All this time she'd worried about poisonous spiders when Elena and her brothers had been concerned about witches? "But witches are not real," she finally said, aware that her statement sounded like one a child would say.

"The klepht there," Alex raised his chin in the direction of the man, "he most likely planned our journey to begin in the afternoon to avoid traveling at midday. Their fear is real, even if it seems unbelievable to us."

He excused himself, and Diana watched Alexandros cross the square, greet the klepht, and depart with him. The more she learned about the Maniots, the more confused she became. Bandits who feared witches, kidnapping pirates that attended church with their families, and a weapons smuggler who behaved like a gentleman and somehow managed to leave her flustered with each encounter. As soon as she returned to the house, she planned to fold some clothing and perhaps line up the pots in the storage room. Thinking of the chores she could perform and the small things she could put into order pushed her emotions back into the proper cupboard. She linked arms with Elena as they walked back through the village.

Chapter 9

ALEX WALKED THROUGH TSÍMOVA WITH the klepht soldier, Private Gerontis. From the corner of his eye, he studied the young man. The private, in spite of his youth, strode with confidence, hand on his weapon and shoulders straight. Though his chin was smooth, lacking a man's whiskers, scars on his arms and face indicated he had seen his share of battle.

"How long have you served under Kapetan Karahalios?" Alex asked.

"Four years. Since I was eleven." Private Gerontis didn't look at Alex but continued to scan their surroundings.

"Where are you from?"

"A small village near Sparti."

"Your family?"

The young man's jaw tightened. "My father was killed when he could not pay the sultan's tax. He had no brothers to marry my mother, and so she remains a widow."

"You became a klepht to fight the people that destroyed your family."

Private Gerontis dipped his head once, his jaw still tight.

Many of the freedom fighters Alex had met had similar stories. He himself—Alex's breath caught in his throat, and he forced away the memories.

The pair passed the house where Diana Snow was staying, and he smiled, glad to think about something that eased the aching in his chest. He remembered her reactions at the church. Her blush. The fluster, the rudeness of her words. He could see bits of her mask falling away, and with each meeting, he understood her better. But so much still remained hidden. Instead of frustrating, the challenge was invigorating. His lips twitched when he thought of her warning to avoid witches.

As he considered the years since all he'd loved had been taken from him, Alex realized he'd focused solely on the rebellion. Revenge and planning had been forefront in his thoughts. Few things had brought him pleasure as his interactions with Diana Snow had. He wondered why he hadn't realized how lonely he'd become—or how single-minded.

That complicated woman with her gray eyes, tight hair, and straight posture had unlocked something inside him. It made perfect sense why a revolutionary remained unattached. Letting himself feel something distracted his mind, so with great effort, he pushed away the images of arched brows framing wide eyes and the curve of her full lips and focused on his duty as an emissary for the brotherhood.

Ahead, where the roads met, Dino and Themis lounged in the shade with another klepht, a man with thick brows and dark hair graying at his temples. As the pair approached, the men rose. Private Gerontis saluted.

"Thank you for waiting." Alex held out a hand.

The klepht took it in a firm grip. "Lieutenant Markos," he said. "*Protopalikari* to Kapetan Karahalios."

The fact that the kapetan had sent his second-in-command was encouraging. Perhaps it was an indication that Kapetan Karahalios would be willing to hear Alex's message.

Lieutenant Markos lifted his chin toward the road leading away from the sea. "The journey to Logastra camp will take two days. We must travel mostly by night, avoiding the main passes and roads. The route will keep us away from the Turks' encampments, but do not expect it to be easy." He glanced at Alex.

Alex blew out a breath, knowing the others did not consider him up to the rigors of the journey. He was quite obviously a man born and raised in a city, wearing peasant garb to fit in, not out of necessity.

In a crowded city, Alex could make snap decisions. Years of study had made him adept at languages and the art of military strategy, but when it came to trekking over rocky mountains, he was sadly ill prepared.

Disguising his educated speech and lack of actual battle experience was impossible, and Alex didn't even try. No words would persuade them of his competency as well as his actions could. Adjusting the pack on his shoulder, he squinted up at the mountain range. He would just have to prove them wrong.

Lieutenant Markos nodded once, then started off.

Not another word was spoken for hours. Alex followed the lieutenant over goat paths, through thorny thickets, down deep gorges, and up steep hillsides. The pace was strenuous, and he could hear the men behind him breathing heavily. He knew he was being tested.

To distract his mind, he studied the man in front of him, specifically his uniform. He'd heard of the klepht's thick woolen kilts, carefully pleated four hundred times to represent the years of Turkish rule. He noted the sturdy clogs with the toe curled to a point covered with a black, fluffy ball. The sleeves of the lieutenant's shirt flowed as he walked, and his stockings were held up by braided, black-tassled knee garters. Beneath an embroidered vest, a wide black sash wrapped around his waist. A red headpiece with a tassel completed the uniform. Alex was certain the man would consider the comparison of his hat with a Turkish fez to be the greatest of insults.

Lieutenant Markos stepped sure-footed over the rocky landscape. The uniform was a source of great pride, even though Alex had heard other Europeans make jokes about warriors wearing skirts, pom-poms, and billowing sleeves. Those same people would eat their words if they witnessed the descendants of Sparta in battle. Even the sultan's elite corps of Janissaries feared the klephts, regardless of their eccentric clothes.

Alex pulled a kerchief from his pack and wiped at the sweat on his face and neck, wishing one of the other men would complain. He would walk until his legs gave out before he asked to rest.

In spite of the breeze blowing from the canyons, sweat rolled from Alex's forehead and dripped from his jaw. He let his gaze travel over the vista. Dark pines covered the mountains above, and below, olive groves and farmland spread over the valleys. Though he was exhausted and aching, he could not help but appreciate the beauty that surrounded him. Bright flowers bloomed from rockrose bushes, and cacti with their pink blossoms provided bursts of color on the drab landscape. He knew brown bears and gray wolves lived in the Taygetos Mountains, but birds, lizards, and the occasional tortoise were the only wildlife they encountered.

The group stopped at a stream, and the private filled a water skin, offering the others a drink before they continued. Alex's relief at the respite was short lived when his sore legs discovered that beginning again after a rest was more painful than the nonstop climbing. After a few hours, darkness fell, but the lieutenant did not slow his pace.

Alex watched the moon rise higher in the sky. This time of month, it was shaped like a lemon. Not full enough to provide much light but waxing. The return journey would be brighter.

In the darkness, Alex's senses heightened, as did his anxiety. The steep hills with their crevices and shadows seemed much more perilous without the benefit of sunlight. He listened for wild animals and enemies but could only hear the chirps and buzzing of insects, footsteps on gravel, and the grunts of his companions, indicating that he was not the only one to feel the strain of the exertion. His legs and lungs burned. He sensed the others waiting for him to complain that the journey was too difficult. He would not.

Though his throat was dry and his feet begged for relief, he pushed onward, distracting himself by reciting the Great Oath of the Filiki Eteria in his mind—the pledge to his fatherland, the sacred and suffering country of Greece, the same pledge he'd taught to Petrobey Mavromichalis only a few days earlier as he'd been initiated into the brotherhood. Alex had sworn to consecrate himself fully to the cause of liberty, and if the price was a few blisters and sore muscles, he would gratefully pay it.

They climbed higher into the mountains, and Alex occasionally caught the scent of wild thyme, lavender, or mint. The familiar smells somehow provided comfort in the darkness. A few times, he caught himself as his head bobbed forward; he'd had no idea a man could feel so tired or fall asleep while walking.

When the sky finally began to lighten, Lieutenant Markos called a halt.

Alex sank to the ground, leaning back against a tree trunk.

Private Gerontis distributed dry mutton and hard biscuits, and the men washed down the scant meal with a drink from the water skin.

By the time they'd finished, the sun had risen, and they could see clearly. Alex's eyes shut on their own; he shook his head to stay awake. He thought every bone and muscle and fiber in his body must ache.

Lieutenant Markos lifted the firearm strap from his shoulder. "Private Gerontis will take first watch, and I the second."

"I—" Dino began, but his words were cut off when the lieutenant shook his head.

"I will not trust my life to a man I do not know. No offense meant." Lieutenant Markos lay on the ground and within seconds breathed deeply.

Dino and Themis exchanged a look. Without a word, Dino rose and joined the private on his sentry duty.

Themis glanced at Alex. "Sleep. We will keep you safe." His words were at odds with his tone. He meant them as an insult.

Alex bristled at his patronizing manner. "I will take a turn."

Themis blew out a puff of air. "Petrobey trusts you, but I do not. You have come to raise trouble where none exists." His mouth was tight and eyes squinted as he spoke. "My people are happy. We are safe, but you seek to get men killed. I am loyal to my clan, not to a stranger from Constantinople." Themis's brows lifted in the center, the smallest movement that an untrained man would have missed, but the quick flash spoke volumes to Alex. The man was afraid.

"You will not always be safe." Alex spoke calmly, not returning the man's angry tone. He lifted his chin toward the sleeping man. "The klepht, he leads us over secret paths, avoiding the roads. He fears the Turks. Here. Not twenty miles from Limeni." Alex rested his arms on his knees, leaning forward. "You will not always be safe," he repeated. "The Mani will not always be free."

Themis looked at Lieutenant Markos and then turned his eyes to the mountains above them. "It is easy for a man with no family to sentence other men to death."

"I realize your sacrifice."

"You realize nothing. You command others to fight but are not willing yourself."

Themis's words were spoken out of fear, but the knowledge did little to reassure Alex. The remark smacked of truth. He closed his eyes, leaning his head back against the tree as bands of guilt tightened around his conscience. He was not a warrior but a planner, a strategist, a leader. Although his training did include combat, his experience was not enough to survive a clash with the Janissaries. His skills were better employed as a gatherer of intelligence. If he were to be completely honest, Alex did not intend to lift a sword in the conflict. Was he also a coward?

"Do not sleep beneath the fig tree," Themis said as he stretched out on the ground. "The shadow is heavy and will bring evil dreams."

Alex glanced up at the tree and moved without question. The conversation had given him plenty to consider, but the moment he lay his head on the ground, he sank into the dreamless sleep of exhaustion.

He awoke in the early afternoon to the sound of men's voices.

"At last you are awake," Themis sneered.

Alex rolled his shoulders and rubbed the back of his neck as he tried to work the stiffness from his muscles. Simply the action of rising to a sitting position made his legs feel as though they had been filled with burning coals.

Private Gerontis offered the water skin, and Alex washed the cottony taste of sleep from his mouth, then gnawed on dry mutton and biscuits as he wondered if his body would possibly obey him after the ordeal he'd put it through the day before.

He rose shakily to his feet and grasped onto a branch of the fig tree when his legs threatened to give out.

The lieutenant shouldered his pack and his weapon and started off. Alex followed behind, pushing the stiffness from his joints with each step.

They would reach Logastra Training Camp sometime that night. He thought over Themis's words and considered how to approach Kapetan Karahalios.

During his time in the Mani, Alex had met with various clan leaders who had been convinced easily with the support of the bey. But what about the legendary kapetan? After the tragic death of Kapetan Zaharias Barbitsiotis, Kapetan Karahalios had become one of the most influential leaders of the klephts. Would he be convinced? Or would he only respect a true warrior?

The day was much the same as the one before. Alex walked until he could not remember a time when his legs hadn't burned and he'd not been covered with sweat. When darkness fell, he hardly noticed.

Lieutenant Markos stopped suddenly, and Alex cast his eyes around, looking for danger. He'd heard nothing. Glancing back, he saw Dino and Themis cock their heads to the side, listening.

The lieutenant hooted loudly, the perfect imitation of an owl. Another hoot sounded from farther up the hill. Lieutenant Markos continued forward. Moments later, a group of klephts surrounded them, seeming to melt from the shadows. They were joined by a man with a torch who saluted when he saw the lieutenant.

They crested the top of a hill, and Lieutenant Markos stopped. "Logastra Training Camp." He spread his hand, indicating a wide valley, high in the mountains. Hills surrounded all sides. The floor of the valley was dark, but Alex could make out the shapes of tents and wide-open spaces he assumed were for drilling.

Alex followed the lieutenant to the bottom of the hill and across the dark valley. When the circle of light reached the edge of the valley, it expanded and changed. Alex blinked, his groggy mind trying to understand what he was seeing, but a few more steps revealed that the torchbearer had entered a cave. The light shone off the walls, casting strange shadows.

Stepping into the cave, he immediately felt the drop in temperature, and the smell of stale water assaulted his nose. The air felt damp. He looked around, but the small bit of torchlight gave only the impression of a living area. A few men lay on sleeping mats, and he saw a table surrounded by mismatched chairs.

The lieutenant motioned him forward, and Alex strained his eyes, trying to see the walls of the cave, but ahead was only darkness. Somehow, he could feel that the cave was much larger than the area he was standing in—perhaps it was because the air did not feel compressed or the small noises did not echo back quickly. He wasn't sure, and his mind was not alert enough to consider how one senses the size of underground dwellings. Following Lieutenant Markos's instruction, he lay on a sleeping mat, and for the second night in a row, his thoughts dropped away as he slipped into a deep pool of blackness.

Chapter 10

"Missno. Wake up."

Diana shook her head to clear away the mugginess of sleep. She glanced at the window. The night was full dark.

"Stella comes today," Elena whispered.

Diana held in a groan. She could not be angry at the lost hours of sleep, not when Elena was so excited. She knew most of the young girl's time was occupied by chores, as she bore the responsibility of her family's household. Diana could not remember the last time she had anticipated anything the way Elena anticipated a day with her cousin.

She rose, and they dressed quietly, hurrying down the stairs to complete the morning chores. Each noise they made sounded even louder as they tried to keep silent. Elena bumped into the table, sending pears tumbling from their bowl, and the young ladies scurried to catch the rolling fruit before it fell to the ground and bruised.

Neither could hold back their giggles. Diana pressed her hands to her mouth and saw Elena doing the same.

Once they were able to keep their laughter in check, they began to prepare breakfast. Elena pounded down the rising dough and shaped it into a loaf while Diana started a fire in the lower part of the brick oven. They whispered as they prepared lunches for the boys. Diana felt like a coconspirator as she put the pears Elena handed her into a knapsack. *This must be what it is like to have a sister.* The thought burst into her mind, and she froze, realizing how much she loved her relationship with Elena and how much she would miss it. This arrangement would not last forever. And then what? Neither the orphanage, nor the finishing school had ever felt as much like a home as did this house in Tsímova.

For the first time, Diana felt as though she belonged. She felt as though she were part of a family. And she felt the force of her longing wash over her so intensely that it overwhelmed her. She pulled in a breath and let it out slowly. This was not her family. It was a fantasy. One that would only result in pain when it ended. The more she allowed Sophia's family into her heart, the more it would hurt when she was forced to leave.

"Missno?"

Diana looked down at the pear in her outstretched hand. A moment passed before she remembered why she was holding it. She slipped it into the sack. "My mind wandered," she said to Elena, trying to force herself to smile. "It must be tired."

She took a deep breath and lifted a stack of thick stoneware plates from the shelf, setting them on the table. She placed a cup beside each plate with the handle facing outward, then a spoon beneath the cup, spacing each object precisely from the edge of the table and ensuring they were an equal distance from one another. Each motion calmed her until she was able to bring her emotions under control, make them small, lock them away, and then feel nothing.

She turned to Elena, folding her hands in front of her waist, as she should, waiting to be assigned a task.

Elena's head tipped the slightest bit, and Diana could see her wondering what had changed. But after a pause, she smiled and pointed toward the door. "Do you think the goats will be more surprised to be awoken early? Or the chickens?"

An hour and a half later, the boys finished breakfast and left for their duties. Diana and Elena wiped off the wooden table, cleaned the dishes, then walked out into the garden.

Elena stood at the wall before her house and looked down the road toward Limeni. "When will she be here?" she complained. "I wanted Stella to arrive early so we would have the entire day together."

Diana crossed the garden and joined her, leaning forward to look up the road. With surprise, she found herself hoping to catch a glimpse of Alexandros Metaxas. She pulled herself back, feeling her face grow warm. She glanced at Elena, grateful the girl couldn't read her thoughts.

Three days had passed since he had departed in the company of the klepht, and Diana had found herself wondering about his journey.

He'd said he would be away for a few days, visiting with the klepht kapetan. He was no doubt offering firearms to the bandits as he had done for the Maniots. Knowing that his career involved selling weapons illegally made Diana's insides feel heavy. Alexandros was not in the least honorable, and it was a good lesson to her. A wolf could wear sheep's clothing and appear to all the world to be a handsome, polite, and even kindhearted gentleman, but appearances were deceptive. She mustn't allow herself to be deceived.

This morning has been filled with unregulated insights, she thought. *I shall attribute my wandering meditations to a lack of sleep.*

"She is coming!" Elena's cry jolted her from her thoughts.

Diana smiled as the girl ran to meet Stella and her brother Kyros.

When they reached the garden gate, Stella greeted Diana and hurried into the house with Elena. Kyros shook his head as he watched the girls enter the house. "I do not envy you today." He rolled his eyes heavenward. "I predict that you and Sophia will suffer from enormous headaches before an hour has passed."

Diana shook her head. "I was a teacher at a school for young ladies. It will take more than two chattering cousins to make my head ache."

"You are a stronger person than I, Missno." His heavy eyelids made his face look sullen.

"Do you have other sisters?" Diana asked as they walked toward the house.

"No. Only brothers. One sister is enough."

Diana wondered how much of his bad humor was for show. Was he simply attempting to keep his soft feelings from showing? She thought he must love his sister, based on the concern he'd shown for her when they'd seen the klepht. Diana had to admit to not fully understanding family associations. She thought if she had a sister, she would never grow tired of her.

When they entered the house, Kyros crossed to Sophia and kissed her hand. "How do you feel today?" His gloomy expression changed to one of concern, and Diana was again reminded how little she knew about being part of a family.

"I hoped you would come with your sister," Sophia said. Diana thought her voice already sounded tired, and she had woken only a quarter of an hour earlier. "I wanted to ask you to carry the sofa into the garden. I have not been out of doors for days, and I fear baking will make the house too hot for comfort."

"Of course." Kyros glanced at the giggling girls. "Stella, Elena, assist me."

Elena helped her mother walk while Stella and Diana lifted one side of the heavy sofa. They followed Sophia's instructions, setting the sturdy piece of furniture beneath a shady tree near the side door, mostly shielded from the road by bushes of flowers.

The girls arranged the pillows, and Diana turned over a bucket, setting a cup of milk near enough that Sophia could reach it easily.

"Thank you." Sophia reclined back with a sigh and a wince as she adjusted into a more comfortable position.

Kyros departed, promising to return in the afternoon to walk his sister home to Limeni.

Diana placed extra pillows beneath her feet, and Sophia smiled in gratitude, her fingers playing over the string of beads as she closed her eyes. Insects buzzed soothingly, and a cool autumn breeze ruffled the leaves, carrying the smell of blossoms and ripe fruit. The spot Sophia had chosen was beautiful, and Diana thought she would not mind napping in the garden herself. She yawned and left Sophia to her rest, promising to return soon to check on her.

The sound of young girls' chatter came from the kitchen.

"Come, Missno." Elena set a burlap sack onto the table. "We have many cookies to make."

"I'm afraid I've never made cookies—or much of anything aside from what you've shown me," Diana said.

Stella's eyes widened.

"Then we shall teach you." Elena opened the sack, showing the almonds inside. "Will you cut up the nuts?"

"Yes." Diana took a knife from the drawer and brought a board to the table. She watched as Elena demonstrated how finely the nuts should be chopped.

"Is it true?" Stella asked. "You have never baked cookies?"

"Very sad, isn't it?" Diana pouted her lip and blinked her wide eyes in a teasing way that made the girls laugh. "In London, I taught reading, arithmetic, German, French, and embroidery, but never cooking."

"But your mother," Stella said, cracking eggs into a bowl, "surely you baked with—"

The shaking of Diana's head stopped her words. "I do not have a mother."

Stella turned her face downward, but not before Diana saw an embarrassed flush. "I am sorry."

"You did not mean anything by it." Diana forced a bright smile. "Now, I have never been to a Greek wedding either. You must tell me all about it."

"The wedding itself is a very beautiful but very long ceremony," Elena said. She puffed out a labored breath to illustrate. Then her face brightened. "But afterward, the wedding party is a grand celebration."

"The square will be swept and decorated with banners and lanterns. And tables are arranged for a feast." Stella whipped the eggs while she spoke.

"A lamb roasts on a spit all day long, and the women bring their favorite dishes." Elena poured a cupful of flour into the bowl. "Men toast the bride and groom, wishing them happiness and health and many babies." She poured in another cupful and looked into the bowl while her cousin stirred. "But the very best part happens after the feast."

The two girls looked at each other and grinned. "The dancing!" they said in unison.

Diana could not help but smile. "And shall you dance with the men at the wedding?"

"Oh no. Men and women do not dance together," Elena said, her brows pinched and her head shaking as if the mere idea were the epitome of indecency. "The men leap and twist, and the women twirl gracefully. You shall see in just a few days."

"Oh, I do not think I'll go to the wedding," Diana said. "I do not know the bride and groom, and—"

"Everybody will go, Missno. Every person for miles around," Stella said. "Even children. Though, perhaps Sophia will not feel well enough to attend." She added soft butter to the mix and continued stirring.

Diana did not want to argue. The cousins continued to speak about the dancing and the wedding feast and the young men who would attend, but she knew she would not be there. She was a servant, even though the family had never made her feel any less than a treasured guest. And dancing in front of people she hardly knew was certainly out of the question. She did not know what to expect with Greek dancing, and though she had to admit to being a bit curious, it did not matter.

She had never had occasion nor inclination to dance. An orphan was not presented at St. James's court. And even if she had been "out in society," she had no reason to attend a ball or assembly. The young ladies at the finishing school attended lessons with a dance master, but Diana had not and was resigned to the fact that such things were never to be part of her life. It was actually a relief, she thought to herself. Dancing seemed an activity fraught with opportunities for a misstep or embarrassment.

"Oh, and I suppose Alexandros Metaxas will attend as well," Elena said. Her lips were pursed in concentration as she tipped the bottle of vanilla into the bowl.

Diana was grateful that Elena had not looked at her. The girl's words had caught her off guard, and she was certain her expression was anything but schooled and polite. Her pulse pounded and warmth crept up her neck. "Oh, I had not even considered it."

"Of course he shall. And I imagine you will be happy to see your friend." Elena smiled as she pushed the cork back into the bottle.

Diana looked closely but saw only an innocent question in the girl's eyes. "Yes, I suppose it will be nice to see him." She hoped her remark sounded off-handed. And why should it not?

Stella continued to stir. "He is indeed handsome, don't you think?"

"Yes." Elena tipped her head and pulled her brows together. "But old."

Diana felt a laugh bubble up inside her throat. "Old? Mr. Metaxas cannot be above thirty."

The girls looked at each other and then at her with wrinkled noses, and she realized that nearly fifteen years separated him from the girls. They could think him old indeed.

Diana turned her gaze back to the almonds, moving the knife up and down with slow motions to keep the nuts from skittering across the board. This was the second time she'd thought of Alexandros Metaxas today, and each time had left her feeling agitated and unsure. How had the mere mention of his name sent her heart racing? She counted each stroke as the knife crunched through the almonds. After a moment, the rhythm calmed her, and she was able to rein in her thoughts.

"I do love a fall wedding," Elena said, breaking the moment of silence. "There is always enough food, and the weather is perfect. Not too hot, nor too cold."

"Perhaps next fall, it shall be your turn."

"Stella!" Elena dropped the cup she was holding. Sugar spilled over the table.

Diana and Elena brushed their hands across the table, sweeping it back into the sugar jar.

Stella smiled. "You should not look so shocked. I have seen Spiros Sássaris stealing glances at you during church."

Elena continued sweeping with her hand, even as a small smile curled her lips. "Perhaps he is simply thinking about something else and happens to look my direction."

"That must be it," Stella said, taking the cup. She poured sugar into the bowl and slid her eyes to the side. "Although he does look a bit like a puppy, wishing for a morsel."

Elena giggled, followed by her cousin. Diana could not help but smile. How lovely to be young and worry free. She adored these girls and their easy friendship.

"We are ready for the almonds now."

Stella and Diana watched as Elena finished mixing the sticky dough with her hands. She demonstrated how to break off a ball and roll it on the table, forming it into a half-moon shape, then place it on a baking stone.

While the girls shaped the dough, Diana cleaned off the workspace. She washed the bowl and spoon, and returned the baking ingredients to their places in the kitchen and storage area. As she walked past the door, she heard a voice in the yard.

She stepped out, surprised by the cool air after spending such a long time in the warm kitchen. After looking to see that Sophia still rested on the sofa, she turned her gaze to the road.

The gypsy woman had returned. She stood at the gate, calling to the house.

Diana hesitated. She was tempted to send the woman away and allow Sophia to rest.

"Let her in," Sophia said.

Diana turned her head. She hadn't realized Sophia was awake. "But . . ."

"Do not worry; she won't stay long."

Diana hurried to the gate, feeling ashamed that her reluctance had shown on her face. Truthfully, aside from wanting to ensure that Sophia rested, she had to admit, the woman unnerved her.

Diana opened the wooden gate, pulling it toward her as the woman walked through. "Good morning."

The woman's gaze traveled over Diana, but she did not speak.

"Sophia is in the garden." Diana lifted her hand toward the side of the house, then followed the gypsy woman as she walked toward the sofa.

Sophia waved and spoke kindly to the woman. She slid her feet from the sofa and invited the visitor to sit. "Diana, would you fetch some milk? And the bread from breakfast."

"Of course." Diana hurried inside and returned with the items. When she stepped out, she saw the woman place a hand on Sophia's swollen belly. She muttered some words that Diana didn't think were Greek but sounded quiet and solemn. A prayer perhaps.

Sophia thanked her.

The woman sat back and accepted the cup and bread from Diana. She ate and drank quickly and with a few muttered words, departed, letting herself out of the gate and walking slowly down the road.

Diana watched until she disappeared from sight.

"She frightens you."

Diana turned her head and saw Sophia watching her. "I learned to beware of people I do not know. London can be a dangerous place, and desperation can cause people to do things they should not."

Sophia nodded, patting the space next to her in an invitation. "I understand. But Miri is harmless."

Diana perched on the edge of the sofa, not wishing to jostle Sophia. "I just want to make sure you and the children are safe."

"You care about them. I can see it in how you treat them—us."

Diana smiled. "I do."

"You must miss your family, your own home, but I do not know what we would do without your help. For this, I am grateful."

Diana patted Sophia's hand. Her heart felt full, and she swallowed against the tightness in her throat. She did love this family, especially Elena. She did not correct Sophia or reveal the truth of her circumstance. If Petrobey were to discover that nobody was coming with a ransom, she did not know what would happen. Would she be turned out and end up wandering from house to house, begging for food? Where would she go? She could not survive in the mountains around the town. "Can I bring you something to eat?" She hoped to change the subject.

"Perhaps in an hour. I am going to sleep a bit longer."

She helped Sophia lift her feet back onto the sofa and arranged her pillows. Sophia lay back and closed her eyes.

Diana paused, brushing a lock of hair from the young mother's forehead. "Rest easy, Sophia." She whispered the words in English; her heart was too full for anything else.

Once the baking was finished, Elena and Stella insisted that Diana accompany them to deliver the cookies to the Michalakiáni home. They carried the trays through the streets, and the girls stopped often to visit with neighbors.

"Calantha will be a beautiful bride," Elena said upon the return trip.

"Yes. Socrates Grigorakiáni is very lucky," Stella said wisely.

Diana smiled, recognizing their mothers' mannerisms in the way the girls spoke.

"I cannot wait to see her perform the Bride's Dance." Elena sighed. "She is so elega—" Her words cut off when they saw Father Yianni leaving Spiros Sássaris's house. The priest stood on the doorstep and crossed himself, then walked slowly toward the garden gate with his head bowed.

When he reached them, Elena and Stella kissed his hand.

"Father, is Costas . . . ?" Elena motioned toward the house behind him.

The priest heaved a heavy sigh. Beneath his graying beard, Diana saw his lip tremble. "Young Costas will not be in pain much longer, my child." He crossed himself again, and Stella and Elena followed suit. The priest walked away with stooped shoulders as if he carried a weight.

The excitement of the day seemed to evaporate, and even the air around them felt heavy. She glanced at Elena and saw the girl wiping tears from her cheeks. Stella's eyes were wet as well.

Diana slipped an arm through each of theirs as they walked back to the house.

Chapter 11

ALEX AWOKE TO A HEAVY silence. The air was cool and comfortable and smelled earthy. Somewhere, he heard water dripping, and the sound lulled him into a daze. He was tempted to return to sleep; his legs practically begged him to remain lying down. But the light at the cave entrance showed that dawn was long past.

Hearing a snore, he turned his head and saw that Dino and Themis still slept. A grin of satisfaction lifted his lips. He was not the last to wake.

A throat cleared.

Alex sat up, stretching out his legs with a grimace, and squinted into the shadows near the cave entrance. Private Gerontis stepped into the light. "Kapetan Karahalios sends his greeting and invites you to help yourself to breakfast." He waved his hand toward the table, where Alex saw three bowls covered with a cloth.

"Thank you."

"He will join you soon." The private left the cave, presumably to inform the kapetan that his guest was awake.

Alex rose, stifling a groan at the aches in his body. He could not fully stand in the cave, but he walked, hunched over, to the table. When he lifted the cloth, he saw the wooden bowls were filled with watery porridge. The fact that it was still a bit warm gave him hope that the kapetan had not eaten too much earlier.

In the dim light, he studied his surroundings. The area of the cave was small, perhaps the size of a cozy parlor. Near the table, he saw mismatched seats arranged in a circle. Some were nothing but rocks, others tree stumps, a few cushions he thought had likely come from raids on Turkish camps, and even a velvet-upholstered chair that looked like it belonged in a fine lady's drawing room. He assumed this was where the kapetan held meetings of his officers. A low opening on one side of the cave led into the darkness, and Alex wondered just how far it went.

Once he'd eaten the porridge, he walked around the space, hoping to learn as much about the kapetan as he could before actually meeting him. Any small bit of information could be an advantage.

Kitchen implements were stacked tidily in a corner. A few trunks lined the wall behind the table. A colorful ikon of St. George slaying a dragon and an elaborate gold cross adorned an alcove. A hearth was cut into the rock, and bending over to look inside, Alex saw a small tunnel burrowed upward to allow smoke to escape. A flat stone jutted out above the fireplace, and he studied the objects atop it. He examined an intricately carved *kilij* with a golden, jewel-encrusted sheath. Alex assumed the saber was a war trophy. Perhaps it symbolized the defeat of a *Yayabasi* or other high-ranking Turkish officer.

Beside the sword were rolls of parchment, likely maps, and an old, leather-bound book. Alex lifted the book and opened the worn cover. *Aesop's Fables.* The quality of the book surprised him—detailed illustrations on thick paper. The Greek lettering was uniform, indicating a superior printer. He was studying a drawing of the tortoise and the hare when he heard footsteps on the cave floor.

A man stepped through the entrance followed by Private Gerontis. "Welcome to Logastras Camp."

Alex closed the book. "Alexandros Metaxas."

"Kapetan Ionnis Karahalios."

Alex noticed a slur to his words. He appraised the warrior quickly. The kapetan's thick hair hung past his shoulders, graying at the temples. His face bore a wide mustache, and the skin was weathered and lined from years of exposure to sun and wind. His dark eyes were calculating as he studied Alex in the dim light of the cave. Even though he was not a tall man, his broad shoulders and straight back left no doubt that he was a man with confidence.

"Thank you for meeting me," Alex said.

Kapetan Karahalios inclined his head, and in the light from the cave opening, Alex saw his jaw muscles quiver, and the lines around his eyes deepen. His lips pressed together. Was the kapetan in pain? "I know why you are here."

"I do not imagine a wise kapetan would permit strangers to a hidden camp without an understanding of their intentions."

"Ah, flattery. You'll find I'm not as easily taken in as the crow in the fable." Kapetan Karahalios waved his hand toward the book in Alex's hand.

Alex raised a brow. The man was direct. "Perhaps I should get to the point, then, Kapetan."

Another snore sounded, and both glanced toward the far side of the cave. Themis continued to sleep, but Dino sat in the shadows, watching the interaction.

The kapetan stepped across the room and sat in the velvet chair. Alex was reminded of his audience a few weeks earlier with Petrobey. The men were similar in their straightforward manner, but Alex didn't sense the same openness in Kapetan Karahalios.

Alex glanced at Dino, then walked to the sitting area, choosing a wooden chair with a seat a bit higher than the kapetan's. He needed every advantage he could get. Alex leaned forward, resting the book on his knee and bracing himself for the burst of pain from his thighs. "You said you know why I am here."

Kapetan Karahalios folded his arms across his chest and stretched his legs out in front of him. He crossed one stocking-covered ankle over the other, the pom-pom on his shoe bouncing as he moved. "Obviously you seek support for a rebellion. Why else would an educated Phanariot dress as a peasant and trek through the mountain to the klepht camp?" He scowled and pressed his fingers against his cheek. "This is not the first group who has tried to organize an uprising."

"This time it will be successful."

He reached for the book. "You are familiar with the fables. Look what happened to the goat when he did not think before jumping into the water. We are wary. Our forces have been weakened, and our great leader, Kapetan Zaharias, murdered. The klephts trust only ourselves."

"And you are opposed to joining with others who share your goals? Kolkotronis himself believes in our cause."

The kapetan brushed his fingers over the book cover. "Petrobey no doubt has been taken in, which is why the Mavromichaleis are here with you." He jerked his head toward Dino and Themis. "The bey is wise, Kolkotronis is great, but in this case, I do not agree." Alex opened his mouth to speak, but the captain shook his head. "Do not waste your time trying to persuade me. The klephts have hidden in these hills for hundreds of years. Already we fight this battle. We do not need leaders from afar to direct us."

Alex felt a wave of frustration but kept his voice calm. "Yes, I understand. But *we* need *you*. A coordinated uprising, instead of the small, erratic—"

Kapetan Karahalios sat up straight. "And you think you're the one to lead us?"

Alex was startled by the anger in the man's voice. "No. I am but an emissary. I seek only your allegiance."

The kapetan scrutinized Alex with squinting eyes. He blinked, appearing as though he made up his mind. "Come, I will show you the camp." He pressed his palm against his cheek as he stood and stomped toward the exit. "Private, feed the Mavromichaleis and show them the training grounds."

"Yes, sir."

Alex glanced toward the Maniots. Themis's lip was twisted in a sneer that showed his pleasure in seeing Alex on the losing side of an argument. Dino's face betrayed nothing. In his typical fashion, he seemed to be considering what he heard instead of voicing an opinion. Obviously neither would jump to Alex's assistance. He wondered why they had agreed to accompany him in the first place. Most likely because Petrobey asked them. And perhaps they were curious to see firsthand the legendary secret klepht training ground. Alex certainly was.

Private Gerontis caught his gaze as Alex passed, then looked away quickly, but not before Alex saw the indecision in the young man's eyes. The worry that perhaps his leader was not making the correct decision. Alex wondered how many others would side with him if their alliance was not pledged to the kapetan.

Stepping into the sunlight, Alex squinted. The valley he'd seen in darkness the night before had come to life. Klephts, wearing their white kilts and red hats, drilled in the different areas of the camp.

In the sunlight, he saw the kapetan's cheek was swollen. His mouth hung slightly open, and the gums inside were inflamed. Few pains were as intense as a diseased tooth. Alex wondered if the man's ill temper were a result of his infection.

Kapetan Karahalios led him toward a group engaged in hand-to-hand combat. The men and boys grunted as they wrestled against each other. The crack of well-aimed blows, grunts of pain, and blood flowing from more than one young man's nose indicated the training was not simply play-acting.

They continued past rows of tents to a shooting range. At one end of the long, flat area, straw dummies were dressed in the bright uniforms and extravagant hats of Turkish soldiers. Klephts stood and knelt, some bracing their weapons on boulders as they took aim and, at the command of their trainer, fired.

Alex pressed his hands to his ears just in time, as the report and echo of gunshots filled the valley. His ears rang, and he shook his head to clear it. The figures at the end of the range lost limbs in a blast of straw. One turban-styled hat blew apart, and the men cheered.

Kapetan Karahalios crossed his arms and nodded as he watched the men hurry to right the dummies and prepare to fire again.

Scanning their weapons, Alex saw few of the klephts carried rifles; most had well-used muskets that he knew were inaccurate and difficult to aim. They would benefit from the British weapons in the hull of the ship heading toward Limeni. If only their kapetan would be convinced.

They approached Lieutenant Markos, who nodded, then barked orders at a group of young boys who were running in place. At the far end of the camp, men lifted heavy logs to build muscles and threw javelins to practice their aim. Some trained with swords and curved knives. The well-ordered camp was filled with the sounds of grunts, gunshots, clashing blades, and leaders calling orders.

Alex saw Dino and Themis studying the sword training with thoughtful expressions. Occasionally one would point out something, but they seemed content to watch.

The kapetan stopped on a rise overseeing the wide mountain valley. He lifted his chin, and his chest swelled as he inhaled a breath. His head dipped in a barely perceptible nod as his gaze traveled over the camp. "We have soldiers as young as nine going on raids. All the men train seven days a week—strenuously. The borders of Logastras are well-guarded and secure. This camp makes boys into warriors, Mr. Metaxas.

They are prepared to fight to the death for Greece." He lifted Alex's hand and placed into it the book he still carried. "But you are not."

"I do not seek to lead your men, Kapetan. Nor do those who sent me. We seek to unite—"

Kapetan Karahalios fixed Alex with a glare, and he stopped speaking, knowing his words were fruitless. He blew out a breath through his nose. "Very well, kapetan. Thank you for your time. I do hope you'll reconsider."

He held out the book of fables.

Kapetan Karahalios shook his head and pushed the book back toward Alex. "Keep it. Few here can read. And those who can have no use for fairy tales."

Alex knew the man meant his words to be an insult. The kapetan considered him to be no more than a soft-handed, city-dwelling scholar with big ideas but no concept of the actuality of war. He would not listen to a man like Alex. Perhaps if a warrior like Heracles or Achilles pleaded his case, Kapetan Karahalios would be convinced.

He ran his fingers over the scrolling design on the leather cover. "Kapetan, more than muscles and weapons are required to win a battle." He held the man's gaze as he tapped the book. "The mighty lion learned this lesson from a small mouse."

Kapetan Karahalios's eyes narrowed, and he placed his hand on the curved knife at his waist.

Alex felt a surge of fear but knew that was precisely the reaction the kapetan was hoping for. He maintained eye contact and kept his expression from showing any strain, even though he was sure the man could hear his heart pounding.

The kapetan pulled his gaze away and called to Lieutenant Markos.

The lieutenant stepped toward him.

"The visitors will leave now. Take them as far as Kalamata. They can find their way from there." He turned and strode toward the cave without giving them a second glance.

Alex saw his hand go to his swollen jaw and knew the kapetan did not want the others to know his tooth was hurting.

Lieutenant Markos watched his kapetan depart. "Come, if we walk swiftly, we will reach Kalamata by nightfall." He started off but turned back. He glanced once at the cave's entrance. "Kapetan Karahalios is an honorable leader. He is simply cautious. After Zaharias's murder, we all are."

"I understand." Although sickening disappointment churned in Alex's stomach, he spoke the truth. He did understand. Zaharias Barbitsiotis had united the klepht bands, turning them into an effective military force. He had been a fearless leader who'd pledged never to surrender until the Turks were driven from the Peloponnese, and his assassination had been a blow to the freedom fighters' morale. "I wish it were otherwise," Alex said.

Lieutenant Markos nodded once, then led Alex across the valley to where Private Gerontis stood talking to Themis and Dino. "Private, fetch the visitors' things. We leave immediately." Private Gerontis hurried to the cave, and the lieutenant started toward the path that led from the valley.

Dino and Themis turned to Alex with brows raised in surprise. If Alex hadn't been so frustrated, he would have found their expressions comical.

"That was fast," Themis said, his lip curling. "It took only an hour for the kapetan to realize what I've been saying from the start."

Dino made a grunting noise that sounded like a combination of clearing his throat and a growl. "Petrobey believes in this." His voice was low and threatening. "And so we believe."

"I envy your blind devotion, cousin." Themis turned away.

Dino's hand shot out, grabbing onto his cousin's arm. "I trust my father. I am loyal to my clan. That is not blind devotion; it is honor." Releasing his grip, he walked in the direction of Lieutenant Markos.

Themis glared at Alex, then stormed after his cousin.

The trek to Kalamata was silent. Alex spent the hours analyzing his meeting with the kapetan from every angle. What could he have done differently? He imagined the disappointment in Xánthos's face. How did one win over a man like Kapetan Karahalios? He respected men of strength, warriors, men who proved themselves on the battlefield. Alex clenched his jaw—frustrated at his failure.

And though he did not want to admit it, Themis's words had left him unsettled. He'd known when he set out from Constantinople that he would make enemies, but dealing with the reality was harder than he'd expected. *I am not here to form friendships.* The thought did not ease his mind.

The group arrived in Kalamata just after dark. The town was larger than Tsímova, with shops and eateries around a center square.

Alex noticed the klephts attracted a few wary glances, but most of the townsfolk simply greeted them as they passed.

"Follow the coast." Lieutenant Markos jerked his chin in the direction of the road. "The journey will take perhaps seven hours—six, if you maintain a good pace." He bowed his head and motioned for the private to retreat.

The thought of walking another six or seven hours produced a wave of exhaustion that nearly made Alex's knees buckle. "We will rest here for a few hours. Lieutenant, Private, please, join us for supper." Alex motioned toward a crowded taverna with tables in the courtyard beneath a canopy.

Lieutenant Markos hesitated. He glanced at the taverna and then at the dark hills ahead.

"Please. You will be my guest. It is the least I can do for your time and effort."

The lieutenant dipped his chin in a nod. "Thank you."

Alex smiled, relieved at the idea of sitting in a chair and eating something other than porridge and dried mutton. His eyes traveled up the street, and he paused when he saw an apothecary shop. "I will meet you there in a moment," he said.

A few moments later, he joined the group at a table in a quiet corner of the patio. He smiled as he slipped into an empty chair, remembering a similar situation a few weeks earlier. The memories of meeting Miss Diana Snow were far more pleasant than sitting with four exhausted, dirty men.

A basket of flatbread sat in the middle of the table. He noticed the men had already ordered drinks, and he lifted a glass, taking a sip of the strong-smelling *raki*. "For your kapetan." He set a small dark bottle on the table in front of Lieutenant Markos.

"What is it?"

"Myrrh oil. It decreases mouth pain and reduces swelling."

Lieutenant Markos lifted the bottle and held it up to a lantern, peering through the dark glass as he shook it. "This will not change his mind."

Alex felt his neck redden and avoided looking in Themis's direction. "I know."

The lieutenant shrugged and slid the bottle into his knapsack. He opened his mouth to speak but stopped when a young man approached their table.

The stranger bowed his head in a greeting. "I want to join the klephts. Please take me with you."

Lieutenant Markos's brows lifted. "What is your name?"

"Iason Solomos."

Iason wore clothing typical of any peasant in Laconia. Alex noticed a crisscross of scars on his forearms, possibly from working with a harvest blade in the fields. But something about the boy's manner seemed off.

"I am Lieutenant Markos, and this is Private Gerontis. How old are you, Iason?"

"Thirteen, sir."

Alex glanced down at Iason's shoes and saw, instead of sturdy work boots, leather slippers with a pointed toe.

"And why do you wish to join the klephts?" Lieutenant Markos said.

"To fight the Turks."

Alex tried to place the boy's strange accent. He was Greek, but something about his pronunciation was wrong.

The lieutenant motioned "Let me guess. The Turks killed a family member and you seek revenge."

The boy's eyes slid to the side as he lowered his head. "Yes sir. My father. I want to become a warrior."

Themis leaned close to Dino and whispered something in his ear.

"Many freedom fighters have the same story, Iason. They arrive, filled with a thirst for revenge, but soon the difficult training takes its toll. You would work hard every day with very little rest, building muscles and endurance, and training with weapons. It will not be easy."

"I can do it, sir. Will you take me to your camp and teach me to fight?"

Lieutenant Markos took a sip of *raki*. "Yes. We leave in an hour."

The corner of Iason's mouth pulled as he glanced toward the road. "I must retrieve my things."

"Meet us at the well in the town square."

"Thank you, sir." The boy departed with a smile on his face.

"A brave lad," Themis said. "His story is tragic."

Alex tore off a section of flatbread. "He lies."

The lieutenant blinked, raising his brows and turning to Alex. "How do you know?"

"He is a spy. I suspect a Janissary."

Themis snorted and took a drink.

"Did you see his shoes?" Alex asked. "His arms are battle-scarred. And listen to his accent. He is educated, but not in Greece."

The men exchanged glances, and Alex saw the truth dawn on them.

"So young," Private Georonitis said. "Why would he . . . ?"

"Can you think of no reason the Turks would want a man inside your camp?" Alex said. "To warn them of your plans, perhaps, or to study your defenses, discover the weaknesses. I would not be surprised if they seek to do away with Logastra Training Camp altogether."

"But even if he communicated with the enemy, our lookouts would see an army approach from miles away." Private Gerontis's voice grew louder, and his face was turning red.

"A small group with inside information could do an enormous amount of damage if they caught you by surprise."

The private slammed his glass down on the table. "We should kill him, Lieutenant. As soon as we're out of town—"

Lieutenant Markos turned to Alex, his voice calm. "What do you suggest? How do we handle the spy?"

Alex was surprised by the lieutenant's question. He glanced at the others and saw Dino and Themis watched him with interest, waiting for his reply. Private Gerontis's jaw was tight. "I suggest you watch him closely," Alex said. "Take him to camp, let him believe he has your trust. But if he sneaks off alone, follow. You'll discover the truth soon enough. And you will have the advantage."

The lieutenant nodded slowly. "It is good advice. I will tell the kapetan of your suspicions. And give him the myrrh."

Alex waved to the serving woman. "Now, enough talk. Let's eat."

The next morning as the trio walked toward Limeni, Alex caught sight of a large spiderweb between two trees. He grinned at the memory of Diana's warning and at the thought of seeing her again. She was such a complicated woman, prim and reserved, nearly rude, and he should want nothing to do with her. She had certainly given him no indication that she was interested in his company.

But he'd caught glimpses of something beneath her detached exterior. Something she tried to keep hidden, but at times, bits of it shone through. She was afraid of allowing anyone to see the real woman beneath her mask, of revealing any emotion that would make her vulnerable, and Alex felt an ache to know why.

"Why are you smiling?"

Alex glanced to the side and saw Themis walked next to him.

"I can read your face as easily as you read the young Janissary's. You are thinking of a woman."

"I cannot deny it." Alex's grin widened.

"You better pray she is not related to me," Themis muttered.

Chapter 12

A KEENING SHRIEK THAT TURNED into a wail pierced the quiet of the waking village.

Diana's heart froze, and the hair at the nape of her neck stood on end. She nearly spilled the pail of milk all over the garden as she whipped around, trying to determine the source of the noise.

Elena calmly set down the basket of eggs and made the sign of the cross.

"Elena, what—"

"Costas Sássaris is dead." Elena held open the door to the house and bowed her head. "It is a day of mourning."

As a child Diana had not been a stranger to death, but funerals were for those with families. The loss of an orphan was not mourned by the directors of St. Luke, Chelsea. It was simply one less mouth to feed and, in the crowded institution, hardly worthy of notice, except by a few friends and, of course, the Reverend Delaney.

The good minister's memorial service was the only funeral Elena had ever attended. The hushed voices, quiet weeping, and enduring smiles had filled her with a deep, aching sorrow. But that gentle ceremony did nothing to prepare her for the Greek mourning rituals.

As they prepared and served breakfast, the wailing continued, joined by other women's voices. The sound put Diana's nerves on edge and her hands shook.

"I wish I could perform the *miroloyi* for Costas," Sophia said in a tired voice from her bed on the sofa. She'd hardly had the strength to climb the stairs to her bedroom the night before. "You must tell me who sings."

Hours later as the villagers followed the procession to the small churchyard, Diana glanced at Elena. The young girl wiped tears from her cheeks and walked with her head bowed. Women wailed loudly, letting out moans, but their noises did not draw a glance from the others. Elena had explained to her that since Costas was a child, the wake had lasted a few hours instead of days.

Costas was wrapped in a shroud and carried on the shoulders of men in his family. Diana hadn't realized that he would not be buried in a coffin, but the Maniots were poor people and wood was scarce, which was why every building was constructed of stone. She saw Spiros wipe his eyes with his thumb and finger as he bore his younger brother's body. His sister, Theodora, walked with her mother.

When they reached the cemetery, Diana hung back.

Elena shot her a questioning glance, but she motioned for the girl to continue. These were her people.

Diana stood beneath a tree at the edge of the churchyard as Father Yianni spoke; then the small figure was laid into the ground.

The mourners stood still, as if they were waiting for something.

Daphne, the boy's mother, began to sing in a high, reedy voice. The melody was in a minor chord, and the tune, instead of offering comfort, was sung in a rhythm that left Diana feeling agitated. The words sounded harsh. She rubbed her arm as goose pimples tightened her skin.

Other women surrounded the grave and joined in the singing, adding their wails and keeping time with the unearthly beat of the music.

Diana glanced around and saw Elena and Stella weeping.

Daphne swayed back and forth as she sang, occasionally letting out a loud sob. The song's intensity grew, as did the singer's actions. The singing became more like shrieking. Costas's mother raked her fingernails down her cheeks and beat at her breast.

Diana darted a look at the other mourners, thinking someone should stop her before she hurt herself.

Nobody looked alarmed at her behavior. The men stood with their heads bowed, and the women swayed with Daphne, adding their moans and cries to the song. One woman tore out a fistful of hair and dropped it into the grave. Another collapsed, writhing as she howled.

The spectacle seemed near to hysteria, and Diana could not believe the others allowed it to continue. Daphne's cheeks bled. Her hair was loose around her shoulders, and she held her scarf by the corners, pulling it from side to side behind her back, keeping time to the music in a way that made Diana think she was nearly in a trance.

The spectacle did not draw strange glances or whispers. She realized it was all part of the mourning ceremony.

Diana fought to hold back a wave of emotion. The display took her by surprise, but it was so desperately moving that her throat tightened, and she drew a jagged breath. She pressed the inside of her wrist against her chest when the pain became too strong and closed her eyes against the tears prickling.

"It is perfectly acceptable to cry, you know."

She recognized Alexandros Metaxas's voice but did not look up—her emotions were not yet under control. She shook her head, squeezing her eyes as she counted and calmed her breathing. Her hands were trembling as she pushed away the tears and finally raised her head.

"A *miroloyi*," Alexandros continued. "Mani women are famous for their weeping songs.

"I have never seen . . . It is so incredibly sad." Her voice quivered, but she held herself tightly and no tears escaped.

He reached out a hand toward her.

"Don't." She spoke more sharply than she'd intended, but her hold on her emotions was precarious and she knew one touch would make her crumble like a sandy wall holding back a river.

"I'm sorry." He tipped his head as he studied her. "Repressing your pain does not make it disappear. It becomes poison inside you." He glanced toward the women at the graveside. "Setting the pain free, it is therapeutic."

Diana clung to her arms, shivering in the shade, though she was not cold.

He turned his gaze toward the graveside. "These women have seen their share of death. They know how to cope with grief."

Tears threatened again, and Diana felt a sob choking her throat. "And you bring more grief." She spoke sharply, using the tactic she was most familiar with, disguising sorrow with anger and pushing away anyone who came too close. "Why do you sell weapons here? To bring war? You pretend to care, but you will cause more death, and for what purpose? To turn a profit."

She turned away and walked hurriedly, heading for the churchyard gate. She did not glance back at either Alexandros or the mourners. Elena was surrounded by friends and family. She did not need Diana to wait for her.

"Miss Snow."

Hearing his footsteps behind her, she quickened her pace.

"Diana."

The sound of her Christian name brought her up short. She whirled around, prepared to deliver a scathing reprimand.

He caught her arm and leaned close. "I *do* bring war, but I do not do it lightly."

The intensity in his expression stopped anything she intended to say. Her pulse pounded, and she didn't know whether it was from her rapid walking, the emotion of the weeping song, or the familiar way this man used her name and stood so close as he spoke.

"Then why?" Her question sounded foolish to her own ears, but she wanted to understand.

"Walk with me." He skimmed his fingers down her arm, catching her wrist and tucking her hand beneath his arm.

Diana felt a trail of heat where his skin touched hers. The sensation left her breathless, and she was tempted to flee, but the unanswered question held her in place. Somehow, understanding this man had become a matter of vital importance.

Alexandros led her to a low stone wall across the square from the church. A bush with bright pink flowers offered shade from the midday sun. He spread his hand, indicating for her to sit, then joined her.

Diana felt an unexpected tinge of loss when he released her hand. The sentiment surprised her.

He turned his knees toward her, arms resting on his legs. "You asked why I bring war. I will tell you. But in order for you to fully understand, you must hear my story."

She folded her hands in her lap, nodding her head.

Alexandros gazed across the square to the churchyard, where the sounds of the *mirolóyi* continued. "Do you know the word *devşirme*?"

Diana pulled her brows together. "*Devşirme*?" She said it slowly, trying to pronounce it the way he had, but her tongue could not form the sounds. "No."

"In Turkish, it means 'collecting.'" He clenched his jaw, and his lip curled beneath his moustache.

A heaviness filled Diana's stomach. The look on his face made her fear what he would say. "Go on," she said tentatively.

"The Turks collect a tax of children, young boys, mostly, to increase their armies. Though girls are taken too. For the sultan's harem."

Diana gasped. "No, they cannot simply steal children." The thought of anyone taking away Sophia's children made panic well up inside her. She needed to hear him say it would not happen. "It is only a story, Mr. Metaxas, isn't it? A rumor."

"Alex. Please call me Alex." He glanced at her then turned his gaze away. The heavy sensation increased, and a foreboding accompanied it when she saw the hardness in his face.

"When I was a child, my father owned a large vineyard outside of Nafplio. It was beautiful. My mother planted flowers and kept an herb garden by the kitchen door. She hummed as she worked. Sometimes my father let me ride on the donkey when he drove into town for market day." A soft smile curved his lips. "In the evenings, Papa would tell us stories from the Bible. I spent my childhood running up and down the rows between vines, playing with my older brother and sister.

"My sister, Dimitria, sang to her dolls. And my brother, Michalis, he loved to read. He would stay awake late into the night with a book and a candle."

Alex closed his eyes and tightened his shoulders. "When I was eleven, a group of men approached the farm on horseback. They were, of course, Turks. Only Turks are allowed to own horses. My father was not a stranger to the local tax collector, but something about these men frightened him. He told my mother to hide me and ran to find my brother and sister." Alex swallowed and drew a breath, letting out slowly before continuing.

"My mother ran with me into the storehouse. She pushed me behind a pile of barrels, against the wall, and squeezed in beside me. I can still remember the smell of wood and wine. She held me against her, and I could feel her shaking.

"Outside, we heard Michalis calling for my parents in a frightened voice. Dimitria was screaming. My father yelled angrily, then was silenced by a gunshot."

Diana pushed her fist against her breastbone. She shook her head and fought back tears when she saw Alex's eyes were wet.

"*Mitéra* pressed my face against her when we heard voices enter the storehouse, but they did not discover our hiding place. We remained there for what seemed like hours. I was afraid, and she . . . I felt her teardrops in my hair." Alex rubbed his eyes.

"Oh, Alex." Diana's heart hurt as she watched this man relive his pain. "I . . ." She could not think of words to comfort him and instead slid closer and placed her hand over his.

He turned his head to look at her, and Diana tried to read the jumble of expressions on his face. Pain, sorrow, resignation, anger . . . He pressed his lips tight and breathed deeply.

"What happened?" Diana whispered.

"I did not see my brother and sister again. I remember, at my father's wake, thinking he looked like he was sleeping, except for the hole in his forehead." He grimaced. "Mitéra and I could not maintain the orchard alone. We moved into a house in the city. She was consumed with fear that I would be taken, and finally, she sent me to school in Italy, where I would be safe. I got word a few months later that she was dead."

"How?"

"I do not know." He turned fully toward her and placed his other hand atop hers. "Diana, for years, anger festered inside me until revenge was my only thought. When I finished school, I traveled to Constantinople with the goal of finding my siblings and killing as many Turks as I could in the process. I concocted a terrible plan involving gunpowder, a disguise, and the sultan's palace. Luckily, a man named Xánthos found me before I got myself killed." His lips pulled slightly to the side. "My death would have solved nothing."

"Xánthos had a similar history, but instead of allowing his anger to poison him, he used it to fuel his goal to free Greece. He learned all he could about the enemy, about intelligence tactics and stratagems. Then he taught me, trained me, and I found a way to make myself useful to my people instead of getting killed on a suicide mission."

"We mean to start a war, Diana. But not for profit, not for revenge. I do not want another family destroyed the way mine was, the way so many are. I do not want another boy to hide in fear while his father is killed and his siblings stolen. I do not want another wife and mother to die of a broken heart."

"And so you bring weapons for people to defend themselves?"

"I belong to an order—I cannot tell you more—but they have sent me to recruit others to the cause. Greeks are fiercely loyal to their clans, especially the Maniots. But if they can work together—if we can all join forces . . ." He cleared his throat.

Diana saw his actions in a new light. The way he'd spoken to Dino and Themis that night on the beach. He was not simply hoping they would be interested in his guns; he needed to win their trust. "It is dangerous. If you were discovered by the wrong people . . ." The thought brought her up short. Alex's mission was a risk. Even among his people. Surely there were those who wanted nothing to do with his group or their plan. Some might even think to report him to the Turks.

"Which is why this undertaking is better for a lone man instead of a person with a family."

Diana's throat was tight, and her eyes burned. "I am sorry I accused you. I am sorry." She could not bring herself to say more. Sobs were threatening to choke her. She felt hopeless when she thought of the pain he had suffered. She had no family and could not imagine how devastating the loss was to Alex and his mother.

"Don't you see? The revenge was poisoning me. When I released my hatred and turned my mind to change instead of vengeance, I was free." He took her other hand, lifting both in his. "You must let it free, Diana. You cannot hold in your pain forever. It will consume you."

"I cannot." She tried to pull her hands away, but he did not release his grip.

"Why?"

"I'm afraid." She tugged and drew her hands from his, pressing her fingers against her eyes and then down her cheeks.

He tipped his head down to capture her gaze. "Afraid of what? Of judgment? Do you think I do not know what it is to weep? You worry I will think less of you?"

She wrapped her arms around herself, shaking her head. Her heart ached, and she felt as if her very soul was grieving—for Costas, for

Alex, for every broken family in Greece. "I am afraid if I let it go, it will hurt." She gasped, swallowing a sob and releasing a shaky breath as she fought down the tears. "It will hurt, and I'll not be able to bear the pain." Diana breathed in and out, counting the bricks in the road while her emotions calmed. She felt like she was gathering soft sand that kept slipping through her fingers faster than she could capture it.

Alex slid closer to her but remained silent, and when she was finally in possession of her self-control, she glanced up at him and saw that he studied her with a thoughtful expression.

She rose, and he rose with her.

"If you will excuse me, I should return." Diana kept the trembling out of her voice. She turned and started toward Sophia's house.

Without a word, Alex stepped next to her, lifting her hand into the crook of his arm.

She was grateful that he seemed to understand her need for silence as she sorted her feelings. Understanding them, analyzing them, and knowing them for what they were helped her put them away. She could not remember ever feeling so much sorrow for another person's pain—even her own. Alexandros Metaxas's burdens weighed on her, and it frightened her. She pushed away the pain and sorrow, and the ache she felt from watching a mother grieve for her child.

She felt guilt for her assumptions about Alex churning like acid inside her. She'd continued to assume the worst about him, even when he had explained his actions on the beach and gave her no reason to distrust him. Why did she do it? She knew the answer rested with the other feeling that she did not want to confront. The one that set her heart beating when she heard his voice and her stomach fluttering when he was near. That feeling was even more frightening than the others. Somehow, Diana's heart had become wrapped up with Alex's, and she knew the only way to cope was to pull it back. She did not know whether it was a matter of days or weeks, but a ship would arrive to take him away, and if she didn't have full possession of her heart, his leaving would tear off a piece of it. And that was a pain she was certain she'd be unable to bear.

Chapter 13

THE DAY AFTER THE FUNERAL, Alex stopped at the roadside shrine on his way to Tsímova, making the sign of the cross and saying a prayer. He opened the door and studied the small ikon of the Most Holy Theotokos and her infant Jesus painted with golden halos and trumpeting angels. Instead of continuing right away, he used the flint and steel inside the box to light a candle.

Memories of his family were close to the surface since yesterday's conversation with Diana. He'd only related the entirety of the story one other time—to Xánthos. He studied the small flame flickering off the figures depicted in the ikon. As much as he ached for his family, he felt as though God had put Xánthos into his path just at the right time. The man had saved his life—in more ways than one, teaching him to release his hatred, instilling in him the belief that his life was not without value, and preparing him to become a member of the order. He crossed himself again, praying for the success of the Filiki Eteria and feeling blessed to be a part of something greater than himself.

He closed the door of the shrine and continued on his way with a feeling of peace. He breathed the cooling air, taking in the smell of rosemary and thyme from the wild herbs along the road. A perfect autumn evening. Patting the knapsack at his hip, he turned his mind to the purpose for his outing. He felt like his conversation yesterday with Diana had broken through some of her walls, and the thought of seeing her again made his chest feel light. An unwelcome whisper of trepidation wormed its way into his thoughts. Would she want to see him again? She had clearly been distressed during their conversation.

Would she revert back to the closed-off woman from before? Had he exposed too much of himself?

He'd hoped sharing a personal piece of his history would make her comfortable enough to do the same. And even though she held her emotions close, he'd seen a young woman who'd been frightened, hurt.

He neared the outskirts of the village, admiring the beauty and simple life of its inhabitants. The rocky land made farming difficult, and it seemed like goats and sheep were the only livestock that adapted to the harsh climate. With few natural resources, the Maniot people eked out a harsh existence. They worked from dawn until dusk with little to show for it, but they were willing to share what they had. He felt grateful and a little jealous of their unpretentious lives. He would miss this place, these people. One in particular.

His ship should arrive within the week, and he'd return to Constantinople, but the thought of leaving Diana to her own devices troubled him. How could he depart without making sure she was taken care of? Surely a British ship would arrive for her soon. The memory of the hurt in her eyes returned. Was she returning to a life that brought her happiness?

He heard the bleating of goats; then laughter and children's voices floated on the air as he neared the farmhouse. He paused at the gate, peering between the foliage and attempting to see the source of the noise.

"Mr. Metaxas!" Elena waved and hurried toward him. She opened the garden gate, and he noticed she carried a wooden comb and pair of scissors. "Have you come for a visit? Missno will be so happy to see you."

The girl's words caught him off guard, but a glance at her guileless expression told him her innocent statement implied nothing out of the ordinary. She knew he and Diana were friends and assumed no more. Was there more to assume? He was momentarily at a loss for words and realized he stood foolishly at the gate, staring at the house with Elena watching him. "Thank you."

She stood aside and closed the gate behind him.

A pair of young boys ran into the garden but stopped when they saw him.

"Iakob and Mikhail, this is Mr. Metaxas. He is a friend of Petrobey's. Mr. Metaxas, these are my youngest brothers."

"*Chaírete*." Alex smiled at the boys.

Iakob, the older of the two, returned the greeting, but the small Mikhail studied him with the unapologetic curiosity of a child. Alex assumed the family didn't receive many unfamiliar callers.

"Miétra, a visitor," Elena called.

A woman's voice bid them approach, and Alex followed the children and Elena around the side of the house.

"We are preparing for the wedding tomorrow," Elena told him. "The boys are all being given haircuts."

The woman he'd seen at church and assumed to be Elena's mother reclined on a wooden-framed sofa in the shade beneath a tree, her fingers moving worry beads along a string. She pulled herself into a sitting position when Alex approached. A boy of about fourteen sat on the ground beside her and rose when he saw Alex. Another boy, a bit younger, was perched on a chair with a sheet tied around his neck. The chair was situated a few feet away in the sunlight.

"Miétra, this is Mr. Metaxas from Constantinople."

"Alexandros, please," Alex said. "I am sorry to impose."

"Not at all. Sophia Mavromichalis. You'll excuse me for not rising." She smiled, and he was struck by the similarity in appearance between mother and daughter. Both had pleasant smiles and laughing eyes, although Sophia's seemed a bit tired.

"My other brothers, Georgi and Chrysanthos," Elena said.

Alex greeted the boys. He estimated the Mavromichalis children ranged in age from Elena, who he thought might be seventeen, to young Mikhail, who he guessed was probably three or four.

He heard the whisper of scissors as Elena returned to cutting Chrysanthos's hair.

"What brings you to our home, Alexandros?" Sophia winced as she shifted against the pillows.

"I—" Alex began but broke off when Diana came through the doorway carrying a tray with grapes and pieces of white cheese.

She froze when she saw him, and pink flooded her cheeks. "Al— Mr. Metaxas. What a surprise." She spoke in English and glanced at Sophia then back, dipping in a curtsey. She set the tray on a low table near the sofa. "How do you do this evening?" This time she spoke in Greek. A small wrinkle appeared in her forehead. Her expression,

though she fought to keep it neutral, seemed uneasy. Perhaps she
thought she would be chastised for his visit. Or she worried he would
renew their earlier conversation.

"I have actually come to see Elena."

He had the pleasure of seeing Diana's usually composed face slacken
in shock, which she hurried to cover by bending down and arranging
the items on the tray.

The oldest brother stepped closer, and Alex realized his statement
might be perceived as inappropriate. He turned to Sophia and
proceeded to explain. "I brought a gift." He pulled the book of fables
from his knapsack.

Elena gasped.

Alex held out the book toward her mother, knowing he needed
parental approval before giving a single young lady a gift of any type.

"It is very kind of you." Sophia's eyes narrowed suspiciously. She
looked down at the book in her hand, opening it and glancing through
the pages.

"I thought she might find it more appealing than the books in the
church. Perhaps a bit easier to understand."

Alex turned his gaze to Diana and saw her expression was soft.
She nodded her head and voicelessly mouthed the words, "Thank
you." Her eyes shone, and her brows rose in the center in a look of the
most sincere gratitude, as though his simple act had been the grandest
gesture ever performed. The fact that his gesture had touched her so
deeply spoke volumes about her affection for the young girl, and Alex's
heart felt full.

He glanced back at Elena's mother. Sophia's expression took on
a knowing look as her gaze moved between the two of them. The
wariness left her face.

Sophia offered the book to her daughter and smiled with a bit of
a smirk, and Alex thought his face may have revealed too much about
his heart's true sentiments.

Elena handed the scissors and comb to Diana and sat on the ground,
her brothers crowding near. She turned the pages reverently. "Oh, thank
you, Mr. Metaxas. It is the most beautiful book I have ever seen."

"Perhaps you will read a story to us?" Sophia said. "Missno, will
you finish the haircuts, please?"

Diana glanced at the scissors and then nodded.

Alex turned toward the gate.

"You will stay, won't you, Alexandros?" Sophia said. "You might enjoy listening as well. If you are not in a hurry."

He glanced at Diana once more, trying to judge how she felt about his presence.

She held his gaze, and the warmth in her eyes sent heat through his core.

"I would be delighted to hear Elena read," he said.

"Come, Mikhail." Diana held out her hand. "Time to cut your hair."

The boy folded his arms. "No. I want my hair to grow long like Uncle Dino's."

"Dino's hair was short when he was your age," Sophia said. Her voice was patient but stern. "And young boys must obey their mothers."

"But I do not want my hair cut."

Elena rose up on her knees. "Mikhail, I will wait to read until you are finished. And I saw a drawing of a lion. We can look at it together . . . once your hair is cut."

The boy seemed to falter as his gaze wandered to the book, but he frowned. "I do not want it cut."

Alex watched the women's frustrated expressions grow as they tried to convince the boy. Sophia sighed tiredly, and Elena looked as though she were bracing herself for battle.

Alex crouched down until his face was even with the child's. "Mikhail, I have a problem. You see, I need a haircut as well, but I am afraid. Will it hurt?"

"A haircut does not hurt."

Alex opened his eyes wide, pulling back his head in a look of astonishment. "You must be very brave. Just like your Uncle Dino."

Mikhail lifted his chin and stuck out his chest. "I *am* brave."

Alex tapped his own cheek. "Perhaps if I watched you get your hair cut first, I would not feel so frightened."

"Do you want Missno to cut your hair?"

Alex grimaced. "I don't know," he whispered. "Would she be gentle?"

He nodded solemnly. "She is nice." Mikhail glanced at Diana, leaned close to Alex, and lowered his voice as if sharing a confidence. "She'll not hurt you. If you like, I will show you."

"You really are fearless." Alex chewed his lip to hide his amusement.

Mikhail climbed into the chair. "I am ready, Missno. Then Mr. Metaxas will have a haircut too."

Alex glanced up to see Diana studying him. The corner of her mouth lifted the slightest bit before she pursed her lips. He thought she was stifling a smile, and he felt a burst of triumph. He would see that woman smile—a full-fledged toothy grin—he vowed to find a way.

He moved closer.

Diana carefully cut off a lock of the boy's hair.

"See, it did not hurt at all." Mikhail regarded Alex with half-lowered eyelids in a look of superiority.

Alex shook his head. "I do not know if I have ever seen such courage." He winked.

Mikhail laughed and sat straighter, enjoying the attention. "Missno is teaching Elena to read."

Diana glanced up, then carefully cut another piece of hair.

"How fortunate for your sister. Perhaps one day you will learn to read as well."

"I would rather learn to fight."

"Fighting is certainly a valuable skill, but so is reading." Alex crossed his arm and grinned at the boy's amusing conversation.

Mikhail glanced up. "Who taught you to read, Missno?"

Diana looked startled at the question. She squinted her eyes and made a snip. "When I was small, a bit older than you, I snuck into a library. I was hiding from . . . some older children."

Mikhail nodded, and she placed a hand on his head to keep it from moving. "The library belonged to a minister—a church man. It was near to . . . where I lived in London. I opened his books and looked at all the words, wishing I knew what they said. I would go to the library when-ever . . . whenever I needed a place to hide." She combed through the boy's hair, looking for spots that were uneven, then snipped another lock.

Alex glanced at Sophia and saw that she was listening. Her eyes squinted, and Alex knew she also understood there was more to the story than Diana revealed.

Diana moved around in front of Mikhail, combing through his thick curls. "I looked at the books for a long time and taught myself to understand the words."

Alex could not help his jolt of surprise. As a young girl, she had taught herself to read?

"The minister found me one day, and I feared he would be angry with me. I begged him not to turn me out. He showed me some books, and when he determined that I was actually reading and not up to any mischief, he allowed me to continue. He encouraged me and discussed with me what I had learned. When I was old enough, he sent me to school."

"Were your mother and father angry with him for sending you away?"

Diana paused, only for an instant, then bent down to trim the hair at his neck. "Come, you mustn't move, or I will slip and your haircut will not look handsome." She spoke in a teasing voice. "Then you will never marry, and all because you wiggled."

"I do not want to marry." Mikhail scrunched up his nose and formed an expression of disgust.

Alex caught Diana's eye and grinned. Diana's lips pursed and pulled to the side again.

"Do you have a husband in London, Missno?" Mikhail asked.

"No." She trimmed the hair above his ears.

"Why not?"

Diana untied the sheet around his neck. "I suppose, if I was married, I wouldn't be living with you. I would have to live with my husband."

"Then I would miss you."

"And I would miss you as well."

She knelt down in front of him and placed her hands on his shoulders. "You look very handsome with your hair cut, Mikhail." She kissed his cheek, then stood and shook off the sheet.

Mikhail slid off the wooden chair. "Mr. Metaxas, it is your turn." The boy stood close, apparently planning to supervise the procedure.

"Do you mind, Miss Snow? I am afraid it *is* long overdue." He spoke in English, hoping she would not feel any pressure and would be able to decline if she was uneasy.

"Are you certain you trust me? I am not an expert at all. I have performed only one haircut, which you just saw."

"And it turned out very well." Alex remained standing, waiting for her invitation.

She spread her palm toward the chair and dipped her head. Once he was seated, she tied the sheet and combed her fingers through his curls. "Now, how shall I cut it?

Alex knew her motions were simply part of the haircutting procedure, but the feel of her fingers in his hair made his scalp tingle and his heart stutter, and it cast all thoughts from his head.

"Mr. Metaxas?"

"I think he is afraid." Mikhail put a hand on Alex's knee. "I told you, it will not hurt."

"Yes." Alex blinked and shook his head in an effort to focus. "What did you say?"

She stepped in front of him and lowered her head to catch his gaze. "How shall I cut your hair?" Diana glanced at Mikhail and winked. "Shorn like a sheep?"

The boy laughed.

"Just trim a little."

Diana moved around behind him. "Are you certain? You would make a very nice-looking bald man."

He had never heard Diana tease and was unprepared for the way her tone made his heart flip like a bird trapped in a cage. "A very little, please." He spoke in a trembling voice, as though he were afraid of what she might do.

Mikhail patted his knee. He'd nearly forgotten the boy stood next to him.

Alex heard the snip and saw a curl fall.

"It did not hurt, did it?" Mikhail said.

Alex shook his head.

"Be careful not to wiggle," the boy advised.

"Mikhail." Elena waved her hand. "Come and listen to the story."

He glanced at Alex with a question in his gaze.

"I will be all right now," Alex assured him.

"I'll read loudly so everybody can hear," Elena said. She pulled her brows together and ran her finger along the page. "The Peacock and the Crane." She glanced up at Diana then continued. "A peacock, spreading its gorgeous tail mocked a crane that . . ." She stumbled over a few words and read slowly but persevered. When she could not decipher a word, Diana crouched down by her and helped with the sounds she needed, then returned to cutting Alex's hair.

He let his gaze travel over the family, the beautiful garden, and the lowering sun. Diana moved around him, at times bending close. Her legs occasionally bumped into his knees, or her arms brushed his shoulders, and his skin remained warm long after her touch. The evening air felt cool, and he closed his eyes. He could not remember the last time he'd spent the evening with a family as they went about their tasks. He'd nearly forgotten how it felt to be among people who cared for each other and was surprised by how readily they accepted him. He let the feeling of comfort wash over him, and for a moment he considered how nice it would be to have his own family, to have a place where he felt safe and cared for. But he halted the thought. He would not risk it. His work was dangerous, and he would not put others in jeopardy. He could not endure having people he loved torn from him. He would not have a family until Greece was safe.

He felt Diana's knees pressed against his. He opened his eyes to see her face was directly before him. She pulled the hair above his ears through her fingers, tipping her head back and forth, making sure the length was even. Her hands moved down to pull the curls at his neck. She leaned close, clipping one side.

Alex held his breath. Surely she could hear his heart pounding. If he were ever to change his mind, this woman might be just the one . . . But no, it was not fair. He was a revolutionary and would never draw her into his dangerous world.

She stepped back, looking over her work one more time. "I am done." She untied the sheet and shook it.

"Miss Snow, you are not completely finished." Alex spoke in English.

She squinted. "Your mustache? Do you want me to trim it?"

He shook his head, blinking and raising his brows as if he were extremely offended. "A man tends his own whiskers, miss."

"Then, what else . . . ?"

"You did not tell me I look handsome. And I believe the previous customer received a kiss." He tapped his cheek and could not help a smile at her shocked look.

She glanced at the family, then back, and he saw her face and neck were pink. "You are very impertinent, Mr. Metaxas." She folded the sheet and walked toward Elena, but not before he saw her lips pulling as she stifled a smile.

"Elena, you did a masterful job reading that story," Diana said.

The young woman smiled. "Thank you."

Alex helped Georgi carry the sofa into the house, then he bid the family good night. He was surprised when Diana offered to walk with him to the gate.

"I cannot thank you enough for bringing Elena that book," Diana said as they walked through the garden. "She was so grateful."

"You're welcome."

Diana held her hand on the wooden gate. "She's so intelligent. I wish she could go to school."

"You see yourself in her, don't you?"

She glanced back at the house. "Maybe a bit. I was much more shy."

"But intelligent as well," he pointed out.

Diana blushed and looked down.

He tapped beneath her chin, raising her gaze to his. "I noticed it the moment I met you. And you taught yourself to read as a young girl? Truly remarkable."

"Thank you." Diana rubbed her arms, and though she attempted to hide it, he could see that his statement pleased her.

"You seem happy here," he said.

Her eyes took on a faraway look. "I am happy, for now, but of course this situation will not last."

He understood what she meant. Her time in the Mani would not be long. "The ship will come for you soon. And will you be happy to return to London?"

She met his gaze and looked away. "I do not know."

Her glance made him uneasy. There was something in her expression, an uncertainty, or even more, a fear. Was she afraid to return home? Or was it something else entirely?

"Good night." She curtseyed and started back toward the house but stopped. She turned back and crossed the distance between them in a few steps. "You look handsome, Alex." Her cheeks flooded scarlet as she whirled and bolted to the house.

He stood at the road long after she'd gone, unable to remove the grin from his face. "*Kalinychta*, Diana."

Chapter 14

DIANA DRESSED QUIETLY AND SLIPPED down the stairs and outside before any of the household awoke. She knew Elena would want to get the chores finished early in order to prepare for the wedding, and Diana hoped to accomplish as much as she could before her friend awoke.

She pulled a shawl around her shoulders against the chill of the early morning, lit a lantern, and set to work.

Humming a tune that Elena taught her, she opened the top of the barrel and spread grain for the chickens. While the birds were occupied, she searched for eggs by dwindling moonlight.

She took the eggs inside and brought out the milking bucket, coaxing the goats with a soft voice. Once the outside chores were completed, she took a deep breath, satisfied at what she'd accomplished. But an unwelcome thought stopped her short, settling in her chest like a lump.

Diana was roleplaying a life that did not belong to her. It never would. This was not her house, and soon enough, she'd no longer be welcome here.

She set down the bucket of milk and leaned her hands against the wooden table as the weight of her self-pity pushed heavily down.

Instead of hiding the feeling away in its small box, she let it expand and cover her until she sank into a chair and held her head in her hands.

What would happen when Petrobey realized a ship wasn't coming? The list of possible scenarios, each worse than the one before, marched in front of her like a parade of carriages through Hyde Park during the fashionable hour. She shook her head, knowing nothing she could do would change the result. But the self-pity didn't disperse. Why was she different? Why did she not belong anywhere? Molly belonged in London with her parties and ball gowns. Alex had found his place in Constantinople, plotting to save Greece. Sophia belonged in her home with friendly neighbors and a family that cared for her. But Diana had never belonged anywhere.

From the very beginning of her life, she had been abandoned with other unwanted children, but even among those like her, she had not fit in. A small, skinny girl who was neither fast nor cunning was a prime target for stronger, tougher children. She'd found refuge in Reverend Delaney's library, but the sanctuary was his place not hers. Once she arrived at school, she discovered the other girls belonged to families who welcomed them home on holidays and sent parcels containing sweets. Diana had nowhere to go and, aside from an occasional letter from the minister, no correspondence. Even as a woman, among the teachers at the finishing school, Diana was an outsider, a person with no connections, no family, and no prospects.

She glanced around the lightening room and thought that this farmhouse in a remote Mani village felt like home more than any place had before. She loved to tidy the shelves in the storeroom, moving jars and bottles into straight, uniform lines. When she pulled a loaf of bread from the brick oven, she felt a thrill of pride, knowing she'd created it and her work would give the family health and strength and satisfaction. The women and children seemed happy to see her each day. They were patient as she practiced the language, and her affection for them was something she could not explain.

Here on the farm, her hands had grown rough, her skin darker. She worked every day until her muscles were exhausted, but the satisfaction of completing tasks, of being needed, and of caring for others brought a contentment she would never have known if she had not been taken by Mediterranean pirates from a rocky beach in Corfu.

"That is quite enough," she said aloud, standing and brushing off her apron. "No one is more miserable than a person who does not realize her blessings," she muttered, quoting the Reverend Delaney. She took out the bread bowl and started combining ingredients for the dough.

She was truly lucky for this time, temporary though it might be. How many people had the opportunity to experience another life? To try it on as one might a new hat?

The room was light, but the sun had not fully risen when she shaped the dough into a ball on the baking stone and slid it into the oven.

"Missno!"

Diana turned to see Elena standing next to the milk and eggs.

"I had hoped to finish the morning chores before everyone woke. But you have beaten me to it." The girl's hands were on her hips.

Diana shrugged. "Today is special. I wanted you to have time to get ready for the wedding."

Elena wrapped her in an embrace, taking Diana by surprise. She had never been hugged like that by anyone before. "Thank you."

Diana's throat constricted as she patted Elena's back.

Hearing a scraping noise, the pair turned toward the staircase. Sophia was leaning hard on the rail as she slowly descended.

Elena hurried toward her. "Mitéra, you must be careful." She slid her arm around her mother's waist and assisted her to the sofa.

Sophia let out a labored breath as she sat. "Breakfast smells delicious."

Diana slid the paddle over the hot bricks and drew out the golden loaf just as the boys entered the room, rubbing their eyes sleepily. She and Elena sliced bread and cheese and served cups of warm milk to the hungry children.

"You must be home early today if you want to attend the wedding feast," Sophia told her sons.

"And will we stay for the dancing?" Chrysanthos asked.

"For a little while. Georgi and Elena will stay. You must bring your brothers home before dark."

Chrysanthos nodded but did not look happy about missing the celebration.

Diana knew not to question Sophia in front of the children. She would speak to the woman later about bringing the boys home, since she had no intention of attending the wedding party.

She and Elena prepared lunch as the boys ate breakfast. Then the women cleaned up the dishes once the younger ones had left.

"Oh!" Elena said. "Georgi forgot his knapsack." She hurried outside to catch him while Diana finished tidying the kitchen.

Across the room, Sophia winced and pressed on her back.

Diana hurried to her side. "Sophia, what is it?"

She let out a heavy breath and relaxed. "Nothing to worry about. It just becomes more difficult near the end." She eased back against the pillows, turning onto her side and moving her beads.

Diana noticed her breathing came in quick gasps. "Sophia, I can fetch the younger boys home after the feast. Chrysanthos wants to stay for the dancing, and . . ." Her voice trailed off when she saw Sophia shaking her head.

"No, you must go to the celebration."

Diana knelt onto the floor beside her. "I do not want to leave you alone. The baby—" She was not sure what words to use to express her worry that the baby might come while she was gone. "I should remain with you. Agatha and Stella will be with Elena. "

A tired smile spread over Sophia's lips. "I have given birth to five children. I know the time is not near—although I wish it were." She winced and shifted again. "You must dance at the wedding, Diana. It is what young women do." She reached for Diana's hand. "And I do not think your life has given you much opportunity for amusement."

Diana's throat contracted. "I do not know how to dance." The confession was humiliating, and she felt a flush fill her cheeks.

Sophia squeezed her fingers. "In Greece, we do not memorize steps and routines. Dancing is not a performance; it is a celebration, an expression. We let the music fill us, and our emotions determine the movement."

The concept filled Diana with dread. "I cannot do that."

"You prefer structure and control. But sometimes you must loosen your hold and just feel."

"That is what Alex—Mr. Metaxas says." Diana was horrified that she'd just confessed something so personal. But Sophia's concern and the intimacy of the conversation drew the declaration from her.

"Then he is wise as well as fine-looking." Sophia winked.

Diana's flush deepened until she was certain her cheeks must be crimson. She searched her mind for a reply. How did one respond to such a statement?

Luckily she was saved from a stammering answer when Elena entered and closed the door with a bang. Her face looked like a storm cloud ready to burst.

"What has happened?" Concern furrowed Sophia's brow, and she groaned as she rose to a sitting position.

"I saw Daphne Sássaris on the road." She folded her arms. "I bid her good morning, and she shouted at me to leave her alone."

"*Po-po-po*." Sophia settled back. "Come, tell me what she said."

Elena stomped across the room. "'Return to your perfect home and do not bother me anymore.'" She crossed her arms as she knelt next to Diana. Tears were in her eyes. "Can you imagine anyone acting so rudely?"

The corners of Sophia's mouth pulled downward. "Do not be angry with her, *paidi mou*"—my child. "You must understand Daphne has endured much heartache. Costas was the third son she lost, and think of how she must feel with the village preparing for a happy day in the midst of her mourning." Sophia's smile was sad. "I have seen the pain in her eyes each Sunday as she looks at my strong sons. And here I am waiting for another. Her own boys have all been born sickly."

"Except Spiros," Elena muttered. "And of course she has Theodora." Her expression was still sad, but she did not look angry anymore.

"It must be more than she can endure," Diana said.

Sophia nodded. "I am sorry for her." She held out her hand, and Elena scooted closer. Sophia brushed her thumb beneath her daughter's eyes, then cupped her chin, bending forward so they were face-to-face. "Remember this, my daughter. If you can understand a person's reasons, you will learn to feel compassion for them."

"Yes, Mitéra. I will remember."

Diana watched the tender moment with a swelling in her heart, admiring the gentle way Sophia taught her daughter. Deep inside she felt a pinch of jealousy. How different would her life have been with a family? She pushed the thought away as quickly as it entered.

Sophia patted Elena's cheek and rested back. "Now, we have work to do. Today is a celebration, and you must both be ready. Elena, please fetch the taupe gown from the chest in my bedchamber."

Elena squeezed her brows together as if she would ask a question, but then her eyes lit up and she hurried up the staircase.

"And bring hair combs and a brush," Sophia called after her. Sophia smiled as she turned to Diana. She glanced at the stairs and spoke in a low voice. "I think my daughter favors Spiros."

Diana pursed her lips, wondering what to say. She did not want to betray her friend's trust. "I do not know."

"His mother is difficult, but Elena wishes to impress her; that is why Daphne's words hurt her today." She raised her gaze to the stairs and let out a sigh. "It will be a good match. I only wish my daughter would remain young."

Elena pattered down the stairs with a gown over her arm. When she reached them, she held it up, smoothing out the skirt. The damask gown was a soft beige color. The fabric was thick and rich-looking. Dark green and gold embroidery detailed the hem and neckline. Covering the bodice was a velvet jacket in a vivid green color with gold fastenings and stitched embellishments around the edges.

"Oh, it's beautiful," Diana breathed. "You shall look stunning, Elena."

Elena glanced at her mother.

Sophia smiled. "This gown is made for a *woman's* body, not a young girl's. It will not suit Elena. And as you can see, I am in no condition to wear it."

Elena held the dress up to Diana's shoulders.

Diana looked down at the full skirt and ornate jacket. "But I cannot. It is yours, and I can see it is special."

"Extremely special." Sophia motioned for the gown, and Elena brought it to her. She ran her hand over the stitching. "My mother made it for me years ago. I want you to wear it tonight, Missno." She lifted it toward Diana. "*You* are special."

Diana's heart felt as if it would overflow. Most of the items in Sophia's home were well used and practical, and the dress must have been quite costly. She lifted the beautiful gown and held it at arm's length, admiring the lovely fabric, amazed that the woman would be willing to share it. "I do not know what to say."

"Do not say anything." Elena gave her a small push. "Put it on so we can see."

Diana hurried up the stairs, and a moment later, descended, wearing the gown. Elena and her mother both clapped. Sophia made a twirling motion with her fingers, and Diana turned to allow her to see the entirety.

"It fits perfectly, as if it were made for you," Sophia said with a nod of satisfaction.

Diana loved the feel of the soft velvet. She had certainly never worn a dress as fine as this one. Swishing her hips, she felt the thick fabric flowing around her legs.

"Perfect for dancing." Elena grinned and clapped her hands again. "Now, wait here, and I will don my dress."

Elena's dress was a soft mustard-yellow with a burgundy velvet jacket. She pranced into the room, twirling and giggling.

"Beautiful!" Diana wished she knew more Greek words to describe exactly how striking her friend looked. Her dark hair and golden skin glowed in the jewel-toned gown.

"Lovely." Sophia motioned for Elena to sit by the couch and pulled a brush through her daughter's hair, separating it into sections and arranging the thick, dark curls into intricate braids. She fastened the braids to her daughter's head with hair combs.

Diana watched, fascinated at how Sophia's nimble fingers created such an elaborate arrangement.

"And now you, Missno." Elena motioned for Diana to take her place.

Diana's first inclination was to protest, but she sat and slid back against the couch. Sophia braided her hair around her head like a crown. "There."

She turned her by the shoulders so that Diana was kneeling. "Enjoy yourself today. You are beautiful." She spoke in a low voice.

"Thank you. I feel beautiful." Diana kissed Sophia's cheek, then stood and clasped Elena's hand. The excitement of attending the wedding party suddenly made her heart flutter. Her hands were shaking.

"And do not worry about me. I shall use the quiet time to rest." Sophia laid back against the pillows, unable to suppress a quiet moan.

Diana felt a trickle of guilt at leaving her.

Elena brought a head scarf in the same beige as Diana's dress. She also handed over a large handkerchief, instructing Diana to keep it in her pocket. The girls bid Sophia farewell and departed.

Elena linked her arm with Diana's as they walked. "What will Mr. Metaxas think when he sees you today? He will not be able to keep his eyes away from you."

The trembling in Diana's chest grew into a feeling of nervous anticipation. She was torn, not knowing whether to giggle and sing or to run away and hide beneath her bed covers. After her declaration the evening before, the second option seemed the most appealing.

Would Alex notice her? Would he even attend the wedding?

She felt beautiful in the elegant dress with her hair braided and arranged loosely. Ever since she could remember, she'd worn simple, light-colored gowns and pulled back her hair tightly. Blending into the background had always been comfortable. A flicker of dread moved over her when she thought of the attention her appearance might draw. She fingered the damask fabric and adjusted her head scarf.

The people of Tsímova, dressed in their finest, greeted each other as they drew near to the center of town.

Elena's arm tightened, and Diana looked to see what had caused her reaction. Spiros Sássaris stood near the church, speaking with a group of men. His forehead was wrinkled and his lips pulled tightly together. When they passed, he met Elena's gaze and dipped his head, but his brows pulled together and he bit his lip with an uncertain expression, turning back to the men.

Elena glanced at Diana with a question in her gaze.

"He is in mourning." Diana patted her arm. "Do not worry."

They greeted neighbors as they joined the crowd walking in the direction of the church. Diana could not help but glance around, searching for Alex, but she did not see him. Perhaps he would come later—or not at all. His presence should not determine whether or not she enjoyed herself. She repeated the declaration in her mind more than once.

Strings of flags were hung between the trees in the town square. Tables were arranged in long rows in the shade. Diana smelled roasting lamb and listened to the excited voices around her. The anticipation in the air was contagious, and she felt a flurry in her middle.

Here in Greece, Diana had the opportunity to be someone she could never be in London. The chance to live a new life was a gift, and although it frightened her, she was determined to enjoy herself, if only for Sophia and Elena's sake. A surge of confidence made her straighten her back and hold up her head as she took a deep breath and walked through the church doors.

Chapter 15

ALEX SHIFTED HIS WEIGHT AS he glanced over the crowd in the church—again. He knew nothing had changed since the last time he'd looked, but he could not keep from searching among those gathered. He stood near the back where he had a clear view of the congregation. Elena had been easy to spot in the crowd. She was near Petrobey and the others of the Mavromichalis clan. She wore a beautiful dress with a wine-colored jacket and stood near the wall on the far side of the room with a woman who must be a relative. Why had Diana not come?

Disappointment felt like a rock in Alex's chest. She had most likely remained behind to care for Sophia and the children. He didn't know why he'd expected anything different. Diana was not in Tsímova for a holiday. Although the family treated her kindly—like a guest—such was not the case.

A breeze from the partially open door blew his hair, and he smiled, remembering the previous evening—the feel of Diana's fingers in his hair, the way she'd brushed his neck, and her shy words before she'd fled into the house. Just the memory made his insides feel as if they were floating.

His gaze was drawn to movement, and he glanced toward the Sássaris men. He'd only made the acquaintance of Sebastianos, the clan leader, and a few of his elder sons. The moment Alex had seen the men gathered in the town square before the wedding, he'd known something was wrong. A tension was in the air, and even though the clan blended in with the others in the church, he saw darting eyes, tapping feet, and tight jaws. The sight made him uneasy.

He turned back toward the ceremony, feeling a warmth at the familiarity of the traditions. The *koumbaro,* the groom's closest friend, lifted the golden crowns from the bride and groom and, ensuring that they remained attached, placed them on the opposite heads.

The woman next to Elena whispered something then turned back, adjusting her scarf. For just an instant, her profile was visible. Alex blinked and looked again. The woman was Diana Snow! How had he not recognized her?

He shifted to the side to get a better view and saw that Diana wore an exquisite gown that fit her curves as if it were made especially with her figure in mind. Wisps of dark, loose hair were visible beneath her scarf. Alex's heart did a slow somersault. She looked beautiful. But it wasn't only the clothing and hairstyle that were different. Diana held herself confidently. Not the forced confidence she typically assumed, but she somehow looked more comfortable with herself. It was obvious in her stance and her movements. He stepped quietly along the wall to catch a glimpse of her face.

Diana watched the ceremony with a pleasant expression. Her head was tipped with interest, and Alex wished he was the one standing next to her, explaining the significance of the bride and groom's candles, the action of drinking from a common cup, and the attached crowns.

If only he knew her feelings about what she saw.

The priest led the bride and groom around the table three times, they switched their gold bands to their right hands, and the ceremony was over. As they left the church, rice was thrown to bless the newlyweds with children.

Alex followed the crowd into the square, where the women busied themselves serving a feast. He took a seat beside Dino and scanned the rows of tables. Diana was assisting Sophia's children with their plates. She sat between Mikhail and Elena farther down the same table as Alex. As if she could feel him watching, she lifted her eyes and locked her gaze with his. Pink colored her cheeks, but she did not turn away. The corners of her mouth pulled, and she allowed it to happen. Diana Snow was smiling, a small smile, yet it warmed Alex from head to toe like sunshine.

Her smile was exquisite.

Mikhail said something that recaptured her attention, and Alex looked down at his plate. He didn't even remember eating the lamb or the rice pilaf. He spread the egg and lemon sauce absentmindedly on the stuffed grape leaf, but his mind was not on food.

Forcibly keeping his eyes from wandering down the table, he glanced in the other direction. The men of the Sássaris family leaned their heads together at one end of the table and spoke in low voices, and this time they were joined by a woman. Alex squinted. He recognized her as the mother whose child had died. She spoke quickly and quietly, her gaze darting, and her face pinched in anger. The feeling of unease returned.

"Cause for concern on what should be a joyful day." Dino lifted his chin toward the group of men.

"What do you think they are discussing so secretly?"

"I do not know. The Sássaris family is strong but impulsive. It will not remain a secret for long."

Alex studied Dino's expression and saw that even though his face was relaxed, the lines on the sides of his mouth had deepened. He was worried.

Voices called for attention, and the crowd quieted as the koumbaro lifted his glass in a toast. The toasting continued, but Alex only listened with half an ear as he glanced to where Diana sat. Mikhail had climbed onto her lap and was holding up his wooden cup with a plump arm each time the adults raised theirs.

Diana's gaze met his again. She raised her brows and darted her gaze to the small dark head and then smiled again. Alex's heart felt soft when he looked at the boy and watched the earnest way he participated.

"Missno is fortunate to be with Hektor's family." Dino gestured in her direction, and Alex knew there was no use in pretending he hadn't been watching Diana for the entirety of the meal. "They are fine children. And Sophia is a good mother." Dino took a long drink of raki.

Alex had never heard Dino engage in small talk, and wondered if his talkativeness could be attributed to the brandy. "And Hektor, he is your brother?"

"Yes." The lines around his mouth tightened further. "He is in Italy, trading . . . merchandise." He blew out a puff of air and tapped his fingers on the table. "But he has been gone too long. I fear misfortune has befallen him."

"And what will happen to his family if he does not return?"

"I will marry Sophia, of course. And raise the children. It is my duty." Dino spoke in a matter-of-fact voice, but Alex could still see the unease in his eyes. He worried for his brother's safety.

"Will you search for him?"

"If he does not return within a week, I will search." He took another long drink and motioned for the bottle to refill his glass.

Alex wondered about Hektor. Was he kind, like his wife? How would he treat Diana when he returned?

Petrobey stood and offered a toast to the new couple, and at last, the music started. A small band consisting of a long-necked bouzouki, a lyre, and a clarinet began to play, and the bride rose to lead the *Kalamatiano*. She walked slowly to the center of the square and spread her arms gracefully, then she began to move in time with the music, twisting her hips and stepping slowly with bouncing steps, first in one direction, then the other. She spun, eliciting applause from the gathered crowd.

A woman joined her, opening a handkerchief and holding one corner while the bride grasped the other. More women merged into a line, linked together by handkerchiefs and facing into the center of a growing circle. The line continued to move, and the music was accompanied by claps and shouts.

Alex watched as Elena tugged on Diana's arm. Diana seemed reluctant but finally followed her to join the other women. Her expression was pinched in concentration as she attempted the steps, skipping along with the line. She stumbled when the dancers changed direction, then stumbled again, trying to understand the rhythm. After a few minutes, Diana appeared to work out the cadence. She stopped watching her feet and smiled at Elena as she was pulled along. She leaned back her head, and her head scarf slipped down onto her shoulders, but she did not pull it back.

The music picked up speed, and the dance became faster.

Following the groom, the men joined the dance, holding onto the shoulders of the man next to them and forming a ring around the women. Alex found a position where he could watch Diana, and his feet moved in the familiar pattern that Greeks from Crete to Constantinople had followed for generations.

Diana grinned at Elena, and Alex nearly lost his footing when her smile was joined by laughter. He felt breathless but could not attribute the sensation to the rapid pace of the wedding dance. A sound had not had such an effect over his heartbeat since he could remember.

The song ended, and the dancers broke off, applauding and moving around the square. Diana walked toward the table, but he intercepted her path, offering his arm.

She squinted in a questioning look but slipped her hand beneath his elbow and permitted him to lead her away from the crowd. The night was cooling, and the area outside the range of the lanterns had grown dark.

The cicadas chirped, softening the sound of voices and music. Alex stopped and turned toward her. Diana was breathing heavily, her face was flushed, her gray eyes bright, and the bewitching smile directed at him. Alex brushed a long curl from her forehead, his fingers following the line of her hair behind her ear. He pulled her gently toward him and pressed his lips on hers. He could not help himself.

Everything about her was soft and warm. She melted against him, sliding one hand along his shoulder and the other around his waist. His thumb felt the pulse at her neck speed up.

Alex drew back and saw her eyes were closed. A soft sigh escaped her lips, and fire heated his insides. "Your smile. It is beautiful." He stroked a finger along her lips. "I knew it would be, but I had no idea that it would enchant me so completely."

His lips smirked as he remembered the woman with the disapproving expression at the Corfu taverna. That was not Diana—not really. This vibrant woman standing before him was the true Diana Snow, and his fingers itched to touch her.

"Thank you." Diana stepped back and lowered her arms. Her expression grew guarded, and the smile faded.

Alex's insides grew cold as he realized the implications in his actions. Once his mind was clear, he regretted immediately that he'd made her uncomfortable. The kiss was a promise he couldn't keep. He grimaced, angry at himself. "I acted impulsively, and I am sorry. Your smile, your laugh, I should not have . . ."

She breathed heavily, and her lips quivered as she watched him.

"You must understand, if circumstances were different . . . But this situation is complicated." He pushed his fingers through his hair. "If we were simply a man and woman living in this village, I would court you. I would walk home with you from church. I would bring you flowers and sing beneath your window."

"I would like that." She spoke so softly that he had to strain to hear. She seemed to realize what she'd said and clenched her jaw. Her shoulders lowered, her chin raised, and her face hardened the slightest bit.

"Why do you hide yourself away, Diana?" He brushed his fingers down her arm to clasp her hand. "Why do you wear a mask?"

"I told you why." She looked down at the ground.

He crooked a finger beneath her chin and lifted her face. "Do you fear that someone will see Diana Snow? Why do you protect her? Has somebody hurt you?" Just the thought made his blood boil and then turn to ice.

"Nobody can hurt me unless I allow it." She pulled away her chin and spoke as if repeating something she'd said often, which he thought she surely had.

"I would never hurt you. Do you know that? Do you trust me?"

She looked up at him, then pursed her lips. "I do not think you would do so on purpose."

Her mask was back, and the sight made his stomach sink. He *had* hurt her, and he did not imagine he would possibly win her trust again.

She glanced toward the dancing. "Excuse me, but I must return to Sophia."

He studied her, but her expression remaind cold. Alex breathed out a sigh. "May I accompany you? You should not walk alone."

She started toward the lantern-lit area and did not glance back to see if he followed. "If you like." She searched the crowd until she found Georgi.

"I am leaving to take care of your mother. Please make sure Elena gets home safely."

Georgi glanced at Alex and then back to her, nodding. "Thank you."

Diana left the square and walked quickly. Her back was straight, her chin up, and her lips pressed together.

Alex lengthened his stride to keep up with her. He wished he could think of something to say that would soften her again, but he feared he'd spoiled the friendship beyond repair. His heart hurt at the thought. "I imagine we do not have much time left in the Mani." It was a pitiful attempt at conversation, but he decided small talk was preferable to silence.

She glanced at him. "Your ship will arrive soon, won't it, Mr. Metaxas?"

"I wouldn't be surprised to see it in the harbor any day now."

"And I imagine you will be pleased to return to Constantinople." She did not glance at him, and her voice was clipped like her footsteps.

"There is a sense of satisfaction that comes with completing an assignment, but I do not think 'pleased' will entirely describe my feelings."

She did not respond.

"Your ship will arrive soon as well. I will delay my return in order to see you safely off. You will be happy to see Molly again, will you not?"

"I'll not be leaving." Her voice wavered, but her face betrayed no emotion. What did her statement mean? Did she think the bey had not kept his word and contacted the navy at Corfu?

"Petrobey told no falsehood. He has sent for a ship."

Diana stopped in front of the garden gate so suddenly that Alex's heart jerked, and he glanced around to see what had caused the abrupt halt.

"Who do you expect to come, Mr. Metaxas?" Diana eyes were red and her voice strained. "Do you think the British navy sends a ship for each person who asks?" She choked and drew in a ragged breath. "I am not a lady or a gentleman's daughter. No ship will be sent to rescue a penniless orphan." She whipped around and fled into the house.

Alex stood on the bricks of the road as if his feet had grown roots. Was there truly nobody coming for her? Did she have no family? No connections? He furrowed his fingers through his hair as he remembered the pink on her cheeks when Molly told him Diana was her chaperone. And now the reaction made sense. "Oh, Diana, what have you gotten yourself into?" He whispered the words. He did not know what the Maniots would do when they realized Diana had been abandoned.

He started back along the dark road toward the music and laughter of the party, his mind spinning as he thought of scenarios. He had friends in Italy who might be willing to help, or perhaps he could negotiate with the British himself.

If only he could take her with him when he returned to Constantinople. But it was impossible. Diana was a young British woman, and he was a Greek revolutionary. She was not strong enough to be involved in that world, no matter how much he wished it.

The memory of Diana kneeling on the beach with a sword to her throat entered into his mind. She had not wept nor carried on but held her chin up bravely. He'd seen her mind working.

He did not allow the memory to linger. The thought of anything happening to her squeezed his chest until he could scarcely breathe. He would have to say good-bye; it was inevitable. Parting would be difficult, painful even. But he was sworn to the cause—and it was *his* cause not *hers*. Diana could not survive in his world. She was not a warrior. He would think of some other way to save her. He must.

Chapter 16

DIANA CLOSED THE DOOR BEHIND her and leaned against it. The house was dark and quiet, and she was grateful for the time alone. Her eyes burned, and she thought she might be ill.

Her emotions felt like a loose ribbon unraveling in the wind, and the feeling terrified her. She struggled to pull them back where they belonged and clenched her fists as she tried to make sense of what had happened.

Alex had kissed her. The memory of his touch, even nearly an hour later sent her heart tripping. But then her insides turned to lead when she thought of his words after. He'd apologized, claiming it had been an accident, then made excuses to explain his impulsive behavior.

Diana was embarrassed and humiliated, and even more, disgusted with herself for enjoying the kiss. For believing, just for that moment, that it was the beginning of something, that Alexandros Metaxas cared for her.

She had not disguised her feelings quickly enough, and he'd seen exactly how she felt.

And on top of it all, she'd lost her temper and revealed something she never should have—the truth about her origins. The thing that had so often been used to hurt her, the truth she hid away. She'd blurted it out without a thought. And why? She knew the reason, and it made her stomach ache. She'd been angry and frightened and had hoped to show Alex how her life was ruined and make him feel as terrible as she did. She'd blamed him for something he had no control over.

A blinding dread rose when she let herself consider what would happen when Alex departed and then later when her ship did not arrive. Facing an unknown future terrified her. And she'd turned her fear into anger, thrusting it at him like a weapon.

Remember this, Diana. Remember what happens when you loosen your control.

She stepped across the dark room, treading lightly on the wooden floor. The moonlight shimmered through the windows, turning the furniture silver, much as it had done early this morning. Had it really just been this morning that she'd risen before Elena to complete the chores? It seemed that so much had happened since then.

Glancing at the sofa, she thought of the kindhearted advice Sophia had given her before she left. Diana had taken the words to heart. She couldn't remember ever feeling so joyful in her life as she had when she allowed her inhibitions to fall away and danced in the wedding celebration. Dancing gave her a feeling of freedom, and for a person who spent her life at the mercy of others, it had been intoxicating.

She stepped up the stairs quietly so as not to wake Sophia or the younger boys. All she could think of was going to sleep and putting this day behind her, but as she passed Sophia's bedchamber, she heard a low moan.

Diana knocked and opened the door. The room was lit only by moonlight. She heard another moan, and when she saw Sophia, her heart turned cold.

The woman was curled up on a threadbare rug on the floor. Tears streaked her face, and her hair and clothes were soaked with perspiration.

"Oh, what is it?"

"Thank goodness you are here." Sophia's voice was a strained whisper that ended in a sob. "The baby is coming. It is early. Something is not right."

"Oh, Sophia. Why did you allow me to leave? What shall I do?" Diana hurried to light a lantern.

Sophia's entire body clenched. She gritted her teeth but could not fully stop a whimper. Diana knelt next to her, pushing her hair back from her face, holding her hand, and feeling utterly helpless.

After a moment, the episode passed.

"The midwife," Sophia whispered.

"Yes, I will fetch her right away." Diana started to rise, but Sophia clung to her hand.

Her eyes were wide. She shook her head. "Please do not leave me alone."

"Then I will send one of the boys." Diana did not know how to assist Sophia with her pain, but she could not imagine the floor was comfortable. She pulled a pillow from the bed and helped Sophia rest her head on it.

"Do not let my sons worry." Sophia's brows drew together in concern for her children. "Do not frighten them."

Diana nodded. "I will send Chrysanthos with a note for Elena. She will bring the midwife."

Sophia's face relaxed. "Yes." She closed her eyes.

Diana glanced around the stark bedchamber. The room contained only a bed, a wooden chair, a chest, and a wardrobe. Upon the wall above the bed hung a cross and a small painting of Mary and Jesus. The first time Diana had seen the room, she'd been surprised at the simplicity. Sophia did not even have a dressing table or a desk. Diana realized she had never seen any paper nor writing tools in Sophia's house. She lit another lantern and carried it down the stairs, searching for anything she could write on.

A thought came to her, and she grabbed a kitchen knife and hurried outside. She sliced a pad from the cactus plant, then carefully broke off the prickly spines. For just a moment she considered what words would be simple enough that Elena would be able to read them, and would accurately convey the urgency of the situation.

βοηθησε *Voithise* help

μητερα *Mitera* mother

μωρο *Moro* baby

ελα ταχεως *Ela Taxeos* come swiftly

She carved the words carefully into the cactus pad, knowing the nouns were undeclined and the verbs conjugated incorrectly, but Elena would understand. She took the message and rushed inside. When she reached the door to the boys' room, she knocked, then opened it. "Chrysanthos? Are you awake?"

"Yes, Missno. Is something wrong?" His voice came from the dark.

She opened the door wider and lifted the lantern. The sound of the children's breathing came from the other beds. "No, but I need you to deliver a message to Elena." She spoke softly.

He sat up in his bed, and his eyes glimmered in the light from the flame. "At the wedding? Mitéra told me—"

"I know, but it is important. Your mother has given her permission." Diana tried to keep her voice calm but felt an urgency to hurry back to Sophia.

He must have wanted to return to the wedding badly enough that he only wrinkled his nose in a puzzled look for an instant. "I need to dress."

She closed the door and waited in the hallway for just a moment before he emerged, then gave him the lantern and the cactus pad. "This is the message. Please be careful with it."

Chrysanthos wrinkled his nose again as he looked at the marks scratched on the green disc, but he only glanced up at Diana briefly before he hurried away.

When she entered Sophia's room, the feeling of helplessness returned. Sophia knelt with her hands on the floor and head bowed. Her damp hair hung in a curtain, and though she could not see the woman's face, Diana could hear her labored breathing.

"Elena will be here soon, with the midwife," Diana said. She crouched down and laid a hand on her friend's back. "What can I do, Sophia?"

Sophia raised her head, and Diana cringed. Her face was pale, and her eyes winced and trembled. Perspiration beaded on her brow. She did not think she'd ever seen a person's expression convey such agony.

"Something is not right," Sophia said. "The baby—"

"They will be here soon." Diana spoke in a soft voice. "Come, I will help you into your bed."

Sophia shook her head.

"Do you . . . can I get you water?"

"Yes. Water." She spoke through clenched teeth and groaned again, tensing back into a ball.

Diana rushed down the stairs and found the water bucket empty.

She hurried outside to the stream, finding her way by moonlight, since she'd left the lantern in Sophia's room. Once she returned to the kitchen, she filled a wooden cup, then started toward the stairs.

The door opened, and Elena burst inside. "Where is Mitéra?"

"In her bedchamber."

Elena ran up the stairs.

A woman entered behind her. She was large and capable-looking. The wrinkles on her face showed that she had seen many years, but she did not stoop nor shuffle her steps.

"Thank you for coming," Diana said. "Sophia is—"

"No drinking." The woman's voice boomed through the kitchen.

Diana glanced down at the cup in her hands. "She is thirsty, so—"

"No drinks for a birthing mother. It will make her vomit. But bring the bucket. We will need water." She walked with purposeful steps up the staircase, and Diana followed.

The woman took charge of the situation immediately. "You two, remove your fine gowns and bring clean linens." She helped Sophia into a sitting position, leaning her back against the wall.

Diana and Elena exchanged a glance, then left the room to do as they were instructed.

"Will Mitéra be all right?" Elena asked while they changed their clothes.

"The midwife seems to know what she is doing," Diana said. She did not want to allow her own worries about what Sophia had said to frighten the girl. "And your mother has had five other babies."

Elena nodded, and the pair returned to Sophia's bedchamber.

The midwife was pushing on Sophia's round stomach with the heels of her hands. She seemed to be rotating the mass inside her. "The baby has not turned," she said.

Sophia's face was tight, her eyes closed and her breathing coming in gasps.

"Sometimes we can—" The midwife paused and prodded gently with her fingertips, then pressed her ear to Sophia's stomach. After a moment, she moved to her other side and listened again. "Two," she said.

"Two babies?" Sophia asked.

The woman nodded her head. "Yes. And both are facing the wrong direction. We must hurry."

Several hours later, Sophia lay exhausted on her bed. Diana got the impression that the birth had been more difficult than normal but had nothing to compare it to. The midwife pulled liquid from the second baby's nose and smacked its backside. The baby made an angry wail that matched the one produced by its twin a few moments earlier.

Diana felt a laugh well up at the sound. She glanced at Elena and saw the same expression on her face, delight, and relief.

"A girl," the midwife said, then wrapped the squirming red infant in a cloth and laid her beside her mother.

Sophia looked back and forth at the two babies lying in the curves of her arms. Tears shined in her eyes. "A boy and a girl. God has been good to us."

Diana wiped her fingers at the moisture that trickled down her cheeks. She'd never seen anything more beautiful than these two miracles.

Elena perched on the edge of the bed, touching the dark hair of one baby. "What will you name them, Mitéra?"

"Apollo and Artemis." Sophia smiled as she gazed at the small faces. "They will likely be called by Christian names as they get older, but for now, they are my miracles, and I will name them after the twins of legend."

"You must rest," the midwife instructed. "I will return tomorrow to ensure that all is well."

"Thank you." Sophia's eyes closed.

"Mitéra, sleep. Diana and I will care for the babies until they are hungry." Elena carefully lifted Artemis.

Diana took the bundle of blankets Elena held toward her. She felt her throat constrict. She'd never seen a baby so small. "I don't know how to hold her." She whispered the words, worried that a loud sound might frighten the helpless infant.

Elena lifted the other baby and adjusted Apollo so that his head lay against the inside of her elbow and he was cradled in her arm. "You're doing it exactly right, Missno. A woman knows how to care for a baby."

Diana sat on the chest, leaning back against the wall. She adjusted the blanket and studied the small face. The baby girl, Artemis, looked like an irritated old man. A tiny hand found its way free from the wrappings, and Diana touched it gently. Artemis grabbed onto her finger with a small fist.

Diana could not stop smiling as she watched the baby's expressions and movements. She felt overjoyed, and at the same time like she would break down and weep.

Elena sat on the chair beside her and turned Apollo so that he lay on her legs. She ran her fingers over his thick hair, then smiled at Diana. "I cannot imagine anything more precious, can you?"

"No," Diana said. And truly, she could not.

>[—]⋯[—]<

Diana jerked at the sound of a gunshot. She glanced down at the baby she held, but Artemis did not seem to have noticed the noise. Her heart pounded, and she held the infant closer to her chest.

She looked across the room at Elena but saw no worry on her face. Just the strain of a long night.

"Visitors," Elena said. "They are here to see the babies." Elena gave the baby she held to Sophia and hurried out of the room.

Diana walked toward the window. Another gunshot sounded, then another. Her gaze darted to Sophia, but she did not seem concerned. "They fire weapons to celebrate my new son."

Diana glanced down at Artemis. Did nobody celebrate a daughter?

Down in the main room, she heard noises: a man's booming voice, a woman's softer tones, and the excited sound of the Mavromichalis boys all speaking at once.

The children had been delighted to wake to find two new babies had been born during the night. They did not even seem bothered when Diana served fruit and yogurt instead of warm bread for breakfast.

The voices grew closer, and she heard the sound of feet pounding on the steps. She saw that Sophia was sitting up in the bed, pushing her hair out of her face, and smoothing down the sheets. *Surely visitors would not come into her roo—* The door swung open, and Petrobey strode inside followed by Dino, Themis, Stella, and Agatha.

"Where is the Mavromichalis clan's new gun?" The bey spoke with a grin on his face.

"Apollo." Sophia held out the boy for the men to see.

"A fine child," Petrobey said. "And he will make a fine warrior."

Diana thought the word *warrior* was the farthest thing from her mind when she looked at the tiny infant's face.

The other adults asked after Sophia's health, and Agatha held the baby. Petrobey looked around the room, his eyes lighting on Diana then dropping to the infant in her arms. He stepped toward her.

"This is Artemis." He spoke softly, stroking the baby's head. "Hello, *kardia mou*," my heart. He raised his gaze to Diana. "She is beautiful, isn't she?"

Diana nodded. Her heart warmed at the gentle way he spoke to the baby girl. Was this man truly a pirate? "Yes. Would you like to hold her?"

He accepted the bundle, lifting her to rest against his shoulder. He hummed a soft tune and rocked the slightest bit. "I saw the message you sent Elena. A cactus plant, very resourceful."

She looked up at Petrobey and saw that he leaned his head back slightly, studying her with shrewd eyes.

"I could not find any paper." She thought her sentence sounded foolish, but his scrutiny made her nervous. What was he thinking?

"She is clever, isn't she?"

"Elena?" Seeing affirmation in his face, Diana nodded. "Extremely."

"I knew it." His lips flattened into a line beneath his mustache, and he bent his head forward in a satisfied nod.

Diana realized his gesture meant the conversation was over. She glanced out the window. Daphne Sássaris stood on the street before the garden wall. She lifted her hand, as if she would open the gate but stopped. She raised her eyes and saw Diana and Petrobey in the window, the baby in his arms. Daphne's mouth drew down, and her eyes hardened. She turned away.

Diana glanced toward Petrobey to see if he had seen Daphne as well.

His brows were pulled together thoughtfully as he looked out the window. But after a moment and without a word, Petrobey walked to join the others at Sophia's bedside, and Diana excused herself to tend to the boys.

As she walked down the staircase, the image of Daphne's expression loomed in her mind. The pain and anger had seemed nearly tangible as she'd glared toward the house. Diana's heart hurt for the woman, and she wondered whether it was preferable to have never cared for someone in the first place rather than to suffer the loss of one you love.

Chapter 17

ALEX SHOULDERED THE RIFLE AND walked with quick steps. From the corner of his eye, he saw that Dino's face was tight and his gaze scanned the road from side to side. Even Themis was quiet for once, holding his weapon at the ready. The journey from Limeni to Tsímova seemed to take much longer than usual. Urgency coursed through Alex's veins, and he was tempted to break into a run.

When the three men arrived at Sophia's farm, he gazed around, relieved that nothing seemed out of the ordinary.

Dino did not stop to announce their presence but strode through the gate and across the garden, opening the door. "Elena," he called, walking to the stairs.

The church bells began to peal, and Dino let out a curse. "Elena! Where are you?"

The girl came down the staircase, holding a small bundle in her arms. "What is wrong?" Her gaze darted behind him as if to see why the bells pealed.

Diana appeared at the top of the stairs, holding the other baby. Her eyes narrowed slightly when she looked at Alex and then widened when she saw his rifle.

"The Sássaris clan, *Gdikiomos*." Dino pushed past her and started up the stairs. "Where are the boys?"

Elena's face turned white. "Georgi is at the orchard, and the others are with the goats in the mountains."

Dino stopped. "Do you know where?"

"No. Yes." She shook her head and took on a determined look. "I can find them."

Dino nodded. "Come, Themis. Alex, remain with the baby."

Themis's eyes narrowed and he looked as if he would argue, but a look from Dino stopped him.

Elena pushed the baby into Alex's arms. The bells continued to peal, their sound foreboding, a signal of alarm rather than worship. She rushed out the door, followed closely by her relatives.

Alex made sure the door was closed tightly. He propped the rifle against the sofa and moved the baby into a more comfortable position in the curve of his arm. He brushed his fingers over the soft hair, and his heart grew warm. "So small. Is this . . . ?" He raised his eyes to Diana.

"Artemis." She took a step closer. Her face was tight, but she spoke calmly. "Alex, what is happening? Are the children in danger?"

He tucked the infant girl tightly against him and lifted the gun. He nodded. "We need to speak to Sophia. Is she upstairs?"

"She is asleep." A crease formed between Diana's brows. She led him up the staircase, stopping at a door and knocked.

Sophia called for them to enter and sat up in the bed when she saw Alex. She rubbed her eyes and glanced at the baby he held. "Alexandros, have you come to see—" Her head jerked toward the window. "The church bells." She pushed aside the blankets and hurried to the window. "Is the town under attack?'

"*Gdikiomos*," Alex said. He moved next to her, looking up the deserted road. "The Sássaris clan."

Sophia's face paled, and she pressed a hand to her breastbone. "Where are my boys?"

"Dino and Themis have gone for them," Alex said. "Elena also."

Diana put her arm around Sophia's shoulder and led her to sit on the bed.

Alex put the baby he held into her mother's arms and stepped back near to the window. There was no movement on the road below. The sound of the church bells must have sent the villagers into their homes for safety.

"I am sorry," Diana said. "I do not understand what is happening."

Alex turned from the window. "The Sássaris clan have sworn a vendetta—a blood feud against the Mavromichalis clan."

"What does that mean?" Diana sat down on the foot of the bed and lifted the baby boy up against her shoulder.

"A vendetta," Alex said the word in Greek, then looked to Sophia to explain, but she nodded for him to continue. He lowered the butt of the rifle onto the floor, leaning the weapon against the wall. "It means they have vowed to kill every male member of the family or die trying. A vendetta such as this will not end until one family surrenders or leaves town, or—"

"Or until they are all exterminated," Sophia finished in a whisper.

"But why?" Diana looked between the two. "Why would they do this?"

Alex rubbed his neck. "Daphne Sássaris claims that a witch put a curse on her family." He winced as he looked at Sophia. "On your orders."

"That is the most ridiculous—" Diana began. But she stopped when Sophia bent down her head and began to weep.

Alex caught Diana's gaze and lifted his shoulder in a shrug. He did not understand the vendetta or the superstitions any more than she did. Believing that intelligent people would willingly endanger so many lives, and all for an irrational belief, was nearly beyond comprehension.

Diana opened her eyes wide in an expression of puzzlement. But the look was gone in an instant, replaced by resolve. "What should we do, Alex?"

"The men will return with your children soon, Sophia." He glanced once more out the window and strode to the door. "We need to be ready when they arrive."

Sophia wiped off her cheeks. "Yes."

"Ready for what?" Diana asked.

"With Hektor gone, they will be safest at Limeni in Petrobey's tower. That is where the Mavromichalis men and boys are gathering. Do you have a cart, Sophia? I don't think you are in any condition to walk the distance."

She stood. "Yes. Missno will show you. I will gather the boy's clothing." She laid Artemis on the bed and started toward the door. "I am so grateful you are here, Missno. Elena will need your help to tend to the farm."

Diana placed her hand on Sophia's arm. "There is no reason for you to go as well. You are not ready for travel."

"We cannot separate a mother from an infant," Alex said.

"Of course not. Elena and I will care for Sophia and the babies."

Alex looked at the baby in her arms, then raised his eyes to Diana's face. He saw the precise moment the truth dawned on her.

She clutched Apollo closer against her chest. "No, they wouldn't. He is an infant. Not three days old. Surely . . ."

"He is a gun, Missno," Sophia said. Her hands were shaking, and tears slid from her eyes. "And he will grow up to seek revenge on anyone who harms his family." She stroked the baby's head and took him from Diana, placing him on the bed beside his twin sister.

Diana's lips pressed together, and she swallowed hard. "I will get the clothing and help Alex with the wagon. You must get yourself and the babies ready." She embraced Sophia and helped her to sit on the bed by her twins. She placed her hand on the mother's cheek. "Do not worry. We will take care of everything."

Her calm manner had a soothing effect on Sophia. Her face relaxed, and she nodded. "Thank you."

Diana straightened up and motioned to him. "Come, Alex. The boys' bedchamber is just down the hallway."

Alex was grateful for Diana's practicality. He knew she would not falter. She could be depended on to do what was needed. He was surprised when he realized there were few men he would trust in an emergency as completely as he trusted Diana Snow.

He stepped outside, holding up his rifle and scanning the area around the house, but all was calm. The church bells had thankfully ceased, and the village was quiet. He moved aside, and Diana came out behind him.

"The wagon is behind the house." She carried a bag stuffed with the children's clothing and extra blankets for the babies. She led him to a small outbuilding, put the bag into the wagon, then helped Alex attach the harness to the donkey. They led the wagon into the yard, leaving it where the animal would have shade as they waited for Dino and Themis to bring the boys.

Diana stepped around the wagon and clasped his arm, pulling on him until he faced her. "You must make certain the boys are protected. Please. If anything should happen to them . . ."

He knew precisely how she felt. The thought of one of Sophia's boys coming to harm made it difficult to breathe. "I will watch over them."

She released her hold and rubbed her arms, looking at the road that led into town. "The Sássaris clan would not really harm a child or a baby." She turned to him. "Would they?" She looked at him with wide eyes, as if searching for reassurance.

He grimaced, wishing he could provide it. "I'm afraid they would. And the Mavromichaleis would not hesitate to do the same."

Her forehead wrinkled. "But these are the people they worship beside, families that they greet in the village and dance with at weddings. I do not understand."

"Nor do I." He glanced up the road, knowing he needed to keep alert for danger. "But the vendetta is an ancient practice here, and they are a proud people."

"They do not truly believe that Sophia put a curse on Daphne, do they?"

"I think they do."

She shifted her position, stepping forward to look around him in the direction of the village. "Sophia cares for Daphne, feels pity for her. She would never—"

Alex nodded. "I know, and you know—and I think deep in her heart Daphne knows."

"Her anger will cost lives, perhaps those of people she loves." Diana's voice rose in pitch.

He glanced toward her from the side of his eyes. "One should not attempt to understand the actions of a grieving mother. Heartache can steal a person's reason."

Diana's lips puckered the smallest bit as she scrutinized him. Her gray eyes were wide and filled with compassion. "You are thinking of your own mother."

Alex knew he could not answer around the boulder that had settled in the back of his throat. He tipped his head forward, swallowing hard.

"It would be unfair to judge Daphne." Diana moved to stand in the shade.

He paced a few times in front of the gate then joined her, leaning back against the cart. Where were Dino and Themis and the boys? He tapped his foot on the ground and tried not to imagine any scenario where Mikhail or another of the children were hurt.

"You care for them too, don't you?" she said. "I can see in your eyes. You are worried."

"Yes."

"Alex, until I came here, I had never felt such . . . I have had friends, people I cared for, students like Molly, other teachers. But these people"—she waved to the house behind her—"this family . . . they are more. I—"

"You love them," he said simply.

Diana tipped her head. "I suppose that is it. The babies, the children, Elena, and Sophia—I feel a closeness to them." She lowered her voice until it was nearly a whisper. "I know I will have to leave them, and it makes my heart feel like it is cracking."

He turned toward her, understanding exactly how she felt. "That is what love is, a risk."

She looked up at him through her lashes and drew in a shaky breath. He had never seen her expression so vulnerable. "Is it worth the risk? Your family was taken from you. Do you ever wish—? Would it have been easier if you did not love them in the first place?"

Her honest question touched on a thought he'd had in his darkest moments. The lump returned inside his throat, but it was not for his family or for himself. It hurt him to see how afraid she was to care. Because for Diana, caring had always resulted in pain.

He set down the weapon and clasped her shoulders, turning her so she faced him directly. "It would have been easier. That is true. But it was worth it. Their memory is everything to me. I assure you, Diana. It is definitely worth it."

She took a step forward, slipping into his arms and clinging around his waist. Alex tightened his embrace and leaned his cheek onto her hair. He felt warm knowing that he could comfort her and wondering if she realized that her action did the same for him. How perfect would his life be if he knew her embrace waited for him whenever he was discouraged? He fought against the thought, knowing there was no use in indulging it.

The bleat of a goat pulled him from his thoughts. He released her, then lifted his gun with one hand and grasped Diana's with the other.

They walked together to the gate. An immense wave of relief washed over him when he saw Dino, Themis, Elena, and the four boys leading a string of animals.

"They are safe." Diana breathed the words as a whisper and met his gaze with a look of relief.

"Missno, Alex!" Mikhail called to them. "We are going to Petrobey's tower in Limeni!" The boy was the only member of the party whose face was not somber.

Diana released his hand and held open the gate. "I have your clothes already in the wagon," she said in a voice Alex recognized as forced cheerfulness.

"Chrysanthos, lock the goats in the pen. Georgi, retrieve your father's weapons." Dino called out orders that were hastily obeyed.

Themis stood in the road with his back to the house. He held the rifle stock in one hand, the other ready to pull back the flint.

"Mitéra?" Elena leaned close to Diana and spoke in a low voice.

"Caring for the babies. She will be ready when it is time to leave."

Elena's young face looked as if it had aged ten years. She nodded gravely and turned toward the house.

Diana put her arm around the young girl's shoulders. "Your uncles and Alex will take care of your family. Do not worry."

Alex saw Elena tip her head onto Diana's shoulder as the pair entered the house. His heart was heavy at the sight of the usually cheerful Elena's sorrow.

Mikhail tugged on Alex's sleeve, and he looked down. "Will you come to Limeni, too?"

"Yes." He smiled at the boy's innocence.

"I am glad."

Diana and Elena lined the wagon with blankets and helped Sophia lie down inside.

Alex watched Diana kiss baby Apollo's cheek before she laid him beside his mother. Her lip trembled. She bid the boys farewell, and Dino led the group toward Limeni.

Elena and Diana waved to the departing family.

Alex stopped at the gate and spoke to Diana in English. "I do not like leaving you and Elena alone, but all the men will be in the tower, and it would not be appropriate for me to remain here."

"I understand." Her lip trembled, and she clamped her hand over her mouth as she watched the others depart.

He leaned close, lifting her chin and capturing her gaze. Her eyes were wide and wet. He moved aside her hand and brushed his finger over her quivering lip. "Remember what I said, Diana. I promise it is worth it."

Chapter 18

A CLOUD OF MELANCHOLY HUNG over both Diana and Elena for the remainder of the day. Diana moved through the motions of the farm duties without noticing what she was doing. More than once, she found herself surprised to see that she'd already performed a task that she didn't remember.

The supper table was silent. Diana picked at her food without really tasting it. She tried a few times to engage Elena in conversation, but neither was able to muster the energy for small talk. Finally Elena announced that she was going to sleep.

Diana remained at the table. She thought of her first morning in Tsímova, how out of place she'd felt and how quickly the family had welcomed her into their circle. The vacant chairs seemed to make the table feel even more lonely.

She replaced the dishes and tidied the kitchen, but putting everything in order didn't bring the calm it typically did. Every sound she made seemed to echo through the empty rooms. She finally gave up and decided there was nothing else to do but sleep.

When she climbed the stairs and entered their shared room, she heard Elena weeping. The sound pulled at her heart. Diana sat on the bed beside her friend and brushed her fingers over Elena's hair until she finally quieted and slept.

Diana undressed and lay on her cot, not tired in the least. Images appeared one after another in her mind, each bringing with it a wave of emotion: Sophia's tears, Daphne's glare, Alex's embrace, the feel of a baby's hand clasping her finger, the sound of the boys wrestling.

The images began to appear distorted and shifted, slipping from memories into dreams, and finally Diana slept.

In the morning, Diana attempted to maintain a pleasant conversation as they worked on the household duties, and the distraction seemed to help Elena's mood.

Without a family to cook for, the chores were finished quickly, and the house set to rights. The two stood outside the goat pen.

"I suppose it is up to us to take them to graze then." Elena made a face.

Diana smiled at the girl's reaction to the task. "It will give us time to read. Bring your book."

Elena's expression lit up. "Yes! I shall."

They packed a knapsack with food and the book, and drove the goats through the winding streets of the town toward the hills beyond. As they passed Spiros's house, Elena glanced up at the tower. Men with weapons stood at the windows, watching the road, but Diana did not see Spiros among them.

Elena sighed and continued. Her mood seemed to sink lower as they climbed over the rocks and searched for shade where they could sit with a good view of the animals.

Diana did not know how the boys managed to keep themselves entertained for an entire day watching over goats among the rocks and scraggly bushes. Elena read for a while, but even Aesop's fables lost a bit of their magic after a few hours. The most interesting thing that happened during the entire day was when Elena nearly sat on a turtle. Diana dreaded repeating the task the following day. Hours later, the pair made their way home, driving the goats before them.

They entered the gate, and led the goats to the pen, then turned to the house.

Elena stopped. "I smell bread." She inhaled. "And souvlaki."

The pair exchanged a look. Had Sophia returned?

Elena's face lit in a grin. She hurried toward the house, but before she reached it, the door opened wide.

Stella bounded out and wrapped her cousin in an embrace. "At last you have come! Mitéra and I have waited for hours."

Diana glanced behind her and saw Agatha in the doorway. Elena kissed Agatha's cheek and pulled Stella into the house. Giggles and chatter sounded from inside.

"Sophia did not want the two of you to be alone," Agatha said. She wiped her hands on a cloth.

"Thank you." Diana was grateful for anything that would make Elena smile.

The mood at supper was a complete reversal from the evening before. Diana didn't realize how hungry she was until a plate of souvlaki and a vegetable salad were set before her.

Elena and Stella talked about the wedding, how beautiful the bride was, whose dresses they admired, which young men impressed them with their dancing, and how well their kourabiedes were received.

Diana caught Agatha's eye and opened her eyes wide, smiling at the intensity of the frivolous conversation. It was precisely what the girls needed during these tense days.

Stella laid her hand on her breastbone and sighed. "And oh, the twins are so perfect. Right now, they are being kissed and cuddled by every Mavromichalis in Limeni."

Elena's face fell. "I miss the babies." She looked down at her plate. "I miss all of my family."

"Perhaps we can go to Limeni soon?" Diana looked at Agatha, not knowing who else to ask if she and Elena could make the journey.

"A splendid idea." Agatha nodded. "After church on Sunday."

"But that is still four days away," Elena said softly. She sighed and kept her gaze lowered.

"Elena, would you read us a story after supper?" Diana asked.

The girl glanced up at her guests' faces. "Would you like that?"

"Oh yes!" Stella clapped her hands together.

Agatha nodded her head. "Yes, that will be just the thing."

Diana could have embraced them for their reaction.

Hours later, after the supper dishes were cleaned, the house set to rights, and three fables read, Elena yawned. "I am ready to sleep."

Diana was glad that the others were willing to sit in the room by lantern light for such a long time and listen to the girl's slow delivery.

Neither seemed to mind that she stumbled over words or needed to pause to analyze the sounds. They were gracious and complimentary.

"Oh! I nearly forgot." Stella jumped up and hurried to a satchel that hung on a peg near the door. She pulled out two small packages and brought them to Diana and Elena.

"What is this?" Diana asked, turning over the bundle in her hands. It appeared to be a grouping of small objects wrapped in a piece of white netting.

"*Koufetas* from the wedding," Stella said. "You both left early."

"They are almonds coated with sugar," Agatha explained. "A traditional favor for wedding guests."

"And if you place them beneath your pillow while you sleep, you'll dream of the person you will marry." Stella grinned and waggled her eyebrows.

"Missno, perhaps you will dream of Alexandros Metaxas," Elena said.

Diana felt her cheeks turn red. "Perhaps," she said, hoping for a nonchalant tone. She set the koufetas in her lap. "Thank you, Stella."

"Off to bed, girls," Agatha said. "We have a farm to maintain tomorrow."

"And you can come tend the goats with us." Elena clasped Stella's hand and pulled her to her feet.

"I'll sleep in the boys' room," Diana said. "So the two of you can be together."

The girls bid them good night and hurried up the stairs. The sound of their voices and laughter drifted down the stairs.

Agatha let out a good-natured sigh and raised her eyes to the heavens. She leaned back against the sofa.

"Thank you for coming," Diana said. "A distraction is precisely what Elena needs. She has been worried about her family."

Agatha's shoulders slumped. "I know." She looked down at her clasped hands.

Diana realized she was thinking about her own family: Kyros and his brothers and her husband, Themis. She moved from her chair to sit beside Agatha. She lifted the woman's hand, a gesture she would have never considered two weeks earlier, but she'd learned that Greeks were much more affectionate than she'd been accustomed to. "Thank you, Agatha."

Each day Diana was in Greece, she learned more about belonging to a family and never failed to be amazed by the sacrifices people were willing to make for those they love. Her heart was soft as she rose and bid Agatha good night.

Later, as Diana undressed, her eyes fell on the wrapped package of almonds. She sat on one of the boy's beds and turned it over in her hands and then, since nobody would know, slid it beneath the pillow. She did not have to fall asleep before thinking of Alexandros Metaxas. Thoughts of him always seemed near. The memory of Alex cradling little Artemis, of him squatting down to discuss his fear of haircuts with Mikhail, and the way his coffee-brown eyes sparkled when he laughed swirled around in her mind, and she barely recognized that she was smiling just before drifting to sleep.

⚊⚊⚊

The next morning, Diana, Elena, and Stella herded the goats through the town. Diana had offered to remain behind, but Agatha thought the girls should not be alone.

When they passed the Sássaris house, Spiros's younger sister, Theodora, was in the garden, spreading grain for the chickens. Diana hadn't noticed before how lovely the girl was. Theodora was probably close to twelve years old. She bore a strong resemblance to her mother, but the bitterness and sorrow that lined Daphne's face were absent. The girl raised her gaze shyly as they passed, looking at them through the long lashes that surrounded her dark eyes.

Elena waved, and Theodora darted a glance at her house before returning the greeting.

Diana's heart warmed at the goodness of her friend. Elena was so like her mother, willing to love and forgive. If only the families were not enemies, the Sássaris clan would be lucky to have Elena as a friend.

Diana was still contemplating on the sweet nature of the Mavromichalis women when she heard a strange noise. It took a moment before she realized it was the sound of horses. She'd not heard any horses since arriving in the Mani.

Somewhere in the village, a woman screamed, and Diana felt a surge of panic when she remembered Alex's words. Only the Turks were permitted to ride horses.

She clasped each girl by the arm. "We must hide." She pulled them onto a smaller side street, looking along the stone walls for a door or a gate.

"But the goats—" Elena began, but she stopped short when a man in a turban appeared around a bend, riding toward them on an enormous black horse.

Diana whirled and jerked the girls' arms, tugging them back to the main road. Her heart pounded so hard that she tasted blood in her throat. Another horseman approached when they rounded the corner. When he saw them, he pointed and shouted something in a strange tongue.

Diana did not stop. She tugged the girls forward. They ran through the winding roads toward the church, the sound of hoofbeats following. But when the road opened wide, they saw that the square was full of people.

The horsemen guarded the roads leading away from the open square. Diana saw a flurry of movement and heard screaming and weeping. In an instant, she realized why. Children were being pulled away from their protesting families.

Three turbaned men stood in wide-legged pants and curled-toed shoes, pointing rifles toward the pleading parents. Men protested loudly. Women fell to their knees, begging for their children's release; neighbors held them back when they moved toward the men.

The Turks were unaffected by the pleas or the weeping as they bound the children's wrists. They may as well have been deaf for all the reaction they showed. Screams and cries for mother and father were ignored as the children strained and tried to pull away.

Devşirme. In her mind, Diana heard the loathing and fear in Alex's voice as he said the word. Another horseman rode into the square, tugging on ropes that bound Spiros and his sister, Theodora.

Elena gasped.

Diana pushed the girls back into a darkened doorway and stood in front of them. "Do not move," she whispered.

The man on the black horse rode back and forth, calling out to the others, using words Diana could not understand. His mustache was curled at the tips in a style that seemed almost comical combined with his bright clothing. The red turban he wore was larger and more ornate than those of the other men. A fluffy yellow feather rose from a jewel in the center of his forehead and bounced with his movements. He scanned the square, and when his gaze reached Diana, he stopped and rode forward.

Panic shot over her skin, tingling her nerves until her fingers hurt. *No.*

The man waved a hand toward Diana and the girls clustered in the doorway, and two other Turks approached.

"No. You cannot take them," Diana said, even as she was jerked away from Elena and Stella and pushed aside.

"Missno!" Elena screamed when the man grabbed onto her arm, pulling her into the sunlight.

The man on the horse nodded and motioned toward Stella.

Diana did not know whether anger or desperation drove her forward. She ran toward the man. "Stop! Please."

The horseman ignored her. His feather swayed as he made a motion for the girls to be taken to join the others.

"No!" Elena cried out. "Mitéra!" She strained against the rope that pulled her forward. The expression on her face showed pure terror. "Help me, Missno!"

Stella fell to her knees and was yanked forward, skidding on her elbows until she was able to stand again. Tears streaked her face, and she shook with sobs.

"You must release them!" Diana tugged on the man's boot, catching a glimpse of the curved saber at his waist. "They are children. You cannot—"

She did not even see his leg move before his kick threw her back onto the stones. She landed hard on her hip. Sitting up, she winced at the pain, then pressed her fingers to the side of her chin, moving her jaw from side to side. It seemed like nothing was damaged.

Elena screamed again, and Diana knew she could not allow her to be taken. She rose, shaking and ran toward the horsemen, but she was stopped short when strong arms clasped her around the waist.

"Let me go! I must—" She wrenched herself around and discovered her captor was Father Yianni.

"Father, release me!" Diana had never felt so angry in her life. Red clouded her vision. She did not care if the curly mustached Turk kicked her face a hundred times, she would chase him down, and—"Father!"

The priest did not loosen his hold, no matter how frantically Diana squirmed. She registered a moment of surprise that the gray-bearded man possessed such strength. He dragged her backward into the church and finally released her but closed the door and stood before it.

"Father, do not do this. I must stop them." Tremors shook her body.

"You cannot." He folded his hands and spoke in a calm voice.

"I must!" She fought back the tears that filled her eyes, knowing that it was extremely disrespectful to yell in a church. "I must, don't you see?"

She sank down onto her knees and images crowded into her mind. Sophia, Agatha, she had promised to take care of their daughters. They had trusted her. And Daphne . . . "Father, Daphne." Her voice choked, and her shoulders shook as she fought down her tears.

Father Yianni's thick brows rose in surprise. "Daphne?" He crouched down beside her. "Yes, I saw Spiros taken when he ran from the house to save his sister." He breathed out. "You are right. Daphne has suffered much."

Diana shook her head, the ache in her chest had grown so strong that she could not speak. She heard Elena's voice in her head, calling for her, begging; saw Stella's tears . . .

She gasped and pressed the heel of her hand against her chest, pushing out her words in a whisper. "I have to go, don't you see? It must be me." She breathed in sharply, wondering if her heart would ever stop hurting. "I am the only person with no family."

"And you would risk your life for these people you have known only for a few weeks?"

"I love them."

He studied her, his shrewd eyes squinting. His lips pursed, and he tapped a finger against them. Finally, he nodded his head and stood, holding out a hand to her. "You will be of no help to anyone if you act rashly."

He was right. She would do no good unless she calmed herself and formed a plan. Diana took his hand and allowed him to help her stand. Her breathing was still uneven. "We need the men. The two strongest clans in the village are hidden away in their towers. If they could put aside this vendetta and—"

"I will speak to the Mavromichalis and Sássaris leaders." He placed his other hand atop hers. "What will you do, my child?"

Diana was taken aback by the tenderness in his voice. She felt tears threaten again, but if she possessed one skill, it was the ability to keep her feelings at bay. She breathed deeply until all of her emotions were controlled. "I will follow them. Leave a trail for the men to know which way they went. I know there is not much that I can do. But I must do something."

Father Yianni shuffled his robes, then pressed something hard into her hand.

She glanced down and saw it was a knife with a curved blade in a metal sheath. The weapon was about as long as her hand.

"It is not much, but maybe you will find a use for it," he said.

"Thank you." Diana bowed her head, and Father Yianni blessed her.

"They rode south," he said. "The horses will be easy enough to follow, they will likely stay to the roads, and they stir up dust." He opened the wooden doors to reveal a deserted square. The sight was almost as heartbreaking as the one she'd witnessed before she was taken in to the church. Despair hung heavily in the emptiness.

"Be careful," he said.

Diana nodded as the weight of what she was doing settled on her shoulders. She waved a farewell and started off.

"Missno?"

Diana turned.

"Never believe your life is not of value or that you are not loved." He made the sign of the cross again and tipped forward his head in a farewell.

Diana tucked the knife into the sash at her waist and hurried away, brushing at the tears that refused her efforts to quell them.

Chapter 19

ALEX LEANED BACK AGAINST THE stone wall and crossed his arms. He slid down to sit on the floor. Spending two days in a tower with a group of angry men and bored boys was not high on his list of interests. He could not help but think of Diana and Elena, and all of the other women trying to maintain their homes and farms without the men's assistance.

He rested his head back and stretched out his legs, crossing one over the other. His gaze traveled over the others in the room.

Chrysanthos, Iakob, and Mikhail sat nearby. The younger boys were making stacks with blocks. Chrysanthos looked on, his elbows resting on his knees and his chin in his hands with an expression of extreme boredom.

On the other side of the tower room, Dino stared out the window facing the harbor. He was still frustrated that his brother Hektor was missing, and now that the family was embroiled in a vendetta, Dino would not be able to take a ship in search.

One of Dino's younger brothers, Argos, leaned against the windowsill and folded his arms. "We could transport the cannon to Tsímova in a few hours. The Sássaris tower would be rubble by nightfall."

Dino shook his head. "The tower is in the middle of the village. The cannon would cause too much damage to other buildings."

"And so we just wait for them to attack?"

Dino turned away from the window and faced his brother. "If that is what Petrobey says we will do, then it will be so."

Argos bumped his fist back against the wood of the windowsill. "And how long will we wait? My wife and daughters are home, trying to manage the harvest season alone. We will lose our entire orchard if this is not ended soon."

Themis entered the room. "Still no movement from Tsímova. The cowards."

The other men and boys in the room muttered among themselves.

Themis strolled around the room, glancing out the windows on every side, then sat in a corner beside Kyros and Georgi. "And what are you boys talking about here in the corner? Is there a girl you fancy?"

Kyros turned to his father. "We are not talking about girls." The similarities between the father's and son's appearances fascinated Alex. Both had the same heavily lidded eyes, making them look perpetually dissatisfied.

"And why not?" Themis said. "When I was your age, there were quite a few pretty girls in Tsímova and even in Kalamata."

Argos kicked Themis's foot. "I'll never know how you managed to convince the lovely Agatha to marry you."

A few of the other men laughed good-naturedly.

"How did you convince Mitéra?" Kyros asked. "Did you speak to grandfather?"

Themis sat back, folding his arms across his chest and getting comfortable. He was a man who enjoyed feeling important, Alex decided. He liked to control the conversation in a room and preferred it even more to revolve around him. "Once I decided Agatha was the woman for me, I waited after church in the town square until the whole town was gathered. I fired my rifle into the air. Then I called out her name. She and her family would have been disgraced if she had not agreed to be my wife."

"You are a true romantic, Themis," Argos said sarcastically.

"I prefer to get what I want. And leave nothing to chance," Themis said with a smug grin.

Mikhail left his blocks and sat against the wall beside Alex. "You should shoot your gun in the air for Missno, then she will have to marry you."

Alex let out a bark of laughter, grateful for the dim lighting in the corner of the room that hid the red flush on his neck. He turned his head and looked down at the child. "It is sound advice, Mikhail. But I can't marry Miss Snow. She will return to London soon, and I must go to Constantinople." He glanced up and saw Dino and a few of the other men watched the conversation with interest.

Mikhail's small brow furrowed. "But she is pretty."

The amusement he felt was joined by a heat in his chest. "That is very true."

"And kind."

Alex nodded. "Miss Snow *is* kind."

Mikhail continued to stare at him as if he were daft for not appreciating what was so obvious, which Alex realized was probably quite accurate. Even though he knew the child did not understand the complications of the situation, his argument was sound. She possessed every attribute that would make her an ideal wife. Truthfully, Alex would like nothing better than to marry Diana Snow. A pang of regret stung his throat, and he covered it with another laugh, mostly for the benefit of the other men. "Perhaps *you* should marry Miss Snow, Mikhail. It sounds as though you are quite smitten with her."

His brothers laughed.

"When I am a man, I will marry her." Mikhail puffed out his chest and gave a crisp nod.

Alex smiled and rested his shoulders back, closing his eyes. If only it were that simple. The regret he'd felt earlier expanded until it filled his throat, and he swallowed hard against it. He would have to tell Diana farewell, and it made him ache.

He was jolted from his thoughts when the door banged open and Petrobey strode into the room, followed by Father Yianni.

Alex noticed immediately that Petrobey's face was drawn. He held his mouth in a tight line, and his shoulders were rigid. His eyes were rimmed in red.

The vendetta—somebody had been killed, Alex thought.

Tension filled the room as the men waited for the news.

"Father." Petrobey nodded to the priest and stepped back, sweeping his hand in an invitation for the man to speak.

Alex did not miss the crack in the bey's voice. His chest tightened.

Father Yianni's posture was strong. His eyes were sharp. If it were not for his black robes, flat *skouphos* on his head, and the silver cross at his chest, Alex would not have taken the man for a priest. He held himself as a warrior—a Maniot, Alex realized.

"A *Yayabaşi* officer with his *sürücu* drovers has taken children from Tsímova."

The men stared at the priest in shocked silence for a few seconds, then the room exploded in noise. *Who was taken? When? We had no warning.*

"They have never come here," Themis spluttered. "The Mani is free."

"The Turks caught us by surprise, sending riders through the streets to drive everyone into the town square." The priest spoke in a strong voice, but Alex heard it waver. "Seven children were taken: the Michalákiani twins, Barnabas and Bartholomaios; Dimitrios Grigorakiáni; Spiros and Theodora Sássaris; and your own kin, Stella and Elena." He glanced around at the stricken faces. "Sophia's servant, Missno, has gone after them."

Alex bolted to his feet. His heart flew into his throat. "What do you mean gone after them?" The memory of seeing his father with a musket ball in his forehead made Alex choke on his own breath.

The men all began to speak at once. Themis leaned against the wall, his head in his hands. Sophia's sons began to cry. Mikhail leaned against Alex, and he placed his hand on the boy's head as the child wept.

Alex's pulse pounded, and his mind spun as he debated his next actions. He would go after Diana, and God willing, he would find her before the Turks did. What was she thinking? Why had she acted so rashly?

He moved toward the door, but Father Yianni intercepted him. The priest laid a hand on Alex's arm and leaned his head close, speaking only for Alex's ears. "Wait."

"Father, I must go. She will be killed."

The priest's hand tightened on Alex's arm until he lifted his gaze to meet the older man's eyes. "I spoke these same words to a panicked young woman a little over an hour ago: You will be of no help to anyone if you act rashly."

Alex felt his hands shaking.

"Trust her. And wait for a plan."

Alex swallowed, seeing reason in the priest's words. He would solve nothing by dashing away after Diana. And she would never forgive him if he did not do everything in his power to help rescue the children. He nodded his head. "You are right."

"Love makes one impulsive, does it not, my son?"

Alex gave a wry smile. He glanced once more to the door and then, with great effort, calmed his reckless thoughts and turned back, brushing his hand over Mikhail's head when the boy stepped close. He did not realize the room had quieted until Petrobey started speaking in a low voice that commanded attention.

"We must call for a *treva*."

"A truce?" Argos spat the word. "Surrender?"

Petrobey's eyes tightened. "We need the Sássaris men if we have any hope of rescuing the children."

Argos turned to the priest. "Father, how many Turks were there?"

"I counted no more than twelve."

"We do not need the Sássaris men for twelve." Argos curled his lip.

"A Yayabaşi officer commands a large unit. We have no idea if more await them at their camp. We need as many Maniots as we can rally."

Argos bowed his head, conceding to the bey's wishes, but he scowled.

"Come, Father. We will meet with Sebastianos Sássaris," Petrobey said. "Dino, Themis." He motioned with his head for the men to join him, then scanned the room. "The rest of you, assemble in the town square—and be ready for battle. The Turks made a mistake when they took our children. And they will regret it."

Chapter 20

DIANA CROUCHED BEHIND A CLUMP of bushes and peered down at the road. A haze of dust told her the horses had come in this direction. In the hours since she had set off from Tsímova, she had seen no one and had decided that a company of Turks on horses dragging crying children was enough to send the local people fleeing into their houses.

She tore another strip from her head scarf and tied it close to the road, where it would be seen, then hurried on. She'd glimpsed the horses ahead of her a few times when she'd rounded a bend too quickly, but so far, she had managed to avoid detection.

Diana was not an expert on military practices, but she did not think the Turks were behaving as if they were afraid that anyone would threaten them. They had not noticed an untrained person following them, and there did not seem to be any scouts or lookouts. The fact that they didn't appear to care whether or not they were seen made her grind her teeth in anger. The Greek people had tolerated the Turkish control and arrogance long enough. And the practice of collecting children had to end.

She saw that farther ahead the road curved back around and decided climbing over the rocky hill would give her a better view. She would at least be able to see the children.

Her weeks of gathering firewood and delivering luncheon to the goat tenders had hardened her hands and firmed her leg muscles, so she climbed, sure footed, over the rough rocks and dusty earth. She did not even wince as she pushed aside a prickly bush that would have scratched the soft hands of a finishing school instructor.

She slipped once on loose rocks and banged her knee but quickly continued scrambling upward. When she reached the top of the hill, she stayed in a low crouch and crept forward, ducking behind a boulder where she could see the road.

The men rode silently, leading the bound children behind. The only noise was an occasional whimper or cough from the dust the horses kicked up.

Diana wished she could catch Elena's attention and let her know she hadn't been abandoned, but she knew the attempt wasn't worth the risk of discovery. The curly-mustached man with the feather in his turban called a halt. He did not even glance back at the rest of his group as he drank from his water skin.

Another man slid off his horse and held a water skin to each child's mouth. Once they'd all drunk, he reached out his hand with the palm down and lowered it, indicating for them to sit. They would rest.

Diana looked farther up the road, but it curved around the steep hills, and she could not see much.

An idea came to her, and she scrambled through the hills in the direction of the road. When she came to it, she glanced back, but the company was still hidden. She did not know how long she would have before their rest ended and they came upon her, and so she ran down the road ahead of them, searching for a cactus plant.

She finally spotted one and climbed the hill to reach it. Using Father Yianni's blade, she sliced off a pad and carefully broke off the needles. With the point of the knife, she carved into the flat pad, each cut standing out darker and moist against the green background. When she finished, she held it at arm's length and scrutinized her work, hoping the letters were large enough to be seen from a distance.

She hurried back to the road, tore a strip from her head scarf, then tied it to a branch she hoped would be too low for a man on horseback to notice. She placed the cactus pad beneath it with the words facing the road.

Μη φοβησου. *Mi fovisou*—do not fear.

Diana glanced back at the message once more and hurried up the hill, finding a hiding spot where she could watch the group pass by undetected.

She did not have to wait long before she saw the man with the yellow feather riding in the lead with his men following. The children were pulled behind.

Her heart felt like it was breaking as she watched them march by. The children seemed so small in the wake of the large animals. Discouragement, fear, and hopelessness showed in the slump of their young shoulders and the emptiness of their eyes. Diana pressed her hand over her mouth, worried she would make a sound and reveal herself.

Elena walked with the others, her head down. When she neared the spot with the message, her pace slowed, and she stared hard at the side of the road, and then she stopped completely.

The man leading her jerked on the rope, pulling her forward, but the difference in Elena's mood showed in her bearing. She walked quickly, her head up. Her eyes scanned the hillside as she looked all around. She'd known the message was for her.

Diana was glad she'd given the girl hope. She knew Elena would pass the word to the other children that they were not given up on.

She did not move from her hiding spot until the party was well ahead down the road. She moved now with a light heart. The Maniot men would follow her trail and arrive soon—they could not be more than an hour or so behind. She felt a bit frightened at what would transpire once they arrived, but the safety of Elena and the others was the priority, and she was certain the men coming to their rescue felt the same.

As she continued onward, she wondered if Alex would be with the men. Of course he would. He cared about the children too. A feeling of worry squirmed in her middle as she imagined him fighting the man with the feather in his turban. The Turk carried a large sword. Did Alex know how to fight? Would he be injured?

She paused where the road branched to tie another strip of fabric. Breathing calmly, she forced her worry away. There was no use in fretting about things she had no control over, especially those things that may not come to pass. For all she knew, Alex's ship had arrived, and he was on his way to Corfu this moment. But she knew the thought was silly. He would not leave without telling her. She was certain of it, although she could not say how she knew. Even though they had hardly put words to their feelings, his heart was connected to hers. And if he left now, without a farewell, they would both feel as though they'd left business unfinished.

Diana stopped short when she rounded a bend and saw the sea before her. She realized the road had brought her atop cliffs that surrounded a cove beneath. She hid behind a large rock and watched as the horses carefully made their way downward on a path.

Lying on her stomach, she scooted forward and watched the company pass on a winding path beneath her that led down to the beach. She slid back away from the edge and searched for a location where she could observe the harbor below undetected.

Staying far enough away to avoid being seen, she followed the curve of the shore around until she reached a cluster of bushes. She scooted closer and saw that the Turks seemed to be setting up a camp on the other side of the harbor, near where they had descended. They stayed back against the rocks, and she wondered if the sea rose during the night, covering more of the beach.

Down below, the horses were led to a nook where two large rocks met. A fence of crooked branches that looked as though it was constructed hastily kept them penned.

The children were taken to another recess, surrounded on three sides by rock face that was nearly fifteen feet high and far too steep to climb. Not that it was even an option with their hands still bound.

One Turk sat on a rock near the opening to the children's area, but he didn't look overly concerned that they would attempt to escape.

The other men rested on the beach in the shade of the rocks. A few gathered driftwood and branches that Diana thought they would use for a fire. She wondered how long they would stay in this harbor. The noon hour was long past, and surely they would remain at least for the night.

She took a chance and moved closer to the lip of the overhang, looking for other paths down to the beach. She saw a few breaks in the rock where she thought a person could lower themselves if absolutely necessary, but she did not think it would be easy to climb back up. Possible, perhaps, but not for a group. The pathway the horsemen had taken seemed the surest escape.

She returned to the place where the road ended and the path began to descend. As she neared, she spotted a structure a bit farther along the cliff. She crept over the rocky ground and discovered an old stone church. She glanced around then entered through the opening where a door must have been at one time.

The sunlight hardly penetrated the interior. She studied the dim room. Soot stains covered the ceiling, and instead of windows, there were uneven spaces high up on the walls where it looked as though rocks were missing. In the center of the floor was a large rectangular column turned on its side. She wondered if it was a remnant from an ancient structure. Lying on the broken column was an old wooden ikon. Even though it was weatherworn, she still recognized the image of Jesus. Beside it were small bundles of dried flowers and a few burned candles. The church must still be used.

At the base of the crude altar, she found a tinderbox among rocks and shoots of grass, and thinking of the dripping candles in the Tsímova church, she lit a candle and murmured a short prayer under her breath. She thought of Father Yianni's blessing and knew he would pray for her and for the success of the rescue mission. Divine assistance would certainly be welcome.

She stepped outside feeling lighter. The children were safe, and soon enough help would arrive. She'd done what she'd hoped to and now had only to wait for the men.

When she turned toward the harbor, terror jolted through her, making her knees weak. She sank onto the cliff and tried to stop the tremors that shook her body.

A ship was sailing into the harbor. A Turkish ship. And the Maniots had still not arrived. If the Turks boarded the ship, they could sail away with the children and any chance of rescuing them would be lost.

Her pulse pounded in her ears, and for a moment she lost herself to panic. She pressed her fists against her temples and bent forward until her forehead rested on the rocks. Father Yianni's words came into her mind. *You will be of no help to anyone if you act rashly.* She shoved away her fear, breathing steadily, and waiting for her heart to calm. Once her mind was clear, she thought of a plan. Not a good plan, but a plan, nonetheless.

Diana stood and let the sound of the waves calm her for a moment as she watched the ship drawing near. She hurried into the church ruin and took the tinderbox, praying for forgiveness as she ran back to the road and found a cactus plant. She sliced off a pad and broke off the needles while she climbed through the scraggy brush toward the rocky overhang above the children.

With shaking hands, she carved a message for Elena: Οταν σημα, τρεχετε προς εκκλησια. *At the signal, run to the church.*

She prayed the children had seen the building on the cliff. Using the last shred of her head scarf, she wrapped the message and the knife, tying them together into a tight bundle. She scooted forward on her belly. A clump of foliage offered some concealment, but she knew it would draw attention if the bushes started moving. She carefully slid around the scratchy branches, stirring them the smallest bit as she scooted toward the edge. Her pulse thundered. So many things could go wrong: if she was seen, if Elena did not find the message, if someone else did find the message, if the children were taken into the ship . . . But Diana was the children's only chance, and she had no other choice.

She peeked over the edge. Elena and the others were directly beneath her.

Spiros sat against a rocky wall, staring toward the sea with his sister sleeping against his shoulder. Elena and Stella huddled together, their bound hands clinging to each other, and three boys stretched out, sleeping on the sand. She looked toward the beach and saw the Turk at the entrance to the alcove. He glanced occasionally toward the children, but his attention was on the ship.

Slowly, Diana slid to the side until she was directly above Elena. She did not dare to drop the bundle while the man was so close. Even if he wasn't looking directly at them, he would surely see the movement from the side of his vision.

Diana remained still and waited, but urgency took hold of her as the ship neared. She bowed down her head and offered a prayer, knowing that Father Yianni and the mothers of Tsímova were doing the same. When she looked back, the man stood, stretched his back, and walked a short distance away. He turned toward the cliff wall and—

Diana pulled away her gaze, horrified that she'd seen him performing a task of a personal nature. Knowing she only had until he finished, she scooted forward, and dropped the bundle, praying that it would not hit Elena in the head.

It bounced off the girl's leg, and she let out a cry of surprise, then hurried to snatch it.

Diana slid back, lying down her cheek against the rocks as her heartbeat slowed.

The man completed his business and walked back toward the mouth of the alcove, resuming his seat on the rock.

Diana did not stay any longer. She'd risked enough by getting so close, and if she was to set her plan into action, she needed to move quickly.

Chapter 21

ALEX PACED, FOOTSTEPS CLICKING ON the flagstone of the town square. His nervous energy made it impossible for him to remain still. He glanced to the closed doors of the church where Petrobey and Sebastianos Sássaris were meeting with Father Yianni. What was taking so long? Didn't the men know precious time was slipping away?

Every instinct screamed at him to run after Diana, to snatch her away and take her somewhere safe, but he knew she would not forgive him for such an action. He needed to wait and plan the rescue mission with the Maniots, or her brave undertaking would be for nothing.

He snatched at a bush that hung over a wall of the churchyard and shredded the leaves as he marched back and forth.

The men of the families stood in two distinct groups, muttering and glaring at each other. The air hung heavy between them, and the feuding Maniots were armed to the teeth with sabers and guns. Other men of the village kept to the edges of the square, glancing between the Mavromichalis and Sássaris families with nervous expressions.

Finally the doors opened, and Father Yianni stepped out, followed by the patriarchs of the two families.

"An agreement has been reached," the priest said. "A treva. The vendetta between the Mavromichalis and Sássaris families is ended."

Petrobey stepped forward. "Our clans will band together now against the true enemy. With our combined strength, we will be more than a match for the child stealers." He motioned to Argos for his rifle, and grabbing onto the stock, he hefted it above his head. "Let us show the Turks that the Maniots will not be trod upon."

"How do we proceed?" Sebastianos asked. The leader of the Sássaris clan was much older than Petrobey. He appeared wrinkled and thin, but his voice was strong. Alex noticed the intelligence in his eyes and saw cruel lines around his mouth. Instinct warned him that Sebastianos would make a deadly enemy. Luckily, the Mavromichaleis could now call the man and his clan allies, and neither family would betray their honor by striking against the other now that a treva was in place.

Father Yianni stood tall, and Alex was again reminded that this was not only a man of the church but a son of the harsh Mani land. "The Turks will not attempt to pass through the mountains. Aside from the threat of the klephts, the journey would be too difficult for both horses and children." He scowled. "They will leave the Mani by sea."

"They headed south," Petrobey said. "Perhaps to Dyros or another uninhabited bay."

Father Yianni raised his chin in a southerly direction. "The woman, Missno, followed them to mark a path."

A few men raised their brows and muttered exclamations of surprise at this declaration. A surge of pride swelled in Alex's chest, and he kept his gaze turned downward until he could school his expression.

"We have only a few hours of daylight." Petrobey shouldered his rifle and without another word started off. He walked with brisk steps.

The men of Tsímova followed.

Alex walked behind Dino and Themis, following Petrobey's steady pace along the road from the village. He typically went about his business for the Filiki Eteria secretively, hiding in the shadows, passing messages, blending into a crowded room as he listened for information. The lifestyle was lonely, and he couldn't help but enjoy the camaraderie of marching with a group of men, all dedicated to the same goal. He glanced back at the Maniots filling the road behind him and felt a satisfaction when he thought that if all went well, someday soon, these same men would march across his beloved country and drive out the invaders.

Petrobey paused at a crossroads, glancing in each direction.

Dino pointed to a scrap of yellow fabric tied to a branch. "This way."

The swell Alex had felt earlier returned and an urgency joined it. Diana had been here. She was close, and they must reach her. *He* must reach her.

Feeling Dino's gaze on him, he glanced to the side, realizing his sentiments were all too apparent. Dino only lifted a brow and turned his gaze back to the road.

The men continued their march, and anytime any question arose as to which direction they should take, a strip torn from Diana's head scarf indicated their route. As they followed the road in a curve around a high hill, Petrobey halted. He stepped to the side of the road and lifted a low bush. A fabric scrap was tied to a branch, but that wasn't what he was looking at. He crouched down and picked up an object from the ground. He studied it, then motioned Alex toward him.

Alex took the object from Petrobey's extended hand. It appeared to be a piece of a cactus plant with words carved onto it. *Do not fear.*

Understanding dawned on him. Diana had left this message here, beneath the marked plant, where Elena would see it. She'd risked being discovered by the Turks to comfort her friend. His throat squeezed, and his chest swelled. He lifted his gaze to Petrobey and saw emotion in the man's eyes.

It disappeared immediately, and Petrobey nodded toward the message. "Clever," he said, and the ends of his mustache moved as his lips quirked, "and cheeky."

Petrobey realized Diana had acted out of compassion but also out of defiance, directly under the noses of the Turks. He met Alex's gaze once more, then continued onward.

Themis and Dino both inspected the cactus pad. Dino's expression looked as close to a smile as Alex had ever seen. Themis handed it back without comment. As much as the man tried to hide his emotions, Alex could see that Themis was extremely close to falling apart. Over the hours of the march, Alex saw Themis's brows waver, then his eyes tighten and his fists clench. He vacillated between anger and fear and the sort of desperation that Alex thought could make him dangerous. He would need to keep an eye on Themis. The man's reckless nature could be a liability on this mission.

The sun was sinking low on the horizon when they saw the sea. Petrobey called a halt, then pointed ahead. "Smoke. They are on the beach."

"Perfect," Argos said. "We know this harbor well. Only one route leads in and out. They are trapped." He grasped onto his sword and moved as if he'd charge down the path, but Dino put a hand on his shoulder. The action looked brotherly enough, but by the way Argos's knees buckled, Alex could tell it was not done gently.

"We need a plan, first," Dino said.

Argos's face was red. "The plan is to charge down the path and kill all the Turks."

Dino shook his head. "We must proceed cautiously. The children are also down in the harbor." He glanced at the other men and at his father, who jerked his chin up in a nod for Dino to take charge.

Alex shifted his feet, knowing they needed to act with caution, but he was impatient to find Diana. He held his hands behind his back, gripping his wrist as he scanned the area but did not see her anywhere. Was she closer to the Turks' camp? Had she been captured? Or worse . . . ?

"Petrobey, Sebastianos, there is a stream about a hundred yards in that direction." Dino pointed with his rifle. "Argos knows the way. Let the men rest and prepare to attack. Themis and I will scout ahead and report back when we have a better idea of what we're up against and where the children are."

"We need him too." Themis nodded toward Alex. Seeing both Dino's and Alex's surprise, Themis frowned. "I do not like you, Mr. Metaxas, but this is my daughter. Assessing a situation is your strength."

Alex bowed his head. "Thank you." He knew the man had not meant his words as a compliment, but he felt relieved not to be waiting by the stream. He would be able to continue on and hopefully discover where Diana was.

Dino led them away from the harbor and over a craggy trail that ran in roughly the same direction as the curve of the shore. He motioned for the two to keep low. They emerged from the rocks and bushes on the far side of the bay, giving them a view of the entire beach.

Keeping low, they moved forward with caution, crouching behind a cluster of rocks. The sight of a ship drawing toward the shore increased Alex's tension, and he was glad for Dino's wisdom in scouting out the situation before rushing in.

He swept his gaze over the spoon-shaped area of the harbor. High rocks and cliffs circled the blue water, and the only scrap of pebbly beach was at the very tip, directly across from the harbor opening.

The horses were housed in a shoddy pen on the side of the beach nearest the cliff. Large rocks came together forming natural walls on the sides of the animals' pen, and a mismatch of branches closed off the opening of the enclosure. He moved his gaze around the curve of the shoreline. The majority of the Turks rested on the far side of the beach, near the path, but Alex could see one man sitting before an opening in the cliffside. There appeared to be no guards watching the path, and he realized the Turks had no reason to fear attack. They were not near the klephts' mountains and had not been challenged by the Greek peasants before. Today, that would change.

"There is a small alcove between the rocks." Dino indicated the opening behind the lone man; the inside was cast in shadow. The children are likely being held inside."

Alex felt Themis stiffen.

He glanced to the side and saw Themis's face was tight and lined with worry.

Alex continued to scan the harbor and the surrounding area, but he still saw no sign of Diana. Hopefully, once she knew where the Turks were making their camp, she had hidden herself away, waiting for reinforcements. He wished he could force his jaw to unclench and the burning to leave his stomach, but until he saw her, he wouldn't be able to rid himself of the worry.

"We would be wise to attack before the ship reaches land and sends reinforcements," Dino muttered.

"What are we waiting for?" Themis shifted his weight, getting his feet beneath him.

Alex prepared to follow him, ready to run back to Petrobey's camp and order the attack. He was sick of waiting. They needed to end this, then find Diana.

"Wait." Dino pointed. "Look there."

At first, Alex could not see what had caught Dino's attention, but then he noticed what appeared to be a large thicket sliding toward the ridge of the cliff. He leaned forward, squinting his eyes.

The clump of brushwood fell down through a crevice that led to the beach.

He glanced back toward the company of Turks, but they had seen nothing. The fissure was hidden on the far side of the horse's pen.

"What—?" he started to ask, but just then, a person peered over the edge, looking down at where the branches had fallen. Not just a person, a woman. *Diana!*

Alex leapt up, but Dino grasped his arm, tugging him back down. "If you call attention to her, she will be killed."

"We must . . ." Alex's pulse was physically painful.

Dino kept his hand firmly clasped on Alex's arm. "Wait. You must trust her." He pointed.

Alex remained tensed, ready to spring to action, but he knew Dino spoke the truth. He pulled his arm away from Dino's grip and watched to see what she would do.

Diana slipped carefully down the crack in the cliffs, pressing her hands against both sides of the fissure. She slipped when she neared the bottom, dropping and tumbling into the pile of branches.

Dino must have anticipated Alex's movement and clamped a hand back onto his arm, holding him in place. Alex frowned but did not take his gaze off Diana.

Below the fissure, Diana crawled from the pile of brushwood and stood, picking bits of wood from her skirt and sleeves and shaking twigs from her loose hair. She pulled and pushed the mass of branches toward the horse pen, carefully staying out of sight behind the rocks as she bunched the mound against the branches of the fence.

Alex's heart was in his throat. He glanced back and forth between the Turks and Diana.

She raised her face toward the exit route, holding up her hand to shade her eyes. Then she knelt on the pebbly beach by the mound of brushwood.

Dino kept his voice low. "She's causing a distraction. The sun will blind the Turks as it lowers over the cliff, giving even more advantage to the escape . . . Clever woman."

Alex's muscles were so tight they ached. "We must do something."

Dino nodded. "Themis, return to the others. Give the order to attack when you hear the horses."

Themis hurried away.

On the beach, Diana leaned close to the branches, and soon, Alex could see a trail of smoke rising from the wood in front of her. She blew on it then set more branches on the flame until she appeared satisfied with the blaze. She ran back to the crevice she'd slid down and started pulling herself up between the rocks.

With the help of a sea breeze, the fire spread rapidly, and within a moment it had grown, flames licking at the thicker branches.

The horses jerked their heads, stomping and whinnying at the wall of fire that trapped them in their pen. A large black stallion reared back, and with his front hooves, broke through the burning barrier and galloped on to the beach. The other horses followed him through the burning opening, running in every direction in their fright. Chaos broke out over the beach as the horses crashed through the camp. Some of the Turks chased the horses, and others ran to put out the fire.

Dino squeezed Alex's arm and pointed. Elena and a young man led a line of children from the crevice. They remained near to the cliffs and ran unnoticed in the confusion toward the path leading up from the harbor.

"How did they know?" Dino muttered. "Unbelievable."

Diana had pulled herself up into the crevice, but it appeared the rock walls were too smooth for her to get a sufficient grip. Finally, kicking aside her skirts, she got a toehold and reached up higher.

Dino sucked in a breath and let out a curse. He raised his rifle.

A large Turk with a feather rising from his turban stepped around the rocks of the horse's pen. He spotted Diana and started toward her, drawing his sword.

Pain compressed Alex's gut. He bolted toward her just as Dino fired.

Chapter 22

DIANA WAS JERKED DOWN FROM the crevice by her leg. She hit the ground hard. Fighting to catch her breath, she raised her eyes to see the Turk with the yellow feather glaring at her. He lifted his curved sword, ready to slash it downward.

Shock emptied her mind, and she threw up her hands.

A gunshot echoed in the harbor. Blood sprayed over Diana, and the man toppled forward, his sword dropping to the sand.

Diana rolled out of the way of his fall and scrambled backward, gasping for air. She blinked as terror rushed through her blood. What had happened? Her hand bumped into something solid and she looked down at the jeweled hilt of the sword. The realization of how near she had come to being killed jolted her mind back into action. She was still in the Turks' camp and could be discovered again at any second. Grasping the sword, she jumped to her feet. Just holding the heavy weapon gave her a swell of courage, and she bolted past the smoking horse pen and over the rocky beach.

The sun had sunk farther. Patches of shadows and twilight played tricks on her eyes as she darted through the confusion of the Turks' camp. She prayed it did the same for her enemies. She didn't dare to stop to assess her route or conceal herself. The time for stealth had passed. Heart pummeling into her ribs, she expected to be stopped at any moment, and the energy that came from fear pushed her on, fueling her speed. She ran directly across the beach toward the path, occasionally dodging a rock or a bounding horse.

Around her, men yelled to one another, horses whinnied, the surf crashed. She thought she heard someone call her name, but she was certain that pausing or looking away from her destination would increase her chance of being stopped.

Diana clasped her skirts with one hand and the sword with the other as she ran up the winding path. At the top of the cliffs, she did not pause or risk a look backward to see if she had been followed. The night was darker now, but the outline of the terrain was just visible. And if seeing was difficult for her, it would be for the Turks as well. She dashed over the rocky ground to the little church. "Elena!" She spoke in a loud whisper. *Please be here.*

"Missno!" Elena's voice was a hiss. She ran from the building, and Diana pulled her in with one arm, pressing a kiss to her friend's cheek. Stella hurried from the church.

Diana embraced her. "Thank goodness," she breathed. "Are you all here?" She shifted the heavy sword into her other hand.

"Yes."

She looked behind Elena and saw the shadows of the other children in the church doorway. Her moment of relief was replaced by a spike of urgency that pulsed through her body. The longer they remained, the better the chance of capture.

She looked back and forth, trying to decide which way to go. If they continued to follow the shoreline past the church, there was minimal cover, and she did not want the children to be exposed. But traveling back toward the safety of the hills would mean nearing the path from the harbor. She debated for only a moment, and since the moon had not yet risen, she decided they would have a better chance of remaining hidden in the hills.

She moved closer to the church where all of the children could hear her lowered voice. "We must run. All of you, link hands."

She heard shuffling and whispers, and the shadows of the children showed they followed her direction. "Spiros, Elena, follow along in the rear. Make sure no one gets left behind." She grabbed on to Stella's hand. "We must be absolutely silent." She pulled the line in the direction of the road.

As they neared the path down to the harbor, shouts, the clang of metal, and the sounds of gunshots echoed from below. Diana did not dare slow. Even if it was the sound of rescue, she could not predict the outcome of a battle. The children would not be safe until they were as far away from the Turks and their ship as possible.

She pulled the group across the road and up into the hills. Climbing a steep, rocky incline hefting a cumbersome sword in one hand and pulling a line of children with the other was more difficult than she imagined, and within a few moments, Diana was perspiring, and her breath came in heavy bursts. The group moved down one rise and up the next, the line jerking when a child tripped or slid on the loose rocks.

Behind them, the sounds of battle grew softer, and Diana started to look for a suitable place to hide. The sky was growing lighter in the east, and she knew the moon would rise soon—illuminating the way but making them visible to anyone searching. Pulling the line of children was becoming more difficult, and she knew after walking for the entirety of the day, they would soon lose the strength to continue. They needed to be secreted away as soon as possible, and then she could speak with Elena and Spiros and determine the best way to get them all home to Tsímova.

After a bit of searching, she found what she was looking for. A shallow bend in a sheer rock face surrounded with a thick clump of bushy trees would at least provide heavy shadows for concealment. The ground beneath the trees was flat, and the rock protected them on two sides.

She led the children into the space, checking each of them for injury. Aside from stubbed toes and scraped arms and legs, they were all unharmed. Elena, Stella, and Spiros helped to soothe the worries of the younger ones. Diana realized the children had probably not eaten for hours, and they must be thirsty.

She surveyed the group. The small children now lay quietly, either asleep or near to it. A day of walking combined with fear had left them weary, and she was glad they could finally rest. The two Mavromichalis girls were seated beside each other with their heads bowed, exhausted. Spiros remained near his sister, leaning back against the rock and stretching his legs in front of him.

"Spiros." Diana knelt next to him. "In a few hours, when the moon is bright, we will need to find water or the children will not be able to make the journey back to Tsímova."

He nodded. "I will find water." His eyes moved over the others and returned to his sister. "Thank you for saving her, Missno. For saving me."

She patted his hand, thinking of Daphne. "Theodora is lucky to have a brother willing to fight for her."

The side of his mouth pulled into a small smile, and Diana could see exactly why Elena was so smitten with the handsome young man. "She is also lucky you were brave enough to follow us and that Elena learned to read."

Diana raised her brows, pleased that he had thought to give credit to her friend. He hoped Spiros would tell Elena that her reading had impressed him.

Spiros bent his head to the side, rubbing his neck. "Sleep, Missno. I will keep watch."

She nodded her head and opened her mouth to tell him good night, but a man's voice stopped her.

"What is this?" A man stood in the shadow of trees. Diana did not know how he had approached without their notice.

Spiros jumped to his feet.

Diana rose and held the sword in front of her. All of her muscles clenched, and her heart raced. Angry tears pushed at the back of her eyes. She should not have stopped the group. "Do not come any closer."

More men joined him, and he folded his arms in front of his chest, tipping his head to the side. He stepped forward.

"Sir, I am in earnest. Do not take another step." Diana could hear her voice quiver but tried to sound confident. She knew she could not fight off the men, and her stomach twisted into a hard knot. The children were trapped.

The heavy sword dipped, her knees felt weak, and her arm began to shake. She grabbed on to the hilt with the other hand, wishing her arms were stronger, and stepped to the side, moving between the stranger and the children.

The man drew closer, and she saw that he wore the white kilt and blue vest of a klepht. His sword remained in his sash. "I'm afraid I do not obey orders unless I know from whom they come. You dress as a Maniot, but your accent is strange. However, I am fairly certain you are not a Turk, even though your weapon would indicate otherwise."

Diana took another step, hoping to keep him away from the shadows where the children were hidden.

The man's brows rose, and Diana realized she had stepped into the moonlight. She glanced down and saw her clothes were torn, her hair full of twigs, and blood spotted her white sleeves and collar.

"I am neither Greek nor a Turk. I am British. My name is Miss Diana Snow." Out of habit, her knees bent to curtsey as she introduced herself, but she decided adhering to propriety was not necessary when one was covered in blood and holding an enemy's sword. "You are a klepht."

He lowered the sides of his mouth and nodded. "Yes. My name is Kapetan Ionnis Karahalios." His stance did not appear threatening. She didn't think a klepht would harm the children, but she would not take any chances and kept the sword raised, pointing it at Kapetan Karahalios.

He did not seem bothered by it in the least.

The moon revealed the faces of some of his companions. Diana's eyes traveled over them. "I know you," she said to the man standing behind the kapetan. "You and another man came to Tsímova and left with Alexandros Metaxas."

The man squinted, then nodded. "Yes. I am Lieutenant Markos." He inclined his head.

Kapetan Karahalios raised his chin. "We actually journeyed to Tsímova for the express purpose of speaking with Alexandros Metaxas, but we were told he was chasing after a band of Turks that stole children from the village." He rubbed his cheek as he studied her, then glanced toward the shadows.

"And if I'm not mistaken, those are the children behind you. So you can see why I might be curious about exactly who you are, Miss Diana Snow."

Spiros stepped next to Diana. "Missno rescued us, Kapetan."

The kapetan raised his brows. "She rescued you?

"Yes."

"From the Turks?"

"Yes."

"Alone?"

Spiros nodded his head once. "Yes."

Diana was impressed at what an exceptional young man Spiros Sássaris was. He did not act at all embarrassed to be rescued by a woman.

"I'll admit I had the wrong conception of British women," the kapetan muttered. He rubbed his cheek again and smirked. "Miss, you can lower your sword. We are on the same side."

Diana slowly let the sword down until the tip of the blade touched the hard dirt. Her arms felt like soft noodles, and she was suddenly exhausted. With the klephts here, she knew the children were safe, and cool relief washed over her. She glanced back and saw that the younger children were still asleep. Elena and Stella stood a few feet behind Spiros. A wave of emotion moved through her at the faith they had in her.

It took all her strength to remain standing long enough to offer the kapetan a seat.

She sat on a rock, holding herself straight, not wanting to show the man any weakness, though she was near collapse. Her muscles felt like all the energy had been drained out and the only thing left behind was jelly. Her head started to feel dizzy.

Kapetan Karahalios stretched out his legs. He looked quite at home in her little camp. He motioned to a man to bring a water skin, then he offered it to Diana.

She thanked him and took a sip before handing it to Spiros.

A man approached the kapetan. Diana recognized him as the other klepht that had come for Alex, the young man with the scar. He leaned forward and whispered.

"No need for secrecy, Private. Speak for all to hear."

He straightened and glanced at Diana. "We are too late for the fight. The Maniots defeated the Turks and took the ship. Now they are searching for a woman and the children."

Kapetan Karahalios tipped his head toward Diana. "Shall I send word of your whereabouts? Or will you threaten them as well?"

She ignored his sarcasm. Truly, she was too exhausted to think of a witty comeback. "Yes, tell them, please." Her mind was swimming with fatigue, but a thought rose into her consciousness. The private had reported that Turks were defeated, but were there any Maniot casualties? Were some of the children's fathers injured? Or killed? How could she tell them? Comfort them? *And Alex.* Diana jolted. Was Alex safe?

The worry she'd felt before returned with a force. She did not doubt Alex's strength. She'd seen the way his shirt stretched over his broad back and felt the bulge of muscles when she held his arm. He was well built and extremely intelligent, but he was not a warrior. She did not know if he'd had any experience in battle. Had he been hurt? Had he—

She pushed the thought away before her mind completed it.

A voice sounded from the darkness. A man called out, but the buzzing of the cicadas muffled the words. The voice came again. "Stella!"

The girl gasped and jumped to her feet. "*Patéras!*"

Themis barged up the hill and swept his daughter into his arms. "My Stella." His voice clogged, and he buried his head in Stella's hair.

Diana heard other men's voices, and a moment later, the hillside was covered with fathers reuniting with their children. She saw Petrobey embrace Elena, and she was nearly certain the moonlight revealed the sheen of moisture in the bey's eyes.

Emotion surged in her throat when Diana watched these same hardened men, who, merely hours earlier, had been entangled in a blood feud, whispering tender words as they held their children.

A man found the young twins, clasping them to his chest, and Daphne's husband embraced Theodora and Spiros. Soon each child had been claimed, but as the moments passed, Diana's heart grew heavier. Where was Alex? The noise on the hillside became a clamor as the men and klephts spoke loudly, some telling about the battle, others showing newly acquired weapons that gleamed in the moonlight or offering congratulations on a fine victory. She strained her ears but did not hear Alex among them.

She wove in and out of the crowd, stumbling over rocks and dodging bushes as she tried to get a view of each face. But still the one she searched for was not to be found.

Finally she stopped. He was not here.

Surrounded by a crowd of happy people, Diana felt completely alone. She let the sword drop, hearing a thud and the scrape of metal when it hit the earth. She sat on the hillside, pulling her knees to her chest. Tears burned her eyes, but she swallowed and stamped down the rush of pain.

"Diana!"

Whipping around her head, she saw Alex's familiar silhouette climbing up the moonlit hill.

The surge of tears pushed harder, and she pressed her hand over her mouth, forcing them back. She shifted to her knees, but the strength to stand had deserted her. She sank back. A sob rose in her throat, and she shook her head, willing it away.

Alex crouched next to her. "Oh, Diana. *Dóxa to theó.* Thank goodness you are safe." His voice shook. He reached for her.

At his touch, something inside fractured, and Diana's emotions burst forth in a torrent.

Alex's arms slid around her shoulders. She pressed her face against his chest, clinging on to his lapels as she gulped and sobbed. The fear she'd felt for the children, the uncertainty about her future, the loneliness, the drain of exhaustion, all the years of holding in her pain and pushing away her emotions—it all grew until it could no longer be contained. She felt as if the tears were being pulled from her. Her face, her throat, her eyes—all were compressed and burning. Her heart split, and it all spilled out in hysterical wails and wet tears.

Alex only held her tighter, speaking soft words of comfort that seemed to spread the opening in her heart wider. Diana choked on the sobs, and her shoulders shook. The precise thing she'd feared and avoided for so long had happened. She had finally lost her tight hold. And the result was not a dainty tear and sniffle. Everything she'd hidden inside was exposed. But instead of feeling uncovered and vulnerable, she felt lighter, like she'd cast off a heavy mass.

She gradually started to calm and realized that Alex's cheek rested on her head.

Her stomach grew hot with embarrassment. "I am so sorry," she panted with a jerky breath once she could manage to form words. "I thought you would not return and . . ." She felt humiliated for coming apart so completely.

Alex cupped her chin and lifted her face. His other hand brushed wet strands of hair from her cheeks. "Are you all right?"

She nodded. "Yes, I am not injured."

"No, Diana. Are you all right?" He spoke each word deliberately. His hands slid to her neck, holding her face toward him. "You told me you feared weeping would be so painful you would be unable to bear it." Even in the moonlight she could see his eyes darken. His head tipped to the side. "Are you hurting?"

"Not anymore." Heat filled her face. Her instinct was to shut him out, lock up her feelings, but her heart was open, and it was much harder to hide it away now. "I—" She drew in a breath, lowering her voice. "I do not hurt because you are with me."

His gaze softened, and he bent his head to touch his lips to hers.

Diana did not hold any of herself back as she returned the kiss. She pressed her fingers into the curls at his neck, and instead of fighting the sensation, she sighed as his touch filled her with warmth. For the first time, she allowed herself to feel without worry of pain because she knew she was not alone.

Chapter 23

ALEX HELD DIANA AGAINST HIM. Her words and her kiss made his stomach turn over, a feeling much like when a ship sinks too fast over a wave. He moved his chin, feeling strands of her hair clinging to his whiskers. He rubbed his hand up and down her back. He'd never have imagined the thing that would finally break through her barriers would be her concern for him.

Finding her safe poured relief over him, flooding cool through his limbs. He said a silent prayer of thanks to St. George—he thought it appropriate to honor the great martyr as his gratitude pertained to the small "warrior" in his arms.

He let a smile touch his lips. He would never have believed Diana capable of the feats she performed today. She hadn't only terrified him, but he thought he had never felt so proud of anyone in his entire life. He wanted to shout her deeds from the rooftops. Tell everyone that it was *his* Diana who had saved the children.

The thought brought him up short. He'd made excuses since the moment they'd met for why he and Diana could not have a future together. He would be returning to Turkey, Diana would return to her family in London, she was not strong enough for the life of a revolutionary. One by one, his assumptions had been proven wrong. He could not help feeling like an element of destiny existed when it came to Diana—and he had to admit, it frightened him. The mere thought of something happening to her shot pain through his chest, fear like he'd not experienced since the loss of his family. He realized that for all the preaching he'd done to Diana, he was every bit as scared of being hurt, of losing someone again, of daring to let himself love her.

Diana lifted her head, pulling back and looking up through her lashes. "I forgot to tell you, Kapetan Karahalios is looking for you."

"The klepht kapetan? He is here?"

She nodded. "Yes. He is near the trees."

He held onto Diana's hand, assisting her as she rose. She clasped the large sword she'd taken from the fallen Turk and motioned toward a copse of trees at the base of a sheer rock wall. The sound of men's voices rose from the area she indicated, and he followed her lead over the hills.

He knew the Maniots were anxious to return to their homes, and he did not wish to linger. But for the life of him, he could not think of what Kapetan Karahalios could possibly wish to speak with him about.

As they neared the trees, the kapetan approached, raising his hand in greeting. The moon shone brightly on his white clothing. Alex saw that Lieutenant Markos followed close behind.

Diana pulled on her hand, but Alex did not release his hold. "Will you stay?" he said in a quiet voice.

"I will if you'd like."

He squeezed her hand in answer, then turned to the klepht. "Kapetan, I did not expect to see you."

"I owe you a debt, Mr. Metaxas."

"Alex."

The kapetan inclined his head. "Alex. You saved Logastras Camp."

Alex blinked, and his brows shot up in surprise. "Sir?"

"Lieutenant Markos told me your suspicions about the new recruit, and it turns out they were entirely correct. Iason Solomos was a Janissary spy."

Alex put a hand on his hip. If he were twenty-five years younger, he would have stuck out his tongue and danced around the irritable kapetan chanting, "I told you so." But he somehow kept himself composed.

"We did as you suggested," Lieutenant Markos said. "Took the young man to camp but kept a close watch on his movements, and within a week, he'd slipped away. So we were ready when he returned with his friends."

"Rather like a flock of lambs wandering into a lion's den, wouldn't you say, Lieutenant?" The kapetan's grin flashed wickedly. "They arrived in a deserted camp, and just when the realization dawned on them that they'd been outfoxed, we pounced. When we were through with them, there was nothing left but turbans and blood."

Alex felt Diana stiffen, and he cleared his throat, tipping his head toward her in a reminder to the klephts that there was a lady in their midst.

Kapetan Karahalios looked at Diana and winced. "Ah. Beg your pardon, miss."

Diana nodded.

"Yes, ah, Alex, the reason I came to find you is I realized nearly as soon as you left that I'd made a mistake. I wasn't myself that day—toothache, you know. And you solved that problem as well." He frowned as he nodded toward Alex. "I was wrong about you, and I hope you will still consider your previous offer to me to be valid."

"Of course, Kapetan." Alex's heart leaped in his chest. His mission to the klephts was not a failure after all. "There are, naturally, details to discuss, but Petrobey will be your point of contact. He will keep you informed."

Kapetan Karahalios nodded. "A good man, the bey." He offered his hand, and Alex shook it, amazed at the difference in the man's disposition now that his tooth no longer hurt.

Around them, the noises changed, and Alex saw that the group was headed toward the harbor. Dino, Argos, and a few others had remained with the Turkish ship. The plan was to sail back to Limeni instead of the children making the return journey on foot.

"It was a pleasure to meet you, Alex."

"Likewise, Kapetan. And I expect we will meet again soon."

"And Diana Snow." The kapetan squinted. He glanced down to the sword she carried, tipping his head to the side with a bemused look. He motioned to his men, and the klephts moved away silently and disappeared into the hills.

"I do not think he knew what to make of you, Diana." Alex smiled.

"When he first appeared, I didn't know who he was. I thought he might be a Turk or a bandit, and I . . . threatened him with the sword."

Alex's smile grew. He lifted her hand to his lips. "That will teach him to sneak up on a warrior woman."

She blew out a sigh. "It was ridiculous. I could hardly hold up the sword. He was not frightened at all."

He held inside the laugh that wanted to slip out, knowing she would take offense. "Come, warrior woman. You have had enough adventure for a lifetime." He pulled on her hand, but Diana paused, her gaze looking far away.

"What is it?"

"What you just said. I said that very same thing to myself . . . once." She closed her mouth and lowered her gaze. Even in the moonlight, he could see color in her cheeks.

Alex knew instinctively not to ask further. "The ship awaits us in the harbor." He glanced down. "Do you want me to carry your sword?"

"Alex, a warrior woman does not allow someone else to carry her sword." Her mouth pulled in the familiar smirk that he wanted to kiss until it softened into a smile.

So he did.

⚓

The harbor was empty and silent. The moon made the pebbly beach shine white, and the tips of the waves glowed with what appeared to be an inner light. Low voices and the soft hiss of the water against the shore made the bay beautiful and peaceful—a far cry from a few hours earlier. A chill ran over Alex's skin as the memory of the battle loomed in his thoughts.

After the conflict, the men rushed to find their children, and Alex had helped Dino and Argos carry and conceal the bodies of the slain Turks in the cavity of the rock where the children had been imprisoned. He was grateful now that Diana and the children did not have to see the aftermath of the battle.

Maniots rowed in small boats from the shore to the ship. Alex rode next to Diana, noticing how her head bobbed with the movement of the boat. She was exhausted. When they reached the boat, he assisted her over the gunwale onto the deck. He glanced around at the Turks' ship.

Dino stood at the helm but strode toward them when they boarded. He pulled an object from the sash at his waist and held out a metal scabbard to Diana. The brass and silver pattern gleamed.

She looked at it, then to Dino with a confused expression.

He took the sword from her hand, pushed it inside the sheath with a swift movement, then handed it back.

"Oh, thank you." Diana took the weapon in both hands, staring down at it. She must have realized that Dino had taken it from the Turk's body. She looked up, and Alex saw that her lip trembled. Her gaze moved to the rife slung over Dino's shoulder. "Did you shoot that man?"

"Yes." Dino kept his chin raised. But Alex saw his eyes waver. Dino was not a man who showed emotion, so the small movement spoke volumes. He'd been concerned for Diana—afraid, even.

"Thank you," she whispered. She held out the weapon toward him and cleared her throat. "You should have this."

Dino shook his head. "I shot the Turk from afar, Missno. You followed the enemy, alone and unarmed. You were the brave one."

"I didn't feel brave at all."

"Which makes your actions all the more remarkable."

Diana pulled the sword to her chest. She bowed her head. "Thank you, Constandinos."

He dipped his chin and returned to the helm of the ship.

Diana stared down at the sword for a moment longer, then turned to Alex. "I am so tired."

"Shall we find you a berth to sleep in?"

She shook her head. "No. I want— Can I remain with you?"

The request must be important if she was willing to speak so openly. He could see by the hesitation in her face that voicing it had been difficult.

And he was glad she did. After agonizing over Diana's welfare for the entire day and then nearly losing her, the thought of leaving her for even a few hours made him feel uneasy. "I will not let you out of my sight."

She smiled, but he could see that it took effort. Her eyelids were heavy, and when they walked across the deck, her steps were sluggish. He lowered her to a spot on the port side aft section of the deck where she would stay dry. He sat beside her, leaning back against the gunwale. He wished he had a blanket or a pillow or something for her to rest on.

She closed her eyes, leaning her head back. The ship's deck rose and lowered as the ship bobbed on the gentle waters of the harbor. The waves whispered as they moved toward shore, and within a few moments, Diana's head dropped. She leaned heavily against his shoulder, and he knew that she slept.

He shifted, lying her down on the deck, her head resting on his leg and swept his fingers over her cheek and back through her hair. Diana's face shone white in the moonlight, her lashes fanned over her cheeks.

His chest swelled, and warmth spread throughout his body as he watched her sleep. He could not resist tracing her jaw or brushing his finger over the dip in her upper lip. The moment was perfect. His earlier thoughts returned, and he made up his mind. If Diana could be brave, he could as well. He was in love with her, and saying good-bye would be like leaving a piece of his heart behind. All of his former arguments were resolved, and no reasons existed any longer as to why he could not be with her.

His eyes grew heavy, and he let his gaze travel around the ship's deck. All of the children slept, except for Spiros, who stood with his father near the bow. The majority of the men sat around the edges of the deck. A few talked together, but most were silent. Alex closed his eyes, listening to the sound of the waves. He did not know that something as simple as making up one's mind could bring such contentment.

⤚⤙

Alex squinted when he opened his eyes and realized the morning sun shone brightly on the ship's deck. He'd not realized he'd fallen asleep. He glanced down and saw that Diana had not moved, so he tried to stretch his stiff back without disturbing her.

Dino stood firm at the helm, and Alex imagined he had not moved from his position for hours. Petrobey, Argos, and Themis were beside him. Alex saw that some of the children still slept. But Elena was awake, walking slowly along the deck with her hand on the rail.

She caught his eye and approached, glancing to her grandfather, who nodded his permission, before she knelt on the deck by Alex.

"Uncle Dino says we will see Limeni soon." She glanced down at Diana's sleeping form, and the girl's mouth curved into a soft smile. "She is a tired hero, isn't she?"

Alex smiled. "Yes, I think that is a perfect description." He glanced toward the Mavromichalis men and saw that they watched Elena closely while she spoke with an unmarried man. He thought he would do the same thing if he had a daughter. "And you are a hero yourself, Elena. We saw you leading the children out of the harbor."

"Spiros too," Elena said. Her eyes darted to where Spiros sat with his father and sister, and color rose in her face.

"How did you know when to run?" he asked the question quickly, trying to dispel her embarrassment. "And how did you untie your ropes?"

"Do you not know? No, I suppose you weren't there when I told the others." She glanced down at Diana again. "Missno dropped a bundle to me from the cliff. A knife and a cactus pad with a note scratched on it."

"And you read it."

Her face colored again, but this time, he knew it was pride, and he did not hurry to change the topic. "You are definitely a hero too then."

"Petrobey said there are many other ways to win a battle beside fighting," Elena said.

"Very true." He shifted again. His one leg was numb and his back tight. "You and Miss Snow proved that exceptionally well."

"He says all children need to learn to read," Elena said. "Perhaps we will even have schools in the Mani."

"That would be a wise thing." Education was the very tool the impoverished Greeks needed to defeat the Turks. Petrobey would make sure of it, and Alex felt both grateful and proud that the Maniot children would learn because of Diana.

A shout came from one of the men at the bow. Limeni harbor was in sight.

Elena took her leave and hurried to the rail where she could get a better view

Alex shook Diana's shoulder, and she sat up. She looked at him, rubbing sleepy gray eyes, pushing away her mussed hair, and smiling with a tired blink that made his heart flip over. Was this the sight that would captivate him each morning? With the other men so near, he did not dare to kiss her, though his fingers itched to pull her into an embrace. Instead, he stood and helped her to rise beside him. "We are near to Limeni," he said, shaking his leg.

Diana leaned her hands on the rail as the ship rounded the bend. "I do not remember so many ships," she said.

She was right. Three ships that had not been there the day before bobbed in the harbor. With a start, Alex recognized his own ship. The sight was a relief—the weapons from Corfu had at last arrived. But at the same time, his stomach grew heavy. The ship was a tangible reminder that that he would soon leave the Mani. He'd become fond of these people, and he would miss them.

"Hektor!" Dino gave a shout that drew glances from many of the men. Such a display was unlike him.

Alex followed Dino's line of sight and saw that he pointed to another of the new ships.

Elena rushed to Diana and grabbed onto her arms. "Patéras has returned!" The girl's eyes were shining. The ship belonged to Dino's brother, Sophia's husband. Alex glanced at Diana and saw the uncertainty on her face.

"Do not worry," he said in English.

She glanced at him, but the tightness in her face did not entirely dissipate.

They neared the village, and Alex's gaze was drawn to the last unfamiliar ship, wondering whom it could belong to. It did not look like a rough trader's vessel or a Turkish warship. The ship was sleek with one mast and a bowsprit. Had it been captured like the vessel beneath him?

Men moved around on the deck of the mysterious ship, and Alex squinted in an effort to get a better look. He glanced at the other Maniots, wondering what their reaction was to the fine ship. He saw Dino's squint as he studied the watercraft. Petrobey tapped his chin, and Themis scowled.

Alex heard Diana gasp and whipped around his head.

A man in the red coat of a British Marine stepped onto the ship's deck.

"Lieutenant Ashworth," Diana said in a choked voice. She pressed her palm to her breastbone. "He has come for me."

As she said the words, Alex's chest collapsed, and his hopes for a future with Diana dissolved, leaving him empty save for an ache. He tightened his grip on the rail. He could see that Diana tried to meet his eyes but knew he could not return her gaze, and so he kept his eyes firmly upon the British vessel that would carry away the woman he loved, and with her, his heart.

Chapter 24

DIANA WALKED ALONG THE PIER of Limeni village with Elena and thought of how altered the experience was after only a few weeks—relief at returning to a place that had filled her with uncertainty and fear.

"I am glad to be back," she said to her companion, linking arms with Elena. She glanced back at the other vessels in the water, feeling a tug of doubt in her midsection.

A boat with Lieutenant Ashworth and other red-coated marines was rowing toward the village, passing another dinghy headed in the opposite direction.

Instead of accompanying her to shore, Alex was in the small boat, rowing directly to his waiting ship. Diana's unease about him had grown from the moment she'd seen the British ship, and he had not met her gaze when she tried to engage him. Alex had become distant and occupied, perhaps it was simply because he had business to tend to. But his reaction felt personal, as if he were avoiding her. Had she disclosed too much? She felt self-conscious about the excessive bout of weeping in the hills. Perhaps she had misinterpreted his reaction, and he had merely tried to comfort her, nothing more.

The others who had come ashore on her boat dispersed, going their own ways.

Elena squealed and ran toward the road.

Diana turned her head and saw Sophia with a tall man who must be her husband. Each held one of the new twins. When Elena ran to them, her parents embraced her. Sophia wept, laying a hand on Elena's cheek. Her father held on to her shoulder. Elena kissed her baby brother and sister.

Diana watched the reunion with a mixture of feelings. She'd missed Sophia and the babies, and the sight of them made her insides feel soft and her eyes swim with tears. But now, things were different. Hektor had returned to his family, and Diana felt as though she no longer belonged. She was certainly not needed as before. She twisted her fingers.

Sophia waved for her to join them. She gave Artemis to Elena and wrapped Diana in an embrace. "Thank you." Her voice cracked. She moved back, her gaze traveling over Diana's clothing, and her brow ticked upward when she saw the sword tucked into her sash. She pushed aside an errant lock of unruly hair in a motherly manner that made Diana's heart warm. "Missno, this is my husband, Hektor." Sophia's gaze was soft as she looked at the large man.

"Pleased to meet you."

Hektor looked almost exactly like an older version of Dino. Small wrinkles fanned out around his eyes as if he was a man that smiled often. Diana was glad Sophia's husband appeared to be a kind man.

He dipped his head in a small bow as he appraised her. "Since my return, I have heard of little else other than the magnificent Missno." He swallowed and cleared his throat. "Thank you for caring for my family. I owe you a debt that I do not know how to repay." His arm tightened around Elena's shoulder.

"You owe me nothing, sir." Diana's throat constricted. "Your family took in a stranger and welcomed me as one of them. I—" A tear dripped onto her cheek. "I am so grateful for that." She wanted to tell them everything, how she had never felt a family's love, and being part of the Mavromichalis household—laughing at the supper table, playing with the children, allowing Sophia to braid her hair, or sitting quietly with a baby—were jewels of memory that meant more than words could say.

Elena handed the baby to her, and Diana was grateful for an excuse to lower her face to brush against the soft hair and breathe in the baby's smell. "I missed you," she whispered to the infant girl.

Hearing voices, she glanced over her shoulder and saw the small boat of British sailors had disembarked and were approaching.

Lieutenant Ashworth raised a hand in greeting.

"I am taking my family back to Tsímova," Hektor said, glancing behind her. "Missno, you are always welcome in our home."

Sophia kissed her cheek and took the baby, joining her husband.

Elena took Diana's hands. She glanced toward the British soldiers, and her brow furrowed. "You are coming home, Missno?"

Diana did not know what to say to ease the worry in her friend's eyes. "I do not know."

"Come, Elena." Sophia held out a hand for her daughter.

"But Missno . . ."

Diana did not think her heart could take any more battering, but the sight of Elena weeping squeezed like a hot band around her chest, and she could not draw a breath.

Hektor took his daughter's hand and gently led her away.

Diana pulled her gaze from her friend when Lieutenant Ashworth reached her, and she curtseyed, breathing out a heavy breath as she calmed herself.

The lieutenant was tall with long limbs. His smile was friendly, and he walked with a confident stride. "Pardon me, miss. Do you speak English?" The lieutenant spoke with slow, clear words. "I am looking for Petrobey Mavromichalis."

Diana blinked. She'd assumed the lieutenant approached her because he recognized her, but it appeared she was just the first person he saw. "Lieutenant, it is I, Diana Snow."

The lieutenant pulled back in a jerk. "Oh, by Jove! Miss Snow, I apologize. I wasn't expecting to find you—"

"No offense taken, Lieutenant. I am certain my appearance is immensely different from the last time you saw me." She swallowed down her emotion, glancing back at the Mavromichalis family.

"I am here to meet with Petrobey Mavromichalis and to retrieve you. I do hope you have been treated well." His brows rose as he glanced over her blood-spattered dress and matted hair.

"Very well, sir." His concern made her smile.

"I am glad of it. My dearest Molly has been quite distraught, you know. She did not rest until we had secured a ship and the . . . means to rescue you."

Diana's face exploded in heat. She knew the lieutenant was speaking of the rescue money. She was embarrassed anyone should have to find the funding to pay for her freedom. And she also felt extremely thankful for Molly. She should never have doubted her young friend's loyalty.

"Petrobey disembarked before I. We just arrived back in Limeni by ship, you see. I will take you to his house."

Diana and Lieutenant Ashworth were shown into Petrobey's library. She sat on a hard-backed chair while the lieutenant paced around the room, studying the pictures, books, and other items.

She knew Petrobey would ask her to remain. Since Alex was still on his ship, there was nobody in Limeni who could translate. The idea of acting as the go-between while the men discussed her ransom—discussed how much she was *worth*—left a bitter taste in the back of her throat. Would the lieutenant attempt to talk down the price, telling Petrobey that she was an orphan, unconnected, and that he had only come to appease his fiancée? Her stomach twisted.

The door opened, and Petrobey strode through. He nodded to Diana and then turned to assess the red-coated marine standing in his library.

"Lieutenant Jonathan Ashworth," the lieutenant said.

Petrobey's eyes squinted as he scrutinized the man. He tipped his head back slightly.

"And you are Petrobey Mavromichalis, sir?"

Diana could tell the bey's silence disconcerted the friendly lieutenant.

He finally dipped his head in acknowledgement. He motioned for the lieutenant to be seated, then sat in his own chair, gripping the armrests. "Missno, ask the man what he wants."

"Lieutenant, Petrobey asks you to state your business, please."

The lieutenant sat. "Please tell him I have brought the means to pay your ransom, Miss Snow." He pulled a leather purse from the inside of his jacket. The sound of clinking coins came from the bag, and heat filled Diana's cheeks once more. "If he requires more, we can—" The lieutenant cut off his speech when Petrobey lifted his hand in a signal to stop.

The bey made a motion as if he were pushing forward with his hand. He did not even drop his gaze to the purse. His words confirmed the gesture. "I will accept no money for Missno."

Lieutenant Ashworth sat up even straighter. Quite a feat for a military man whose posture was already rigid. "Sir, it is unacceptable for you to keep a citizen of the crown as a prisoner. I do not wish to threaten you, but it is in my power to give a command to sink the ships in your harbor, for starters. His Majesty's Navy has been extremely understanding up to this point, and if you think you have the force to engage the most powerful nation on earth, you have another thing coming." The lieutenant's face was flushed, and Diana was quite shocked by the anger in his eyes. She had never seen anything but good humor from the man, and she realized she was getting a glimpse of him as a military officer.

Petrobey leaned forward in the chair. He did not ask for a translation, for which Diana was grateful. "Missno has repaid her debt to us a hundred times over. Your money does not even come close to compensating the way her actions have done."

The lieutenant raised his brows and leaned his head toward her, asking Diana to translate.

But her eyes swam, and she turned to Petrobey. "I cannot say that. You see, it is not true. I fear I have deceived you." She wiped away her tears with the tips of her fingers. "The reason the lieutenant has come is because my friend is engaged to him. The navy did not send the money, she did. I am not anyone of importance to England. I have no family. I am nobody. And I am sorry."

Petrobey's shrewd eyes studied her until Diana could not hold his gaze any longer. She felt like a fool, an imposter. Two men were arguing about her, but one did it at the bidding of his beloved. The other, because he had been misled.

"What did he say to you, Miss Snow?" Lieutenant Ashworth's voice was low and dangerous.

She shook her head and pushed her words through a tight throat. "He was not unkind. He just did not understand."

"Missno," Petrobey said. "Do you know the meaning of Mavromichaleis?"

She had not thought of it. *Mavros*, black. "Black Michael?"

"It means my ancestor Michael had no surname. He was an orphan, in mourning, and was called Black Michael. And look at the Mavromichalis now. The most powerful family in Laconia. That orphan did great things with the little he was given. As have you. The Mani people will forever be in your debt. You will always have a home among us, Missno. You are family. And to Maniots, family is everything."

Diana did not trust her voice. She bent down her head as tears fell into her palms.

"Did he threaten you, Miss Snow? What did he say? On my word, if that man—"

"No," she pushed out the word. "He said I am welcome to stay or leave; it is my choice."

"Stay?" Lieutenant Ashworth's eyes opened wide. "You would consider staying?"

She looked up at him, realizing that he must be extremely confused by her reaction. "I have been happy here. The people—I love them."

Lieutenant Ashworth tipped his head and gave a soft smile as if he understood. "What will you do?"

"I do not know."

"Well, if you please, make up your mind soon. I would like to return as soon as possible to my dearest Molly."

"Yes. I understand, Lieutenant."

The lieutenant took his leave, and Petrobey only glanced in his direction when he departed.

Diana rose. "Thank you, Petrobey," she said. "I need to make a decision."

He squinted his eyes and dipped his head. "Yes. You do."

Chapter 25

Diana sat on a low wall at the edge of Limeni Village, dangling her feet and watching fishermen unloading their catch in the harbor.

She looked at the British ship, still unable to believe that it was here for her. That someone cared enough to send for her and that she could be on it in a moment and back to her life teaching young ladies at Elliot's School in London within a matter of weeks. The idea did not hold any appeal.

She turned her head, letting her eyes travel over the stone houses of Limeni. She did not think it would take much to convince Petrobey to start a school. She could live here among the people doing what she loved. Now that Hektor had returned, things would not be exactly the same. She was certain she could see Elena and Sophia and their family any time she wished, but still, it would be different. And she felt like something would be missing.

She let her gaze linger on Alex's ship, knowing exactly what that something was.

Finally, she rose, feeling unsettled as her mind vacillated between her two options. She walked along the road, the low wall between her and the drop down to the harbor. Glancing back, her eyes followed the road that led to Tsímova. She continued, passing a taverna and stepped onto a path that wound in switchbacks down to the beach.

She made a turn and stopped when she saw Alex walking along the path toward her. He smiled, but his eyes were missing their regular mirth.

"You are leaving." She said it as a statement not a question.

He nodded, offering his arm. "And you are leaving as well."

Diana placed her hand in the bed of his elbow. "I do not know."

He turned to her with wide eyes. "You would remain here?"

"I have not decided." She continued to walk, and he kept pace with her until they reached the rocks of the beach. Diana searched until she found a flat rock and sat, scooting to the side. "It is difficult to choose. I love both London and the Mani. But neither quite feels like my place."

He sat beside her and did not speak. He seemed to be considering something, but since he was not speaking and she found often it easier to put words to her thoughts, she continued. Perhaps he was listening, perhaps not. "My entire life, I have done what I was told, taking the path another chose for me. But there have been three times I acted purely on impulse, making a decision for myself. Each has set my life on a new course."

"Hiding in the library," Alex said.

She glanced at him. He *was* listening. "Yes."

"And when you followed the Turks yesterday."

Diana nodded.

"And the other?"

"When I chased after a strange man in the middle of the night, hoping to return his gloves." She shrugged and gave him a wry smile.

Alex lifted his head. "Ah yes."

"Those times, the way seemed clear, almost as if I was led in the direction I should go, but now . . . Neither choice feels more right than the other."

"Diana, why did you follow me that night?" Alex's voice was lower than usual, and she turned to him, noticing that he watched her intently, as if her reply were important.

"I told myself it was to return your gloves. But that was only an excuse." At this point, she had nothing to lose by telling the truth. "That day when we met at the inn—in that brief moment, I felt a connection to you, something I didn't understand, and I wanted to see if it was still there." She thought she would feel embarrassed confessing something so personal, but the way Alex studied her made her feel as if her silly words were important.

He nodded and turned his gaze toward the ship. "Yes. I know. I felt it too."

She glanced at him, but he was not looking at her.

"Are you glad you followed me?"

"Well, obviously not at first. But I am glad. I found myself here in the Mani. I discovered Diana Snow and who she really is." She lowered her voice to a whisper. "I learned that I can be braver than I would have believed and that I should not be afraid to feel. I learned what it is to belong to a family and what it is to love." Her blush rose full force as she thought of his kiss, and she did not look at him. "I am grateful that I had that chance."

Alex continued to watch the ship, and she thought he was waiting for an opportunity to say good-bye. Very well. She braced herself for the words.

But they did not come.

He squinted but did not look at her. "What if there was another choice?"

"I beg your pardon?" What was he talking about?

"Besides Tsímova and London." He turned to her; his eyes darkened and looked into hers. "What if you had another choice?"

Diana's pulse sped up at the intensity of his gaze. "I—I don't."

"There is another ship in the harbor." He slid his arm across her shoulder, moving her closer as he pointed toward his ship.

Diana followed his gaze.

"What does your heart tell you?" His voice was a whisper in her ear, causing a shiver to spread over her skin. "Is your life ready for a new course?"

Diana closed her eyes. The sound of her heartbeat drowned out the noise of the waves. "My heart says yes," she squeaked.

His answer was a kiss that sent the breath from her lungs and made stars explode behind her eyelids. A promise that she would always belong somewhere and that her life would never be lonely again. His touch was tender, his fingertips brushing on her arms.

Diana wove her fingers into the curls at his neck, returning the kiss with every bit of her heart. She sighed when he pulled away and pressed his forehead to hers.

"I do not know what lies ahead, Diana. But whatever the future brings, we will face it together. And I promise it will be worth it."

Author's Note

Occasionally as I've researched an era, a particular person in history will stand out to me, becoming more than just a name on a paper. Such was the case with Petrobey Mavromichalis. Finding much information about him was difficult, but it seemed like every time I turned up a new fact, my appreciation for the man and for his character grew. Petrobey was known from a young age as a man who settled disputes, reuniting warring families—something uncommon for Maniots. His reputation grew as he sheltered revolutionaries and klephts, helping them escape, often right beneath the Turks' noses. He believed in education and wrote letters, asking for help and funding to start schools in the Mani. Sometime between 1817–1818, an emissary from the Filiki Eteria left Constantinople to recruit Petrobey to the society. From then on, his loyalty was to the revolution. In 1819, he brokered a formal pact between the Maniot clans, uniting them and working out a truce to end the vendettas that were so common. Two years later, he raised the flag of freedom in Tsímova, the town that was later renamed Areopolis (city of Ares, the ancient Greek god of war) in his honor. Flags with the motto "victory or death" were raised all over Greece. Petrobey, leading the Maniots, joined the klephts and Kolkotronis's army as they marched against the Turks, eventually driving them out of Greece altogether. During the war, no less than fifty of his family members were killed. My heart has been so touched by his sacrifice, and I hope that through this small effort, more people will know his name and remember him as the hero he truly is.

About the Author

JENNIFER MOORE IS A PASSIONATE reader and writer of all things romance due to the need to balance the rest of her world, which includes a perpetually traveling husband and four active sons, who create heaps of laundry that are anything but romantic. Jennifer has a BA in linguistics from the University of Utah and is a Guitar Hero champion. She lives in northern Utah with her family. You can learn more about her at authorjmoore.com.